SECOND TIME AROUND

SECOND TIME AROUND

MELODY CARLSON

THORNDIKE PRESS
A part of Gale, a Cengage Company

LIBRARY OF CONGRESS CIP DATA ON FILE.
CATALOGUING IN PUBLICATION FOR THIS BOOK
IS AVAILABLE FROM THE LIBRARY OF CONGRESS.

ISBN-13: 979-8-88578-847-2 (hardcover alk. paper)

Published in 2023 by arrangement with Revell Books, a division of Baker Publishing Group.

Printed in Mexico
Print Number: 1   Print Year: 2023

Second Time Around

1

Everyone moves on.

Everyone except for Mallory Farrell. At least that's how she felt as she drove home after her daughter's wedding. Mallory sighed. Dear Louisa had made such a beautiful bride and, thanks to all of Mallory's careful planning, it had been a gorgeous wedding. Picture-perfect down to the tiniest detail. Well, almost.

Mallory had suppressed the urge to growl when her ex-husband, dressed in a sleek black tux, escorted their youngest child down the aisle. Vince, who'd been mostly absent from their lives for nearly twenty years and now had a new wife with two young kids, had the gall to take center stage with the daughter Mallory had raised by herself. And when asked, "Who gives away the bride?" he proudly proclaimed, "I do." Oh, sure, he'd added "on behalf of the family" in a quieter tone, but Mallory had felt the sting.

Despite her pasted-on smile throughout the day's wedding festivities, Mallory was left with a bad taste in her mouth. She'd only learned Vince planned on coming during the wedding rehearsal. After she'd been so pleased to see her older son, Seth, practice-walk Louisa down the aisle, she'd imagined a repeat performance for today. But as they left the church, her younger son, Micah, had spilled the beans.

"Dad just texted me that his flight was delayed," he'd whispered, "but he'll be here in time tomorrow." She could tell by Micah's half smile that he'd felt conflicted too.

When her kids had questioned why her boyfriend wouldn't be there to share in the nuptial celebrations, Mallory had feigned nonchalance, saying she and Marcus were taking a break. After all, she didn't need her personal life to detract from Louisa's limelight. She sure didn't want them all to feel sorry for her when the truth was that Marcus, after almost four years, had suddenly decided he, too, wanted to move on. Just three days before the wedding where he was supposed to be her plus-one.

Despite Marcus's usual bad timing, Mallory had told herself it was for the best. Sure, the relationship had been handy when

8

it came to social functions. Marcus was charming and attractive and well-connected, but he'd always been more about Marcus than Mallory. Was it possible he'd viewed her as nothing more than the consummate escort? And maybe she deserved that. After all, everyone moved on eventually.

Mallory felt a weight fall upon her as she pulled up to the house she and Vince had purchased when Louisa was still in diapers. She'd loved this house then and loved it even more now. She'd been the one to urge Vince that it was a fantastic deal "for a fixer-upper." But the once-neglected property had quickly evolved into a serious money pit. Still, they'd been young and strong and motivated . . . at first. But this house put their unrealistic DIY dreams, as well as their marriage, to a severe test. A test that first drained them — and their bank account — then thrust them into two different directions and two completely new career paths. Well, that was water under the bridge now. Mallory was beyond this. Wasn't she?

Still, she felt an indescribable lostness as she unlocked the massive front door and walked into her big, lovely, *lonely* house. By now she'd fixed and renovated every square inch of the stately old Victorian. Her friends called it a showplace, which came in handy

9

for her interior design business. In her effort to be a stay-at-home mom, Mallory had converted the basement into a workspace years ago. But she'd always welcomed clients at her front door in order to show off the fruits of her efforts in her own home. Vain perhaps, but useful too.

She set her handbag on the cherry buffet in the foyer and picked up the small stack of mail she'd tossed there this morning. But before thumbing through it, she paused to admire the sunflowers, cosmos, and ferns she'd arranged in a bottle green vase. Sweet but simple perfection. Although this house had been built in the overly frilly Victorian era of gingerbread and fussy frills, Mallory had given it a more "grown-up" style — something all its own. People were usually surprised to discover her historical home wasn't filled with floral wallpaper and ornately carved antiques. Oh, there were a few well-selected old pieces, but the overall feel was more clean and sophisticated than fluffy and stuffy.

She'd offered to host the wedding reception in her home, especially since it had an early end time, but Marshall's parents had packed the guest list so full that everyone agreed a hotel reception was more practical. Still, Mallory had handled all the decorations, at both the church and the hotel, and she suspected some of the guests were still talking about it.

She kicked off her shoes and sighed. Life was good . . . *right*? She strolled through the living room where the last of the evening sunlight filtered through the massive maple tree outside. The yard looked so pretty in late May. But there was no one but her to enjoy it today. Mallory's sons and significant others had opted to stay over in the hotel. They hadn't said as much, but she imagined it was so they could whoop it up late into the night without bothering her. And that was fine. After all, everyone moves on.

"Oh, get over yourself," she said aloud as she opened a legal-size envelope. Talking to herself was a habit she'd acquired after Louisa had left home for college six years ago. "Be grateful your children have their own lives now and that they're not living under your roof, raiding your fridge, cluttering up your house — not like some of your friends' kids." But even as the thought crossed her mind, she wondered which was worse.

She turned her attention to the letterhead she'd pulled from the envelope. It was from an attorney named Lloyd Henley, from a law firm in Portside, Oregon — the town

11

Grandma Bess had resided in for most of her life, before passing away several months ago. Mallory had attended the funeral, which had been arranged by her mother's sister, Aunt Cindy. According to Aunt Cindy, all Grandma Bess left behind was a " 'worthless' little tourist shop and a mountain of debt." Not that Mallory had cared about any of that. Mostly she'd regretted not having spent more time with Grandma Bess in recent years. Especially since there was no good excuse.

Portside had felt like a second home during her childhood. How many summers had Mallory spent with Grandma Bess after her mother had died? She'd even taken her own children to visit when they were young — before adolescent lives grew too busy. Prior to her grandma's funeral, Mallory hadn't been to Portside for nearly ten years. She tried to maintain contact with cards and notes and phone calls on Grandma's birthday, but she regretted not making it over there more often.

Mallory reread the letter more carefully. According to Mr. Henley, Grandma Bess left Mallory her small tourist shop, including the small apartment above it. Mallory, pacing, reread the letter a third time. Aunt Cindy must've been wrong about Grandma's assets. Mr. Henley's letter claimed he had the title and keys and some paperwork and would present them to Mallory when she came to pick them up in the near future.

How strangely intriguing. Mallory was now the owner of a beachy tourist trap. Oh, she'd loved that dusty cluttered shop as a child. She'd laughed over the silly gag items, played with the cheap plastic toys, and been completely charmed by the seashells and glass balls that Grandma had wisely displayed on a higher shelf. Mallory had even worked in the shop as she'd grown older. Dusting, stocking, and sweeping until she was old enough to run the old cash register. What fun she'd had waiting on customers. She'd sometimes dreamed of having a shop just like Grandma's when she grew up. But then she grew up and things changed.

Still, the idea of taking a trip to the coast was surprisingly appealing. And if she hadn't invited her sons for Sunday brunch tomorrow, she'd take off right now. But all things in good time. She would spend the day with her boys and their girlfriends tomorrow. Then on Monday morning, she'd reschedule this week's appointments, make a hotel reservation, and leisurely venture on over for what she hoped would be an interesting trip down memory lane. It might even turn into a much-needed vacation. Perhaps she could pretend that, like everyone else, she was moving on too. At least for a week anyway.

Because she had no doubts that after her restful week in Portside, she'd come back here and get her nose to the grindstone again. That was what she did. And she had a long list of impatient clients with high expectations. Mrs. Denton wanted her entire house finished by early August for her family reunion. Sunshine Estate Realty wanted a bid to redo their lobby, and Alice Moore was still waiting for her high-end kitchen appliances to arrive. Perhaps Mallory would track those down from the coast.

Mallory was aware she'd inherited more than just her father's dark brown eyes, height, and prematurely gray hair. She ran her fingers through her thick, shoulder-length hair. It took her years to give up the dark brown dye she'd hidden behind since her late twenties, but ironically now that it was shiny and silver, people often assumed she had it done at the salon!

Besides Dad's physical looks, Mallory had been "blessed" with his workaholic ways. Early on she'd blamed her obsessive work ethic on being the only breadwinner, after Vince's disappearing act, but she suspected these habits went deeper than that, and although she'd always promised herself she'd slow down after the kids were launched, she was still going strong. And her clientele list was as demanding as ever. And growing. She'd get one client satisfied and, like Whac-A-Mole, two more would pop up. More people than ever wanted their homes redone these days.

Sometimes, usually around three in the morning, Mallory grew worried. What if she continued this hectic path — would she work herself to death and follow her father into an early grave? Sometimes, again only at three in the morning, she'd even feel her heart fluttering frantically, imagining it was giving out on her. But her last doctor's visit had confirmed she was in generally good health for her age.

Although death was one surefire way to move on, it wasn't something she felt ready for. Despite knowing fifty wasn't too far in her distant future, she still felt fairly young and fit. And if Louisa and Marshall had children as soon as Louisa hoped, Mallory could become a grandmother. Perhaps it was time to slow down some and reevaluate her life plan. And perhaps Grandma Bess was offering her the opportunity. God willing and the creek don't rise, she planned to check it out!

2

Mallory drove the old route to Portside, cruising along the rolling countryside where several new vineyards had popped up, then over the rugged Oregon Coast Range until she reached the first coastal town. Surprised to see how it had changed over the years, she continued southward, passing through more towns, each of them slightly smaller than the one before it. But they all had one thing in common: all appeared to have grown and improved. Finally, Mallory arrived in Portside, where, it seemed, nothing had changed. Although the familiarity was refreshing, she wondered why this small sleepy town felt somewhat left behind.

Not so unusual on a hot summer's day inland, the afternoon heat was quenched by a wide band of fog rolling in off the ocean. She turned off the AC in her SUV, opened a window, and inhaled the sea-scented cool air. It felt like being home again and she

17

suddenly missed Grandma Bess more than she imagined possible.

Instead of heading to her hotel like she'd intended, she drove straight to the attorney's office, just a block from her grandmother's old tourist shop, and picked up a folder containing the paperwork and keys to both the shop and the apartment above. Then, feeling slightly like a child on Christmas morning, she strolled down to the shop and let herself in the front door.

She was greeted with musty smells of old wood and damp cardboard and something else — had Grandma kept a cat? She flicked on the overhead lights, listening to the hum of the florescent tubes warming up. Then, taking her time, she strolled down the aisles of the funky old store. Nothing much had changed here either. Even the merchandise looked the same.

She picked up a plastic shark on a stick, testing to see if she could still make its jaws open and shut to the beat of the *Jaws* theme music. She ran a finger over a cribbage board with faux whale bone inlay and shook the dust off of a boxed puzzle of undersea creatures, absently wondering if some of these items might be considered "collectables" by now.

"Grandma Bess," she whispered, "what

do you want me to do with all these treasures?" She continued to peruse the narrow
aisles, exploring the cluttered shelves, laughing at some of the oddities she remembered,
and scratching her head. Seriously, what *did*
her grandmother expect her to do with this
merchandise? This shop? Why, when
Grandma had one living daughter and two
other granddaughters, had she left this shop
entirely to her youngest grandchild?

Mallory set the large envelope on the
counter, extracting the contents, and carefully examining the title and deed, insurance papers, tax papers, and a copy of her
grandmother's one-page will. Everything
seemed legit and official. According to
Lloyd Henley, Grandma Bess's second
mortgage, which she'd taken in order to
keep her shop afloat, would be covered by
the equity in her house on Second Street.
And since Grandma had already agreed to
sell it to a cash buyer, it was all taken care
of. So this shop and its entirety belonged to
Mallory. According to Lloyd, that had been
her grandma's last wish.

"Hello?" a voice called from the front of
the store, startling her.

"I'm sorry," she called back, "the store
isn't open for business."

"I'm not here to shop." The silhouette of

19

a tall man waved from the opened door. "May I come in?"

She peered curiously at him. He looked harmless enough in a pale-blue chambray shirt with the sleeves rolled up. "Sure," she said. "Just leave the door open a bit to allow some fresh air in."

The stranger took a few steps toward her then stuck out his hand. "I'm Grayson Matthews. I assume you're Bess's granddaughter Mallory."

"Yes." She shook his hand. "How did you know that?"

"Lloyd Henley's a friend of mine. He mentioned you'd be coming today."

She studied him more closely. Not bad-looking. Dark hair tinged with gray, easy smile, nice eyes. "You seem familiar."

"That's because you used to know me." He grinned. "I used to go by Todd, but for some reason that name seemed childish in college, so I started going by my middle name."

Todd Matthews? She blinked. "The lifeguard at the community pool?"

He chuckled. "Yeah, that was a long time ago. Haven't saved any lives lately."

She glanced down at his left hand, which was in his faded jeans pocket, then immediately regretted looking. What business

20

of hers was it whether he was married? Her cheeks grew warm to remember the teenage crush she'd nurtured on him at the tender age of fourteen. Thank goodness she hadn't faked drowning like other girls had done.

"I can't believe you still live here," she told him. "Have you stayed in Portside this whole time?"

"Guilty as charged." He shrugged, then smiled. "I just happen to love this little old town."

"I was surprised with how much the same it seems. It's like nothing changed."

His smile faded. "Yes, but that comes with its own set of problems."

"Such as?"

"Mostly the local economy. Lack of growth and tourism is hard on a lot of businesses." He waved his hand around the cluttered shop. "Like your grandmother's, for instance. Just not enough tourist traffic to keep everyone afloat. Bess made out okay because she didn't have a mortgage. But others have struggled."

She nodded. "I assume that means commercial real estate prices aren't too strong."

"Not right now. But" — his face brightened — "I'm a member of the chamber of commerce, and we've been developing some big plans for this town. Things might be improving if all goes well."

"Really?"

He nodded. "I'm not at freedom to announce anything, but it could be a game changer for Portside businesses."

"Well, that's exciting. I'm glad for you — and for Portside."

"So what are your plans?" he asked.

"Plans?" She wondered if he meant for dinner but suspected that was her stomach talking.

"You know, for this shop?" He crossed his arms. "Will you be listing it?"

"I, uh, I'm not entirely sure. I guess that's the best plan."

"Well, before you list it, would you consider selling it to me?"

She hadn't been expecting that. "I, uh, I'm not sure —"

"For fair market value, of course. I'm not looking for any special favors. But I'm very interested in this particular property. I think it has potential to become . . . well, something special." A gleam sparkled in his eye. "Something that would really help this town."

She didn't know what to say, which must have shone because Grayson continued, "I'm sorry. I probably overwhelmed you by bursting in on you like this. Corrina is always warning me I come on too strong. But when I'm enthused about something, well, I just don't keep it in."

She wanted to ask who Corrina was but knew that would sound nosy. "I do plan to be in town throughout the week," she said in her coolest business tone. "So perhaps you should decide what you'd like to offer for this property and, in the meantime, I'll think about whether I want to sell or not." For some reason his "enthused" interest in the shop ignited her own. What was she missing out on here?

"Yes, that's a good plan." He pulled out his cell phone. "Can we exchange numbers?"

She retrieved her phone from her bag and entered his number, resisting the urge to put the name Todd in place of Grayson. "It's nice to see you again." She smiled politely. "After all these years."

His blue eyes twinkled. "You're still just as pretty as ever, Mallory."

She pursed her lips doubtfully. "Do you seriously even remember me?"

He laughed. "Of course. Tall skinny girl with the long brown braids? A too-big T-shirt with a red-and-white bikini underneath?"

She tried to cover her shock — he *did*

23

remember her!

"And you always hung out with Sandi Brower."

"That's right. I'd nearly forgotten about Sandi. Her parents used to own the ice-cream shop. Is that still there?"

He nodded. "Sandi runs it now."

"So she stayed here?" Mallory remembered them sharing their big dream ideas over sundaes with hot fudge. Sandi had wanted to live in Paris.

Grayson grimaced. "She came back a couple years ago . . . messy divorce."

"Oh. That's too bad."

"Anyway, I remember you and Sandi weren't as obnoxious as some of the other girls. You know the ones, always flirting and teasing and pretending to drown just to force me to jump into the pool."

She couldn't help but laugh.

"You might not have known, but I was painfully shy back then. My parents kind of forced me into the lifeguard job. I didn't have much confidence and that first year was pretty intimidating."

"I never would've guessed."

Grayson checked his watch. "Well, sorry to take up your time. I'll call you later this week to find out if you plan to sell or not."

She felt herself softening. "I can't say for

sure just yet, but I'm fairly sure I'll sell. And if you offer a fair price, I see no reason not to sell to you."

His face lit up as he stuck out his hand. "Great. It's a deal."

They shook on it, but before he released her hand, she felt an odd tingling sensation running up her arm. Once again, her cheeks grew warm and she was relieved that he had turned away, reaching for the door before abruptly spinning around.

"Hey, how about joining me for a meal? Doesn't have to be dinner. Maybe just a cup of coffee?" he asked in an uncertain tone.

"Sure, why not." In the back of her mind, she still wondered who Corrina was . . . and why she even cared.

"Great. I won't trouble you anymore today. You probably have things to do and need to get settled. How about tomorrow?"

"Tomorrow works." Her eyes went to his hand on the doorknob. No wedding ring.

He nodded. "I'll shoot you a text in the morning."

After he left, Mallory locked the door then leaned against it to catch her breath and steady herself. *Todd Matthews.* Well, Grayson Matthews now. But still good-looking. And he seemed genuinely nice. And he

25

wanted to get together with her tomorrow. And he didn't seem married. Although how could one be certain? She took in another deep breath. How was it, after all these years, she felt like a fourteen-year-old again?

But who was Corrina? In need of a distraction, Mallory decided to venture up to the apartment. Grandma Bess had always kept the space rented out and had always been emphatic that Mallory respect the tenant's space. Of course, this only made Mallory more curious. According to Lloyd Henley, there'd been no tenants for the past few years. He'd also warned her that the apartment was in need of serious repair.

As a young teenager, Mallory had been fascinated with the idea of a living space above Grandma's shop. She'd even imagined ousting the tenant and taking up residency there herself after she turned eighteen. So one time, while her grandma was getting groceries and Mallory was minding the shop — with no customers about — she'd sneaked the brass key Grandma kept hidden under the change tray in the register, then tiptoed up the narrow staircase and let herself in.

The apartment had a sickeningly sweet musky aroma. Maybe it was incense or maybe something rotten. The place was wildly colorful with brightly painted walls and fabrics, but it all looked messy. Empty bottles of booze and fast-food packages were littered about, as well as some scanty clothing and a few other curious items. She felt so weird being up there that she couldn't even force herself to go into the bedroom. Mallory didn't put two and two together at the time, but she suspected now that the woman living upstairs had possibly been a prostitute. Which could've been the reason her grandma so adamantly forbid Mallory to go up there.

Now Mallory turned the brass key in the door, bracing herself for a sleazy stinky bordello. Instead, she saw an unkempt, neglected apartment, with the most hideous wall colors. Lloyd Henley had been right — it was definitely in need of some serious repairs. But instead of writing it off, like some would do, she put on her designer cap and started to toy with the idea of fixing it up. Gut the kitchen and bath. Save the old baseboard and trim and what looked like pine plank floors. Replace and enlarge the windows to capitalize on the ocean view. She looked up to the ceiling, which was nearly ten feet tall but was covered in ugly circa 1950 panels. Hopefully there was no asbestos.

Of course, it would take a team of carpenters, plumbers, electricians, tile installers, cabinet makers, painters, and so on. And who knew what was available in this one-horse town? But with the right touches, and a boatload of money, this space could be amazing. She pulled up the broken mini blinds and peered out the dirt-encrusted window to spy an ocean view! Suddenly this apartment became much more valuable. But did its real value equal the investment? Probably not.

"What're you thinking?" she asked herself. "Just sell the kit-n-caboodle to Grayson Matthews and get out of town. That's what any sensible person would do."

Still, she wondered, hadn't she been a sensible person her entire adult life? Maybe it was time to stop being sensible. But that would mean telling Grayson Matthews no — that she wouldn't sell to him. And for some unfathomable reason, Mallory wanted to make Grayson happy. She wanted to see his clear blue eyes light up again. But maybe that was just childish.

3

Although the air was cooled by the fog, Mallory had a hankering for ice cream. Pulling her fisherman knit cardigan more snugly around her, she hightailed it to Brower's Ice Cream Parlor two blocks down. Of course, by the time she got there she was more interested in a hot cup of coffee than ice cream, but the tattooed teenager behind the ice-cream counter didn't seem to care.

"If ya want ice cream, ya come here. If ya want coffee, ya go down the street to Portside Brew," she said with an eye roll.

"Right." Mallory glanced around. "Is Sandi Brower around?"

The girl leaned her elbows onto the glass case. "Ya mean Sandi *Simmons*?"

"She used to be a Brower. Yes. Sandi Simmons. I believe she's your boss." Mallory gave her a warning look that floated right over the girl's head.

"Sandi!" she yelled over her shoulder.

"Someone here wants you."

Mallory walked over to the door that led to the back room.

"What is it?" a short blond asked.

"Sandi?" Mallory didn't even have to ask. "Remember me? Mallory —"

"Mallory Harris!" Sandi threw her arms around her. "I can't believe it."

Mallory hugged her. "It's Mallory Farrell now."

"Yeah, I was Sandi Simmons, but I'm going back to my maiden name."

"I heard you got divorced." Mallory grimaced. "Me too. But mine was almost twenty years ago."

"You were smarter than me and got out quick." Sandi wrinkled her nose. "What're you doing in Portside?"

"Right now I am looking for a cup of coffee. No offense, but ice cream sounds too cold for this weather."

"Let's go to Portside Brew." Sandi was already grabbing a parka from a hook by the door. "I could use some caffeine too."

The wind was starting to blow as they hurried down Main Street. "After growing up here, I still get caught by surprise when we get these cold summer days," Sandi said. "Probably the result of living in Southern California for too long."

30

"I heard you've been back here a couple years," Mallory said as they went into the coffee shop.

"Not quite two years." Sandi rubbed her hands together to warm them. "Mom had been running the ice-cream parlor by herself after Dad died. Then my marriage fell apart, and I thought, Why not go home?" She paused to greet the young man behind the counter and order her coffee. Then she turned to Mallory with a grin. "I guess it's not true what they say, you *can* go home again."

"What'll ya have?" the barista asked Mallory.

"Uh, a latte with whole milk. Thanks." She glanced around the mostly empty coffee shop as she paid him. "Kinda quiet in here."

He shrugged. "Pretty typical afternoon."

Sandi made a face. "Pretty typical of this whole town. It's always quiet." She led Mallory to a table by the window that looked out over the ocean.

"It's such a great location. I can't believe it's not packed in here." Mallory gazed out at the amazing view and sighed. "But to be honest, I'm glad it's not. I get tired of waiting in lines in the city. And that's for places with no view like this. But you can just walk in here, get a table and a coffee, no problem.

31

Makes no sense."

"Yeah. When I first got back, I was stunned that Portside hadn't grown more. Mom just takes it in stride, but a lot of businesses are having troubles."

"I've heard that, but I don't get it." Mallory paused as the barista set down their coffees.

"It's because of city codes," Sandi said. "Back in the late 1990s they got all worried about expansion and growth and created all these rules and restrictions to keep it in check."

"Well, I guess it is kind of nice that Portside hasn't changed much."

"I know. I felt like that when I first got here. But then I see how our ice-cream parlor is barely hanging on . . . and I get worried."

Mallory considered this. "You know, I only got here this afternoon and I already got an offer to sell my grandma's shop."

"Is that why you're here?" Sandi asked.

Mallory nodded, then explained her inheritance. "I came here planning to sell it, but I want to stick around for the week and just think about it."

"Who offered?" Sandi leaned forward with interest.

Mallory smirked. "Our old lifeguard friend."

"Grayson Matthews, aka Todd Matthews?"

Mallory grinned. "Yes."

"I like Grayson better. Sounds more sophisticated." She sipped her coffee. "So, is that who you're selling to? Grayson?"

"He's very interested. He said he has a plan for it. Something that will help this town."

Sandi frowned. "Did you ask him what his plan was?"

"No. But I promised to consider his offer." She took the lid off her latte and blew on the steaming liquid.

Sandi shook her head. "I don't trust him, Mallory."

"Seriously? Why?"

"I'm worried he's trying to make a fast buck. Rumor has it he's talking to some big developers that want to turn Portside into a giant indoor mall."

"What?"

"I know, I know." She held up her hands. "It sounds crazy. But that's what I heard. And your grandma's shop might be the only thing standing in his way."

Mallory felt a rush of indignation. "Well, he can't do that. I won't sell to him if that's

33

his plan."

"Good for you." Sandi nodded, taking a sip of her drink. "What a relief."

"I'm not sure what I'll do, but I will *not* let him take Grandma Bess's shop," Mallory said, getting worked up. "He'd probably want to demolish it for his stupid indoor mall."

"We've been holding out too. But our ice-cream shop isn't exactly a kingpin location. We're on the fringe, and he could easily develop without our cooperation."

"What about the other businesses?" Mallory tried to remember what flanked her grandma's shop. "Is the shoe shop still there? And the Chic Boutique?"

"The Chic Boutique nearly gave up during the pandemic, but Caroline Kempton still keeps it open. Mostly for her employees' sake, I think. I've heard they're hanging on by a thread. Or maybe it's a shoelace." She smiled.

"And the chamber really thinks an indoor mall would help?" Mallory cringed to imagine an ugly mall in this town. "Why?"

Sandi pointed out the window where the thick fog was enveloping the street. "The weather. They think indoor shopping would be a draw."

"But the weather is part of the charm. I

happen to like the fog. And a lot of tourists come here just to escape the summer heat."

"Maybe, but for some reason they're not coming often enough." Sandi frowned. "I get that businesses are hurting. I just don't think an indoor mall is the answer."

"No. Portside isn't that kind of town," Mallory declared. "It needs its small shops with their big personalities. That quaintness alone should be a tourist attraction."

"It *should* be. But the chamber doesn't see it that way."

"I hate indoor malls." She picked up her coffee mug. "Honestly, didn't they go out in the past millennium?"

"Apparently not." Sandi held up her coffee mug like a toast. "But here's to you keeping things in check, Mallory. Looks like you got here just in time."

Mallory clinked her mug against Sandi's. "Here's to Portside staying the same, but only better."

"Better?" Sandi seemed to consider this. "What do you think we could do to improve things?"

"Not an indoor mall. But it does make me wonder . . . what *would* make Portside better?" Of course, Mallory had to ask herself, what difference did it truly make to her? And what possible difference could she make to the small town? Oh, she loved this place and her childhood memories from visiting here, but what could she do in just one week?

Mallory couldn't remember when she'd slept so well in a hotel, but she attributed it more to the sound of the ocean than the firm mattress or amenities of the hotel. The next morning, after refusing the offer of complimentary coffee in the lobby, she found herself talking to the hotel clerk. "Usually I find hotels noisy" — Mallory pulled on her cardigan — "but yours is so quiet, I could easily hear the waves."

"That's because we're running pretty low for the summer season. Hopefully it'll pick up soon." He frowned as he did something on his computer. "Otherwise, we might go under."

"Really?" She glanced around the lackluster lobby. "That would be sad."

He shrugged. "It's been a rough few years. We're hoping this summer will turn things around."

She resisted the urge to run her finger across the dusty oak coffee table in front of a faded sofa, and she had to hold her tongue from suggesting that the fake palm tree in the corner should go or that a mini makeover to freshen up the lobby probably wouldn't hurt. Instead, she told the clerk to have a nice day and set out on her way. Her plan was to walk through the small town's business district, which would take only a few minutes. But she wanted to study things . . . and think. Despite her conversation with Sandi yesterday, she was having second thoughts about talking to Grayson about selling her property. Just talking. But first she wanted to do her research.

Several businesses were boarded up and vacant, and a couple of new ones seemed to be doing okay, including Darma's Deli and the Port Wine Shop, but they were beyond the section of town that Mallory suspected Grayson was most interested in for his indoor mall. Several businesses she remembered from childhood were still there. She passed the Red Hen Café, where Grandma Bess used to take her for lunch, and Fisherman's Wharf Restaurant, which had been only for special occasions, but both were closed. Not that unusual for a Tuesday.

She strolled back to her grandma's shop, pausing to look at it from across the street. If she were a tourist, would she cross the street to check it out? Of course not. Besides looking like a cheesy tourist trap, it was dowdy and run-down and basically uninviting. Definitely not her cup of tea. She tilted her head to one side and, squinting her eyes, tried to imagine it differently.

The stucco siding needed a good paint job. Maybe a creamy white with black or charcoal trim around the big windows that were worth keeping. Canvas awnings could give the storefront some charm, as well as a place for tourists to shelter when it was raining. But would canvas take a beating in a storm? Maybe a metal awning that looked like canvas would be wiser. Then she'd place a big handsome planter on each side of the doors, filled with well-maintained plants. And perhaps an attractive metal bench on one side to keep it from feeling too symmetrical.

Pleased with the design she'd created in her head, she decided to continue with this imagination game by going inside. What would she do in there? As she unlocked the old wooden door with its glass window, she wondered what might lie beneath all those layers of paint. It might actually be pretty.

Inside the shop, she felt overwhelmed by all the shelves and clutter. Closing her eyes for a moment, she imagined wiping it all away, creating a clean slate. Opening her eyes, instead of being distracted by what she saw, she followed the lines of the walls and realized the shop was actually larger than she thought. She wished she had a tape measure. "You need to clear all this stuff out," she told herself as she walked to the back. "But how?"

She'd seen liquidation sales before. When they involved interior design items, she was always glad to pick up some pieces at reduced prices. She wasn't sure this merchandise had any real value, but why not try? At the very least, she could give it all away. But why not hold a liquidation sale first? She pulled out her phone and did a quick search. There was a liquidation company in a nearby town. Out of curiosity, she called them and when a friendly sounding woman named Phyllis answered, Mallory explained the situation involving her grandmother's business.

"The challenge is that I'm only in town for a week," Mallory said. "But I'd really like the place cleared out."

Phyllis asked a few business questions, confirming that Mallory wasn't too concerned with the value of the merchandise. "It's mostly just tourist junk," Mallory admitted. "Of course, one man's trash is another man's treasure."

Phyllis laughed. "That's true."

"It's what my grandma used to say." Mallory gazed around the shop with a pang. Was she wrong to liquidate everything?

"I have an idea." Phyllis paused. "I have a friend with a tourist shop right here in my town. Claudia was just saying how much difficulty she's had with some of her usual orders. Some imported items have gotten harder to find. I wonder if she might be interested. Can I take your number and call you back?"

Mallory eagerly agreed, and after ending the call, she shot up a quick prayer — asking God to lead her. Then she began walking through the shop. Despite her emotional ties to her grandmother, she knew she couldn't hold on to all these things. But was there anything in here that she might want to save? Just as a memento? Something she might want to pass on to future grandchildren some day?

She got a cardboard box and filled it with some funky toys and curious items, then stopped in front of the shell shelf. Although everything was covered in a layer of dust, she knew at once that she wanted everything on this shelf. After locating a large box, a dust rag, and some tissue paper, she cleaned and wrapped all the shells and glass balls and carefully packed them away. She was just taping the box closed when her phone rang.

"My friend is very interested," Phyllis told her. "And since her shop is closed on Tuesdays, she asked if she could pop on down to Portside to take a look today."

"Yes, of course."

"Great. I'll give Claudia your phone number."

Mallory thanked her then, feeling delighted with this possibility, she shot up another prayer. This time she asked God to direct her through this whole process. "If it's not your will for me to continue in this direction, please, dear God, just close the door."

She decided to poke around in the back room while she waited for Claudia to arrive. Perhaps there were things back there that needed to be saved. But mostly she found more boxes of the same merchandise that filled the shelves out front. T-shirts and trinkets and junk. The only thing that interested her was a tape measure she unearthed in a drawer. She grabbed a child's drawing pad and a set of pencils from the coloring books section and went to work measuring and drawing a makeshift blueprint of the shop. Before long, she was playing with elevations. She was just sketching in the windows when her phone rang. Seeing it was Grayson, she was tempted to ignore the call, but thought the grown-up thing was to answer it and gently but firmly let him down.

"Hello, Grayson," she said in her business voice. "How are you?"

"Just fine, thanks. Even better now that I have you on the other end."

The warmth in his voice caught her off guard.

"So I was hoping we could meet for coffee this morning."

"Oh, I'm sorry. I'm here in my grandmother's shop, waiting for a liquidator."

"Really? You're certainly a woman of action. I'm impressed."

"It seems a good idea to clear things out." She studied her rough elevation sketches, wishing for a drafting ruler and T square.

"Although I should've told you I'm fine with purchasing everything as is, Mallory. I don't want to make work for you. I can hire someone to handle the liquidation. I know you only planned to be here for a week and liquidations take time."

"The woman I'm waiting for isn't exactly a liquidator. She's a shop owner who might be interested in purchasing the inventory."

"That's even better. Good for you. Now

I'm even more impressed."

"So, anyway, as far as coffee goes . . . well, I'm sort of tied up this morning."

"How about lunch?"

She rubbed the back of her neck. "I think I'll be busy for most of the day."

"How about dinner then?"

"Well, I —"

"You have to eat, don't you?" He sounded slightly hurt. "Or maybe you're trying to give me a subtle hint. I've been told I can be socially dense sometimes. I'm sorry, Mallory."

She softened up again. "Okay, you're right. I do have to eat. I'll have dinner with you."

"You will?" His tone brightened. "That's great. We can make it whatever time works best for you. Early, late, you name it."

"How about six thirty?"

"Perfect. Where can I pick you up? Your hotel?"

"How about if we meet at the restaurant?"

"Yeah, that works. How about Fisherman's Wharf at six thirty?"

"Sounds great. I'll see you then." As she told him goodbye, she suspected this was a mistake. Was she leading him on regarding her interest in selling? It's not like this would be an actual date. He wanted her property — not her. She wondered if she should just tell him up front that she didn't plan to sell to him. Then if he still wanted to share a meal with her, she'd insist on Dutch treat and do her best to keep it impersonal.

4

Claudia turned out to be surprisingly fun. Although she probably wasn't much older than Mallory, she reminded her of Grandma Bess as she went up and down the aisles, exclaiming with delight at every new discovery.

"Oh, I love these." Claudia held up a clear bag of miniature plastic sea creatures. She pointed to a stack of ocean-themed jigsaw puzzles. "And I just had a customer asking for a seascape puzzle. All I had were dogs and cats."

When it came time to strike a deal, Claudia wasn't sure she could afford everything, but she clearly wanted it.

"What if you make a down payment, take everything, and then make me payments?" Mallory said, leaning against one of the old shelves.

Claudia reached out and grabbed Mallory's arm. "You'd let me do that?"

"Sure." She smiled. "You remind me of my grandmother. I think it would make her happy to know all this stuff is finding a good home with you."

"Oh, that would be fabulous." She touched a rack of books. "What about your fixtures? Do you want to sell those too?"

"I'd be glad to." Mallory studied the woman. "But would your shop have room?"

"No, but I could use them in our warehouse, you know, to help with storage."

"That's great! How soon would you be able to pick everything up?"

"Well, Phyllis told me you were in a hurry to liquidate. I could have my husband and sons get a rental truck and drive down here this week. My husband's retired, but he helps me with my business. And my boys owe me a favor or two."

They shook hands on the agreed price and, after Phyllis made some calls, she offered to have everything cleared out by Thursday. As Mallory walked her to the front of the store, she could hardly believe what she'd just done. In two days, the store would be cleared out. Amazing. But then what?

It wasn't until she was back in her hotel room that Mallory began to question herself. She had no intention of selling to Grayson and planned to make that clear tonight. But what would she do with the property now? Would it have been easier to sell it as a tourist shop? Maybe to someone like Claudia, who would enjoy selling trinkets the way Grandma Bess had? Had Mallory moved too quickly? Didn't her grandmother always say "haste makes waste"?

Mallory pulled out the drawing pad, opening it up to look at her sketches and measurements. She'd spent the afternoon going over and over them, even drawing an artistic elevation of the front of the shop to show how charming it could be. She'd even tinted it with colored pencils. *But why?* What was the point? Why was she still so obsessed with these drawings?

Seeing that it was already five thirty and she felt as dust-encrusted as the back room of the shop, she decided to take a shower and get ready for dinner. Not that she was looking forward to breaking the news to Grayson. She still hadn't decided whether she'd tell him before or after dinner. After sounded less stressful, but what if he pressed her while they were eating? Oh, why had she agreed to meet him at all? Perhaps she should just text that she was bailing. She could claim a headache, but she didn't like to lie. She could say she was tired, but truth

47

be told, she felt highly energized from all the creativity that had been flowing through her today. Although she felt like she was keeping a lid on a pot that threatened to boil over, she knew a silly old dream was simmering there. Something she was afraid to seriously consider.

Distracting herself by carefully dressing for dinner, Mallory tried on several combinations before deciding on a simple ensemble of sleek black pants topped with a pale-gray silk blouse. She accented the modest outfit with silver and pearl beads, silver hoop earrings, and a silver bracelet. Casually elegant. She glanced at the clock and noticed it was already six thirty, and she was about to be elegantly late.

As she drove the short distance to the waterfront restaurant, she rehearsed various conversation topics. She would inquire about his family, career, hobbies, and anything else to keep him talking. If that didn't work, she would talk about herself. Anything to get them through dinner without having to discuss her decision not to sell to him. If that were even possible.

She was ten minutes late by the time she told the pretty hostess she was meeting someone. "Grayson Matthews?" the woman asked with interest.

"Yes." She nodded. "That's right."

"This way." The woman led her through the dimly lit restaurant. Just like Mallory remembered from her youth, the tables had white cloths, glowing votive candles, and miniature and slightly boring flower arrangements.

"Good evening." Grayson stood to welcome her. He was dressed in a navy sports jacket, pale-blue shirt, and dark tie. Like a gentleman, he even pulled out her chair.

"Sorry to be late." She smiled nervously.

"No problem. I took the liberty of ordering a bottle of wine. I hope you like rosé. They say it goes with almost anything."

"I'm not much of a wine drinker," she said as he began to fill her glass. "But sure, I'll have some. Thanks."

They made small talk while perusing the menu. Then the server came, and Grayson asked if she liked steamer clams. When she said yes, he ordered them for appetizers. Then he asked if she liked lobster and again she said yes and he ordered the lobster dinner for two. She thought of protesting, but then decided not to rock the boat. Besides, she was hungry.

After the server left, Mallory told Grayson about the first time she came here. "It was with my grandmother on my twelfth birthday. For some reason I'd gotten it into my head that twelve was quite grown up and that I deserved a fancy dinner. Unfortunately, I was still a pretty picky eater back then. I didn't like any of the seafood items on the menu. Finally, Grandma asked if they could make me a cheeseburger. And they did."

He laughed.

"But they brought me a complimentary dessert that I'll never forget. The richest, moistest, most delicious piece of chocolate cake ever."

"They still have a killer chocolate cake here. Can't remember what it's called." He sipped his wine. "Did you ever come back here after your twelfth birthday?"

"Not until I was sixteen. I'd acquired a slightly more sophisticated palate by then."

"Was that with your grandmother too?"

"No, that was with Sandi." Mallory smiled at the memory. "We dressed up and acted as if we were very grown up. Sandi even tried to order a martini, but they asked for her ID and that was that."

He held up his wineglass. "Well, here's to being old enough to order a martini without ID."

"Yes, there's definitely no problem with that now." She clinked her glass against his.

"I haven't been asked for ID since I stopped coloring my hair."

"I must say, I think your silver hair is very attractive."

Her cheeks warmed with pleasure. "I'm surprised you recognized me. Sometimes old friends are taken aback when they see the silver. The first time my ex saw it, he had the nerve to call me Grandma Mal."

His brows arched. "So you have an ex?"

She shrugged. "Yes. For almost two decades now." She told him about raising her three kids on her own. "But my ex is happy. He remarried about ten years ago, has a couple kids, lives far enough away that we don't have to bump into each other." She didn't mention his surprising appearance at Louisa's wedding.

"You say you supported your children. What do you do?"

Hoping to pass more time as they started on the steamer clams, she told him about her career in interior design. "I had an art degree when I got married, but no plans for how to use it." She explained about fixing up her Victorian home. "My friends loved what I did, and suddenly I was doing design work for others. Finally, I realized I needed more training, so I took a correspondence course, learned a bit about drafting, and then my business really took off."

"Good for you." He nodded. "You mentioned three children. I assume they're grown?"

Mallory took a sip of her ice water. "Yes. My baby Louisa just left the nest and got married. Not that she'd been back home for long, but it had been nice having her around after she finished college. My sons Seth and Micah are twenty-seven and twenty-five, respectively." She dabbed her mouth with her napkin. "How about you? Any children?" Although still curious about Corrina, she didn't want to ask about a wife. Seeing no wedding ring, she assumed that he, like her, was likely divorced.

"I have a son and daughter. Lindsey is twenty-four and Garret's twenty-two."

"Do they live in Portside?"

"Garret's in the Navy. Stationed on the East Coast right now. Lindsey lives in town. She's a grade school teacher. Just like her mother." He sighed. "In so many ways."

Mallory didn't know how to respond to that. Unless she was mistaken, there was a longing in his voice. Perhaps he and his wife were separated.

"And your career?" she asked in an effort to segue the conversation.

Grayson cleared his throat. "I've been in

construction most of my adult life. My dad was a contractor. I worked for him then got my own license and took over his company when he retired. In recent years, I've tried to get out of the actual construction and more into development. Easier on the body." He grinned. "But I kept my license. Just in case."

"Probably smart. You never know what's going to happen in our economy." She paused as their entrées were set on the table. As they ate, she told him about the various contractors she'd worked with over the years. Some she greatly respected and some not so much.

"I could probably echo that with some of the designers I've worked with." He chuckled. "There's this old gal — Elizabeth Jones — who recently retired. And I swear she was at least eighty and possibly suffering from some memory issues. I hated to work with her. She was always changing her mind but acted like she hadn't or like it was my fault. Like I'd forgotten something. Some called her Queen Elizabeth because she acted like the queen of Portside, but take it from me, that woman was a royal pain."

Mallory laughed. "Then why did you work with her?"

"What could I do if my client had already

committed to her?"

She forked a piece of lobster. "Yes, that is tricky."

"Now there's only one active designer in town, Vicki Strong. She's not half bad."

"Not half bad?" She shook her head. "That's not too flattering."

"Well, at least Vicki doesn't change her mind. But sometimes I wish she would. It's like she does the same thing over and over. Everything is midcentury modern with her. No matter what kind of house. Gets boring after a while."

"I can imagine."

"What kind of style do you lean toward?"

"That's a good question." She paused to think. "My personal style leans more toward traditional with an artistic edge. But I try to get to know my clients and their homes and their goals . . . . and then I try to create something that fits their sensibilities."

"That sounds nice."

"Yes, it keeps me from getting bored with my work. I know it sounds cliché, but I like to think everyone's home has a story. I like to help them tell their story."

"That doesn't sound cliché to me."

"Probably because you don't hang out with a lot of designers. Sometimes our vocabulary gets overused." She smiled. They were both finished with the meal and so far not one word about purchasing the shop had come up.

The server came to refill their water glasses, then asked if they wanted to see the dessert tray. "What about that fabulous chocolate cake?" Grayson asked. "Have you got any of that?"

"Of course. It's our specialty."

Grayson looked at Mallory, but she waved her hand. "I've already had too much."

"Bring us one piece," Grayson told the server. "Two forks." He winked. "And how about some coffee? Do you have a fresh pot of decaf?"

"We will," the server promised.

"Two cups," Grayson told him.

Mallory wanted to protest, but a good cup of decaf actually sounded amazing. And perhaps just one bite of that chocolate cake, just to see if it was as good as she remembered.

"I hope you don't mind that we're not discussing your property," Grayson said. "I don't enjoy talking business over a good meal."

"I don't mind at all." She sighed in relief.

"But perhaps we could do it over coffee? Tomorrow?"

Her stomach tightened. "I have a lot going on tomorrow," she said quickly. "I need to get things ready for Claudia."

"Who's Claudia?"

"The woman who's purchasing all the old merchandise. I want to go through everything more carefully, make sure I'm not letting go of anything I'll regret." She frowned. "To be honest, I'm a little worried I've moved too quickly. I really liked this woman, and her enthusiasm reminds me of my grandmother, but then I started wondering what Grandma Bess would think. Would she be sad to think I'm getting rid of everything?"

"If Claudia reminds you of your grandmother, it seems she would approve."

"I don't know." She slowly shook her head. "I still can't figure out why Grandma left it all to me. She has two other granddaughters. And a daughter too." She told him about losing her mother as a child and how Grandma Bess kept her in the summers. "So I guess I was closer to her than the other girls."

"She must've loved you a lot." Grayson's expression grew more serious. "Enough to trust the future of her shop with you."

Mallory studied him closely. Did he suspect she was having second thoughts about him too? Did he have any idea she had already decided not to sell to him? And, in that case, what did she actually plan to do with the soon-to-be-empty shop? But the server was bringing their coffee and chocolate cake now. She would have to think about the future of her grandmother's shop later.

5

Mallory was able to keep Grayson at bay for the next day. True to her word, she did spend the day poking around, organizing, cleaning — *and dreaming.* Then on Thursday morning, Claudia's crew of young men showed up.

"Does everything go?" Claudia's husband looked around the crowded room.

"Everything you see in here," she told him. By now she'd put the things she wanted to save in the back room, though it wasn't very much. Silly as it seemed, she'd decided to hold on to the old cash register. It wasn't exactly an antique, but it was old enough to be interesting. And the fact that she'd used it as a teenager made it feel a bit special too. She would decide what to do with it later.

With the three men working together, it didn't take too long to clear the place out. Claudia's husband gave Mallory the check for the amount they'd settled on and promised that the additional payments would be made monthly for the next year as agreed upon. As they shook hands, she realized that although she trusted him and Claudia, she wouldn't actually care if she never received another payment. She was just glad those things were finding a good home and she now had an empty space.

After Claudia's movers were gone, Mallory went to work washing the windows. Then she swept and even mopped the wood floor, using a lemony soap that almost eradicated the musty aroma and made the worn pine planks gleam. With a coat of stain and sealer, they would look like a million bucks. She even ran a damp rag over the six-inch baseboard. Like the window trim, the wood appeared to be old growth fir. It looked like it had never been painted and was in surprisingly good shape. It gave her hope for the old door. Perhaps the wood beneath that gummy paint had potential too.

Despite the obnoxiously flickering florescent lights, she could almost imagine this space being transformed into an attractive shop. If it wasn't already midafternoon, she'd be tempted to run down to the hardware store for a gallon of paint to clean up the walls. Maybe tomorrow. Or not.

Really, what was she trying to accomplish here? Even if she got the store looking fabulous, there were other vacated properties that hadn't sold. Other than Grayson, it was possible that no one would make her an offer. And yet, she felt compelled to keep working on it. Maybe it was the designer in her, that simmering dream, or simply that she wanted to "move on," but she felt determined to keep improving Grandma Bess's old store. And with each step along the way, she silently prayed, begging God to direct her path.

She was just dumping the dirty mop water in the backroom sink when she heard someone knocking on the front door. With a strong suspicion of who it might be, she took a quick glance at her rather disheveled image in the cloudy mirror above the sink, then wondered why she should even care. Wiping her damp hands on her jeans, she went to open the door.

"Hello, Grayson." She smiled brightly. "What can I do for you?"

"I noticed that moving van had come and gone. I tried your phone, but you didn't answer, so I thought I'd just pop in." He held out a white paper bag. "And I brought treats."

"Treats?" Her stomach grumbled and she

realized she had skipped lunch.

"Just cranberry-orange scones and coffees." His dark brows arched as he glanced around the shop. "Wow, this doesn't look like the same place at all."

"No, it's quite transformed." She jerked a thumb backward. "We could use the checkout counter as a table."

She led him back and watched as he carefully arranged their makeshift table with napkins and scones and coffee. "Very nice," she told him as she popped off a lid.

"Well, I thought you might need a break." He removed two creamers and sugar packets and a stir stick. "I remembered you don't take your coffee black but couldn't remember about sugar."

"No sugar, but I do like a little cream. Thanks."

He picked up his coffee, then looked around the space again. "I honestly can't believe this is the same shop."

"It has some exciting potential."

He nodded without saying anything, then sipped his coffee.

"I think my grandmother would be happy to see it cleaned up like this." She broke off a piece of her scone. "I wonder if this is how it looked when she first started the shop, after World War II, when everything was fresh and new."

"She had it for that long?"

"Yes. Her husband was a war veteran. He was about ten years older than her, and she was only sixteen when they first met. But they got married when she turned seventeen. And he bought the shop for her. It might sound corny, but it was her dream to have a tourist shop."

"That's a good story." He took a bite of his scone.

"I never met my grandfather. He died when my mom was a teenager. But Grandma still had her business as a means of support."

"Well, he must've been a good man to have supported his young wife like that in her business venture."

She nodded. "I always liked hearing about that from her. He really was a good man." She didn't mention that she'd been disappointed to marry a man who was nothing like her grandfather when it came to supporting his wife, financially or otherwise.

"So you've invested a lot of time and energy cleaning this place up. . . ." His voice trailed off like there was a question behind the statement.

"Yes, and you're probably wondering why." She stirred her coffee.

"It's crossed my mind. But how about if I take a wild guess?"

"Go for it."

"You've decided not to sell, after all."

She shrugged. "I'm not totally sure yet. But I have made one decision." She felt slightly guilty for finishing off the scone he'd so kindly brought to her. But she reminded herself, he was just trying to win her over in order to get this property. "I decided that I cannot sell my grandmother's shop to you, Grayson. Not because you're not a nice guy. But because I don't like what you plan to do with it."

He frowned. "What does that mean?"

"It means, I've heard of your plans to create an indoor mall."

"Who told you *that*?"

She considered this. "I don't think my source matters. Unless the information I received is wrong." She looked into his eyes. "Do you plan to turn this property, and the ones around it, into an indoor mall?"

"It's not how it sounds, Mallory." He swiped some crumbs from the counter.

"But it's true, right? You do plan to knock down the existing shops to build a mall?"

He simply nodded.

"Besides not wanting to see my grandma's shop demolished, I'm not a fan of malls.

No offense, but I thought they went out with video stores and arcades."

"That's not exactly what I had in mind. I have some sketches in my truck. It's a very attractive mall, with a courtyard outside and covered walkways and green spaces and planters. It could be a fantastic asset to Portside."

She sighed. "Well, if that's true, I hope you get to pursue it. But not at the expense of my grandma's shop."

"Without this space, it will be very difficult." He set his coffee cup down.

"I'm sorry, Grayson, but this space is not for sale."

"Not for sale to anyone? Or just me?"

She thought for a moment, gathering her resolve. "Not to anyone. I think this shop deserves to go a second time around. Maybe I do too because I'm considering using this space myself."

"What for?" His brow creased.

She took in a deep breath. "I've always had this little dream. Or maybe it's a big one. I've never actually told a living soul — well, besides God." She made a shaky smile. "But I've dreamt of running an interior design shop in a quaint neighborhood. An attractive backdrop to fill with my favorite things."

He looked doubtful. "And you would run this shop?"

"That's right."

He blinked, then slowly shook his head. "It's a nice dream, Mallory. But do you have any idea of how many home design shops have come and gone in this town?"

Her heart sank. "No, not exactly."

"Well, I've been here to see it up close and personal. Those shops come and they go. For whatever reason this town just doesn't support that sort of thing. And the tourist traffic doesn't come. That's why we need that indoor mall. To improve traffic for everyone."

"Well, I really hope you can find the right spot and make that happen."

He pursed his lips. "I don't mean to rain on your parade, but I predict your little dream shop will be out of business in less than a year."

She stood straighter. "And I predict that it won't."

"Well, if your business venture does fail, and if we still haven't secured the property we need to create our mall, would you be willing to sell then?"

"Maybe." She squared her shoulders. "But I don't think it will happen like that. If it does, talk to me then."

"Fine." He cleaned up their napkins and empty paper cups, stuffing them into the bag. "Good luck, Mallory." Just like that he walked out. And for some reason, she felt like crying.

But instead of crying, she pulled out her phone and called her best friend from back home, Kara Whitworth. "You won't believe what I've done, or what I'm about to do. Oh my goodness, I feel like I need to breathe into a paper bag." She laughed nervously.

"What's going on?" Kara asked. "Are you okay?"

"Actually, I am. In fact, I maybe have never been better." She explained about inheriting the shop and how she came to Portside to sell it. "But I'm not going to do that. I'm going to turn it into a home decor shop."

"Really?"

"Yes. It's all come together in my head. And in my heart too. I honestly feel like God is directing me, Kara. Does that sound crazy?"

"Not at all. It actually sounds very exciting. Do you have anyone to run the shop for you? Looking for any volunteers?"

Mallory suspected Kara would jump at this opportunity. She was a good designer

66

but had never gotten her own business fully off the ground. "I'm going to run the shop myself," Mallory declared. "I'm moving to Portside."

There was a pause. "You can't be serious."

"I'm totally serious."

"But what about your business and your home and —"

"My house is too big for me," she interrupted, wondering if she truly meant her own words. "The market is strong right now. I'll sell it."

"What about your design firm? Your clients?"

"I need a partner," Mallory said. "That's why I'm calling you, Kara. What do you think?"

"What do I think about what?" Kara's voice was filled with excitement.

"About becoming my partner?"

"Are you kidding? Of course! I'd love to be your partner!"

"That's great. There's no one I'd rather partner with. Besides your design talent, I love that we're both believers."

"Oh, Mallory, this is so thrilling. But I'm still confused. What does that actually mean? How does it all work?"

"For starters, it means we'll need an attorney to write it all up. Unless you're opposed, I'd like it to be a fifty-fifty partnership. At least for starting out. We can always renegotiate later. Does that sound okay?"

"Absolutely. How could I say no to that? But are you sure about this?"

"I am. I don't think I consciously realized it. Not until I got here. But it's time I moved on, Kara."

"I've never been to Portside, but it must really be something if you're willing to make this huge leap."

Mallory couldn't help but laugh. "You're right, it is *something*. But even more than that, it feels like God is pushing me toward it. He's helping me make this huge leap of faith."

"Well, that's even more exciting."

They discussed a few more details and ideas, then agreed to meet up the following Monday to go over everything. "I'll call my attorney and see if he's available," Mallory said. "I wouldn't do something like this with just anyone, Kara. But I honestly think you're ready for this."

Kara thanked her again. "And if you want, I can let the word slip out that you might be selling your house. I know several people who might be interested."

"Thanks. That'd be great."

As Mallory put her phone into her handbag, she felt slightly numb. Was this for real? Was she honestly doing this? Was it what she truly wanted or had she been goaded into a crazy decision by Grayson's disbelief? No, she told herself as she started to turn out lights and lock things up. This dream had been simmering for years. This was her chance to finally chase it. And, really, it was about time!

Friday was what some people might call a real estate day in Portside. The sun was shining, the air was calm, and there was no afternoon fog. In an effort to calm her spirits and clear her head, Mallory started the day with a leisurely walk on the beach. When was the last time she'd done something like that? If she planned to reinvent her life and relocate to Portside, she might as well start establishing some good habits.

After her walk, she went to Portside Brew for coffee and there at the table by the window sat Sandi. Mallory carried her latte over. "Mind if I join you?"

"Not at all." Sandi smiled. "I thought maybe you'd blown out of here by now."

"Nope. In fact, as it turns out, I plan to become a permanent resident."

"Are you kidding?"

"Totally serious." She shared her decision

to transform her grandmother's property into a home interior shop. "I can already see it in my mind's eye." She described some of her vision for it, including metal awning that would look like canvas. "Sort of an old-world feeling."

"Wow, that's very adventurous." Her brow creased.

"You mean adventurous as in risky?"

"I guess it depends. If you can afford it, then you should go for it." Sandi held up her coffee mug. "Here's to you and your shop. I hope it's wildly successful."

"I do too." Still, she felt uncertain. "When I told Grayson Matthews about it — you know, when I said I wasn't selling to him — he predicted it would fold within a year."

"Well, that does happen around here." Sandi perked up. "Was he terribly angry about you not selling to him?"

"Not angry. But disappointed. Maybe a bit surprised." Mallory didn't want to elaborate on how he'd wined and dined her in the hopes of securing the sale.

"Well, that will definitely put a damper on his silly mall plan."

"You know, the way he described it to me didn't sound too terrible." She reiterated what he'd told her about a courtyard, covered walkways, and open spaces.

Sandi cocked her head to one side. "That actually sounds kind of interesting."

"Grayson needs to communicate his vision better. He'd probably get more people on board."

"Maybe. But I still think Portside is better off without it."

"I agree." Mallory sipped her coffee. "There must be better ways to improve it."

"Hopefully your shop will help some. Anyway, it sounds like it'll be pretty. What are you going to call it?"

"I have this old idea, but I'm not certain it's right." Mallory wasn't sure she wanted to say it aloud just yet.

"What is it?" Sandi urged. "Now you've got me curious."

"Well, it came to me years ago when I dreamt of having a shop like this." Mallory looked out over the water. "The shop would be full of lovely things that would make a home feel cozy and beautiful and romantic."

"Ooh, I like the sound of that." Sandi nodded.

"I imagined calling it Romancing the Home."

"I love that!"

"Seriously? You don't think it sounds silly?"

"No! I think it makes me want to shop

71

there." Sandi's eyes lit up. "In fact, my bungalow over on Fifth Street needs some serious romancing, and I can't even decide on a paint color. I'll be your first customer."

"It's a deal." Mallory felt a surge of hope. "Just don't tell anyone the name until I get it all set up and ready to hang a sign."

"These lips are sealed. But, seriously, how long until that happens? You've got me all-in now. I'm imagining my neglected bungalow all romanticized."

Mallory considered this. "Well, I already have a lot of inventory back at home. Things I've collected for my design business. More than enough to fill a shop that size. But I want to stage it all carefully. And, of course, I have to sell my house. And there will be things in there I can use too." She thought of all her rooms filled with wonderful furnishings. Some could stay with Kara to be used in the design company, but some would be great in the sort of shop she was imagining. "I'll make space in the back room to store things, but I'll probably need to rent a storage unit as well."

"My cousin runs the U-Store place on the edge of town. He can set you up with a space." She checked her watch. "Where do you plan to live once you move here?"

"I'll renovate the apartment above the

shop," Mallory told her. Of course, this was the first time she'd actually thought of this. The place was a wreck. But it did make sense for several reasons, starting with finances. Even if she got a good price on her house, the second mortgage she used to pay off three sets of college tuition would eat most of her equity.

Whatever was leftover would need to go to the apartment remodel. But living above the shop would also save rent money, not to mention gas money. And looking ahead, she realized she'd need to be frugal. To keep her shop thriving, she'd have to regularly reinvest in good inventory. And she wanted it to sparkle and shine and hopefully draw in lots of clients. So to start out, she'd have to be careful.

And if Grayson's gloomy prediction turned out to be right, she could be pinching pennies a year from now. Even Sandi had hinted that the business Mallory had in mind was risky. But determined to make this work, she would do everything possible to keep her dream afloat.

6

The next morning, Sandi called to share the name of a contractor. "Thomas Norton is a great guy," she said. "He's my neighbor and has done a lot of repairs on my bungalow. Very easy to work with and not too hard on the eyes, if you know what I mean." Sandi giggled. "I've been hoping to get better acquainted, but so far he hasn't taken the hint. Anyway, I bumped into him this morning when I took out my garbage, and I used you as an excuse to strike up a conversation."

"Really?"

"Yeah, I mentioned your plans to redo that apartment and that you might be looking for a contractor. He seemed pretty interested in helping you out."

"Awesome."

"I can text him your number if you want."

"Absolutely. I'd love to get someone in here while I'm gone."

"I'll let him know — that gives me another excuse to connect with him."

"Glad I can help." Mallory laughed.

"I'm so excited you're moving here. I've only been back a short while, but it's been a little lonely. Seeing you back here is encouraging."

"And you'll be seeing a lot more of me," Mallory warned.

"Perfect!"

It wasn't long after she hung up that Mallory's phone rang again. After a quick conversation with Thomas, who actually did sound like a nice guy, she invited him to drop by and check out her apartment. "It's not a big project, and a lot of it is more of a gut job. But there's a lot I want to save, and I think the bones are good. I already have a bunch of ideas."

"Sounds like fun to me. I'll pop in before noon."

So, distracted from working on the downstairs, she grabbed a notepad and tape measure and hurried up to do some straightening and planning above. Wouldn't it be amazing if Thomas could get some big things done while she was gone? The more she looked around, the more she realized that other than widening the opening between the kitchen and living room, which didn't appear to be on a weight-bearing wall, there wasn't any structural change needed. The size and layout of the bed and bath were adequate, and hopefully the rough plumbing could stay in place since it all seemed to be in working order. That would save a few bucks. She wasn't sure about the electrical. Work had been done on it, but she knew the building was old. . . . What lurked beneath those walls?

She heard a voice calling from down below and invited Thomas to come up. An attractive man with sandy hair, probably in his forties, came up the stairs. He appeared strong and capable. He shook her hand, gave her his business card, then glanced around. "Well, this does look like quite a project."

She pulled out her tablet and began showing him what she wanted done. "Obviously, everything needs to be repainted. And there's some gutting to do, but I'd like to maintain as much of the original plaster work as possible. I'm not sure about the electrical, but I'm hoping the plumbing can stay."

He flicked a light fixture on and off. "Don't see why the electrical can't stay put. These cabinets look like they're from the sixties or seventies. I'm guessing everything

76

was updated then."

"Great. And you'll get a better idea once you start to work on it." She walked him through the kitchenette, explaining her goal to keep things simple. "I'll do measurements and order cabinets from the guy I usually work with. I won't change the layout for sink, fridge, and stove, I think it works. We might as well leave the sink and its cabinet in place until it's closer to cabinet time, but that ugly fridge and stove can be removed." She pointed to the open space beside the sink. "And I bet we can squeeze a small drawer dishwasher there."

He just nodded, making more notes.

She rocked a loose base cabinet. "You can go ahead and remove all these cabinets." She pointed to a rickety-looking upper cabinet that had been painted fire engine red. "And these can go. I might even put open shelves up here. Mostly I want to keep the whole process simple and easy so I can get moved up here as soon as possible."

Thomas crossed his arms. "Keeping it simple should save money too."

"I don't need a state-of-the-art kitchen. It's not like I plan to do a lot of cooking up here." She tapped her toe on the vinyl-covered floor. "I peeled a corner of the living room carpet back, and it looks like pine

77

tongue and groove beneath. Same with the bedroom. I'm guessing it goes throughout. I'd like to keep and restore as much as I can. Just sand and stain and seal. Hopefully they'll look even better than the wood floors downstairs." She led him to the bathroom, which also housed a decrepit washer/dryer stack. Both were painted a bright orange color that reminded her of road crew vests. She almost wanted sunglasses every time she went in there.

"I wouldn't be surprised if you find some dry rot in here." She bounced on the floor by the toilet. "It's kind of spongy. Anyway, I want it all gutted. We'll replace that tub with a tiled shower of the same dimensions. It's such a small space, I'd like tile throughout. Sort of like a wet room. So you'll need HardieBacker everywhere. I assume you've got connections with a good tile installer."

Thomas shrugged. "I can actually do tile myself."

"Even better. And you probably have a good lineup of plumbers, electricians, painters, and all that."

"Of course." He was making his own notes and measuring.

"And I want to keep and restore all the old doors, windows, and door trim."

"Nice." He nodded. "With the price of

wood these days, that's a smart move."

"So what do you think?" she finally asked.

"Looks like a cool project."

"Not too big? Not too small?"

"Just right." He laughed.

"Can you get me an estimate before I leave town tomorrow?"

"No problem."

"And you're not busy with another job?"

"Your timing is perfect. I'm between jobs right now so I can give this my full attention. I'll get my crew going, and we should wrap it up pretty quickly."

"That's fabulous." She smiled. "The only other contractor I know in this town is Grayson Matthews and he'd rather tear this place down than fix it up."

"That sounds about right." Thomas scowled. "Mr. Development."

His reaction piqued her curiosity. "So you know him?"

"Not to work with, thankfully." He shook his head. "Grayson isn't into restoration, but you probably figured that one out."

"I sort of got that impression."

"I think old things are worth saving." He patted the doorframe. "Like this woodwork and the doors. They could be stripped and stained and sealed."

"I totally agree. Even if it doesn't look

picture-perfect when they're done. I like that the place has history and tells a story."

"Me too." He nudged the baseboard with the toe of his boot. "Old growth fir wood like this is hard to find nowadays."

"Well, I believe you're a true godsend and I look forward to working with you." She caught herself. "Well, I guess I shouldn't speak too soon. Naturally, I need to see your bid first. Then I'll let you know."

"Totally understand. And you got it."

"And can you check with your subs — your electrician, plumber, painter, and so on . . . maybe get a bid from them too? Or incorporate it into yours. At least give me a ballpark?" She sighed. "Because, unfortunately, I do have a budget."

"Don't we all?"

She stuck her hands in her pockets. "And just so you know, I'm a designer. I do renovation projects all the time, so I have a pretty good idea of what something like this would cost. At least back in the city. I can't imagine prices differ too much here." Except, she hoped, maybe small towns were less expensive.

"Yeah, I could tell this wasn't your first rodeo." He chuckled. "Plus, Sandi gave me a heads-up. She's pretty excited about you relocating to Portside."

80

"So am I. And Sandi highly recommends you." She shook his hand again. "So unless your bid is outrageous, I think we can proceed."

"Great. I'll have your estimate ready in the morning." He glanced around. "Do you mind if I do some more measuring and run some numbers while I'm up here?"

"Not at all. I'll just be downstairs." She held up a finger. "In fact, if you have a good painter to recommend, I would appreciate a bid for down there. Both inside and out, and some trim work too."

"Send me the details of what you want done and I'll include that in my bid."

She was about to head down to the shop when something else popped in her head. "By the way, I'm not familiar with local building codes."

"Don't worry. I'll handle all that. And since you're not changing the footprint of anything, this should be pretty easygoing with the city."

"Wonderful." She thanked him again, then went downstairs to do some more thinking and imagining. She could hardly believe that within one week she'd not only made a life-changing decision but nearly secured a contractor to help her get it done too. And, really, it wasn't a complicated job. She was intentionally keeping it simple. If time and money were no objects, she could dream up a lot of high-end things she'd love to do upstairs. But she also knew that a simple backdrop with all her beautiful pieces and design skills would be lovely.

She had all the measurements to draft a scaled blueprint that she'd take home with her to use for planning which furnishings she could use up there. But she planned to pour most of her energy and creativity into the shop. That was what mattered most in the long run. If she didn't make it look inviting down there, it made no difference what happened up here. Especially if Grayson became her buyer next year. She cringed to imagine him sending in a crew to tear the place down. Bulldozers didn't care if your appliances were state-of-the-art or your countertops were marble. But, God willing, she wouldn't let it come to that.

By Sunday, Thomas had already texted Mallory a bid to review. After going over it a couple times, she decided although it was less detailed than what she was used to, it looked good. His estimate seemed very reasonable too. Maybe working with contractors in a small town would be simpler than in the city.

She'd spent most of Saturday making drawings and lists and photocopies down in the hotel business office. She worked late into the night putting together everything she felt Thomas would need to get started. She sorted it all out and put it into a canvas beach bag that she'd saved from her grandmother's shop.

They arranged to meet for coffee to go over the details the next morning. Mallory got there first and was already arranging the table with samples and drawings, as well as photocopies of fixtures and appliances. Perhaps this wasn't as professional as she would be with a client at home. But since she was the client, she felt no need to impress herself, or Thomas.

She started by showing him her paint and stain samples for both the interior and exterior of the first floor. "I'm highly motivated to get the shop ready first." She fanned out the samples — each one clearly marked to avoid any confusion. She pointed to a photocopy. "These are the light fixtures I want to replace those horrid fluorescents. And these are the awnings I want out front." She pointed to her dimensional drawings to make sure he understood. "And here's my hit list for everything I want done down there. Hopefully before I come back. As you can see, it's not a complicated list." She pointed to the awnings photo. "Of course, these won't arrive for a few weeks, but you get the picture."

"Yeah. Nice though." He looked it all over, flipping through the pages, then neatly stacked them. "It's all very doable."

"Now for the upstairs apartment. Naturally, that's more involved." She pulled out the larger folder, removing her photocopies of appliances, plumbing and light fixtures, even hardware. She pointed to her hand-written notes. "These will give you the dimensions and direction so you can have spaces prepared, but I'll order the items from my own suppliers and have them shipped here." She pulled out the copy she'd made of the scaled kitchen design for the layout of her cabinets and appliances. "I've already talked to my cabinet guy. He's busy but promised to squeeze me in and possibly get them done by late June."

Thomas rubbed a hand down his cheek. "That's impressive."

She smiled. "He owes me a few favors."

"Well, this all looks great. Can I keep these?" he asked, pointing to the stack of papers.

"Absolutely, I put this together for you."

"Cool."

84

"It's not a complicated project. As you can see, the living room and bedroom only need paint and the floors refinished. And I've kept the paint and stain color the same throughout just to keep it more simple. I want you to tackle those two rooms first so I can store a few things up there when I come back."

"No problem." He made a note of this.

"I've tried to keep things as simple and easy as possible, but do you have an estimate for the timeline? I plan to stay in the hotel while it's in the heavy construction stage, but I'd like to sneak in as soon as possible to save money. I don't mind if the cabinets aren't up yet or if the tile work's not finished. If I just have floors and walls and electricity, I'll be okay. And I can always use the bathroom downstairs. I know it'll be campy for a while, but I can handle it."

"I'm guessing we'll have it in good enough shape for you to be fairly comfortable in, say, about three weeks." He handed her what appeared to be a standard contract. "I put this together for you."

She read through it, relieved to see it was a much simpler version of what she was used to, and not as costly as expected. As she signed both copies, she felt even more appreciative of small-town living. "I've tried to keep everything pretty straightforward," she said. "But I realize snafus can happen. Just let me know if they do, I'm good at problem-solving and thinking on the fly."

"You will definitely be in the loop," he assured her.

Now she handed him the check for half of his estimate, the duplicate keys she'd had made for the property, then shook his hand. "This is so exciting," she said as they both stood. "I've done lots of renovations, but for some reason this one feels very special to me. I guess because this one is personal."

"It's going to be a fun project." He nodded eagerly.

"And if you have any problems, any questions, just call."

"You got it."

Satisfied that she'd given him everything necessary to get started, she checked her watch. "If I want to get back in time for a meeting with my new design partner, I better get moving." She picked up her handbag as he slid the paperwork back into the canvas bag.

"I can't wait to get started on this." He walked her to the door, politely opening it for her.

"Good luck." She stopped in the doorway to see that Grayson was just about to enter the coffee shop. "Oh, hello," she said awkwardly.

"Hello." He smiled, then, glancing at Thomas right behind her, his smile faded.

"We were just going over the plans for my property renovation," she told Grayson, perhaps a bit smugly.

"So you're really moving forward with your improvements?" He slowly shook his head. "I hope you're not investing too much into the place, Mallory. You might be sorry down the —"

"I will *not* be sorry," she declared. "I'm not only investing in my future, I'm investing in the future of Portside." She stepped past him and, without looking back, hurried on toward her car, pausing to wave goodbye to Thomas, who looked highly amused.

As she started her car, she thought that Grayson might eventually see what she was doing and understand. Perhaps he'd even begin to appreciate the sensibility of rescuing and restoring historic buildings and preserving a charming commercial neighborhood. One could only hope. As she drove back toward the city, she imagined what her grandmother's building might look like by the time she returned. Already, she'd greatly transformed the shop portion. She couldn't wait to see how much greater it would look with fresh paint and freshened-up wood trim and doors. Not to mention how fabulous it would look filled with her merchandise and touches of design. Romancing the Home would soon be more than just a dream. She could hardly stand to wait two whole weeks. After she got it all perfectly set up, she would have a beautiful open house. Maybe she could get Sandi's help setting up a special promotion. It was all so exciting!

7

Transitioning her design business into a partnership with Kara went much more smoothly than Mallory had imagined. Although she almost felt guilty for the fifty-fifty split. It felt like Kara would be doing most of the work, but Mallory would be getting half of the profits. However, Kara kept reassuring her it was fair.

"You built this business and clientele," Kara said when they met for a working breakfast a few days after signing the papers with the lawyer. "I never would've been able to do this at this stage of my career without the foundation you built."

"And I would never have done this with anyone but you," Mallory told her.

Kara poured cream into her coffee. "I secured the warehouse I told you about and can start moving inventory whenever you're ready."

"Great. I've already started to sort through

what I've got. I'm tagging the items I want to keep so there's no confusion when the movers come."

"That must be a chore."

"You got that right." Mallory sighed. She was embarrassed to admit what an emotional challenge it was to go through all her things. After all, they were only furnishings . . . just stuff. Why should she suddenly feel so attached to everything?

"I'm almost done revamping your website with my tech guru," Kara said brightly. "We won't let it go live until you approve it. Probably in another week."

"And I've already called my current clientele to explain the transition."

"How did they take it?"

Mallory pursed her lips. "Well, it was a mixed bag. Some were initially mad, but I assured them that you and I were partners and that I'd still be involved. Just from a distance. Mostly they wanted to know their projects would be completed on time and, of course, done wonderfully."

"I will bend over backward to make sure that happens."

"I know you will." Mallory smiled. "I think this is going to be great for both of us, and for all of them. I'm making a letter of recommendation for you that I'll send to everyone on my mailing list. Speaking of lists." Mallory scanned the list of details she'd jotted into her Day-Timer these last few days, going over each item with Kara.

Finally, it seemed they'd covered everything. "And if I've forgotten anything, you know I'm just a phone call or text away."

"Yes, it's not like you're going to the moon." Kara peered curiously at her. "You're not having any regrets, are you? Any second thoughts?"

Mallory carefully spread marmalade onto her toast. "Not exactly. I'm glad to move to Portside. It really does feel right to me. But it's feeling a little bittersweet. I'm excited about what my shop and apartment will be like, but it's sad saying goodbye to my big old house."

"I can imagine." Kara held up a finger. "But that reminds me. My mother's best friend has a daughter and she and her family are moving here this summer. She's been looking for a house but not just any house. She wants something with historical value."

"Send her my way. If she buys before I list, I'll give you a finder's fee."

"Speaking of selling your house" — Kara's brow creased — "what do your kids think about all this?"

Mallory sighed. "Their first reaction was a

little unexpected. Surprisingly, Louisa seemed okay, but the boys both got pretty worked up about it. For different reasons. Seth was worried I was taking too big a chance. Micah didn't want to give up the family home."

Kara nodded. "That understandable."

"Anyway, I invited them all home for the weekend." She checked her watch as their server dropped off the check. "Which reminds me, I still need to get groceries."

"I'll tell Mom she can give her friend your number." Kara snatched up the check. "And I'm getting this. You go ahead. I'm sure you still have a million things on your list." She pointed to Mallory's ever-present Day-Timer. "Honestly, you're the only one I know who still uses one of those."

Mallory smirked. "This is my brain."

Kara held up her phone. "And this is mine."

"Yes, but if yours falls in the toilet, you're sunk. I learned that the hard way once." Mallory shuddered. "If this one takes a dip, I have indelible ink and a hair dryer."

Kara laughed. "Well, have a good weekend with your kids."

Mallory thanked her, but as she left the restaurant, she wondered what kind of weekend they would have.

Mallory was determined to have her house picture-perfect before her kids arrived on Friday night. Mostly because she didn't want to upset them with all the items she'd tagged to take to Portside. So she either concealed the tags or moved the items to the holding area she'd created in the basement. She just hoped this weekend would be a relaxing family reunion that could make up for the time they hadn't spent together during the crazy rush of Louisa's wedding. She wanted to give the kids a chance to say goodbye to their family home and collect any personal items from the attic.

To that end, she spent Friday afternoon cooking, cleaning, arranging flowers, and making the spare rooms inviting. But at four o'clock, she got her first call. It was Micah.

"Mom, I totally forgot that this weekend is Haley's best friend's wedding. Haley is maid of honor and I have to be there."

"Oh?' Mallory tried not to replay their previous conversation, where Micah was worried selling the house would break apart their family. And now he wasn't coming at all?

"I'm sorry, Mom. But you know how girls are about weddings."

"Of course. And June is a big wedding month."

"The wedding is over at the coast," he told her. "Too bad you're not in Portside, we could've met up there."

"Does that mean you're warming up to the idea?"

"Well, Haley and I talked about it. Like she says, it's your life, Mom. You shouldn't let us kids stand in your way."

"I'm liking Haley more and more," she said.

"I probably won't tell her that."

"Why not?"

"Because after Louisa's wedding and this one tomorrow night, she'll probably be hinting more than ever about us getting hitched."

"Getting hitched?" She laughed. "Do people still say that?"

"Of course."

"Well, you and Haley are both still young. Plenty of time to get hitched."

"I'm sorry about missing this weekend, Mom."

"Maybe you can come next weekend?" she said hopefully.

"I'd love to, but Dad got Mariners' tickets

for Seth and me."

"Oh?" For some reason she felt like shaking Micah but kept her tone calm. "Well, that's nice. Sounds like fun. I guess I'll just move anything you've got left in the attic to my storage container and you —"

"I've already gone through all that stuff, Mom. I got what I wanted. The rest of my junk is just that" — he laughed — "junk."

She ignored the sting of his words. "So the giveaway pile?"

"Sure. Bless someone else with it." He laughed. "Or trash it. I don't care."

"Okay then. You and Haley have a good time at that wedding, and at the beach. The weather is supposed to be nice over there."

"Thanks! Love you, Mom."

"Love you too!" Despite her aggravation at Micah's wishy-washy-ness, she felt relieved. His initial argument for keeping the house had resonated with her the most. Now it seemed he had moved on so she had only Seth left to persuade. He was her practical son, always watching the bottom line, planning for the future. She needed to convince him she was going about this carefully, which was why she'd put together a small spreadsheet just to show him.

As it turned out, Mallory didn't even need her spreadsheet. And she didn't need to go to all the trouble to make her children feel at home. Louisa, worn out from the wedding and honeymoon, now had a summer cold and begged out of the visit just before dinner. And although Seth showed up for dinner, he simply glanced at her spreadsheet, then gave her a short lecture about finances, investments, and the stock market in general before he gathered what things he wanted from the attic — just one box! He set the box by the front door, then made his excuses.

"Since Micah and Louisa didn't make it, I think I'll head out too." He was already on his phone. "Jacob just texted that he and Riley are headed to McAllister's. If you don't mind, I'd like to meet up with them. I haven't seen Jacob in a couple of years, and he's only here for the weekend and Riley is —"

"Of course. Tell Jacob and Riley hello for me." She patted his back. "Thanks for coming for dinner."

"It was delicious, Mom." He grinned sheepishly. "And I know you're a good businesswoman. You'll be just fine over in Portside. In fact, I want to come visit. Do you have room for guests?"

"I plan to have a pullout bed in the main room, but the space is small so it'll be cozy."

"That's okay." He kissed her cheek. "Maybe I can pop over for the Fourth."

She considered this. "I'm not sure the apartment will be done by then, but I'm hoping."

"Well, keep me posted." He waved as he jogged down the front steps with his box in hand. The sight gave Mallory a flashback. Seth had been only nine years old but turning into an "old" homebody. Of the three kids, the divorce had hit him hardest. Worried that he was getting stuck, Mallory had practically kicked him out the door to go meet his good buddies Jacob and Riley in the park to kick around the soccer ball. Over the years, those three boys had maintained their friendship and, really, she was glad they were still getting together now, which only proved that her conclusion that everyone moved on was exactly right.

And she was moving on too.

Despite her canceled family gathering, Mallory was glad she'd gone to the effort to make her home welcoming when she got an interesting call from Kara the next morning.

"Jenna is in town for the day. That's Mom's friend's daughter, the one who's house-hunting, and she'd like to see your house. I told her your kids are there and it might not be a good —"

"No, it's perfect." Mallory explained the change of plans.

"Wonderful. I'll bring her around eleven if that works."

"Eleven totally works." Mallory gazed around her now-immaculate kitchen, which she'd obsessively cleaned after Seth left last night. Her frenzy had been partly from irritation that all three kids had bailed on her and partly from angst as she started to consider what she was actually embarking on.

By the time she'd gone to bed around midnight, she was having serious second thoughts and felt close to a real panic attack. Maybe this was all a huge mistake. Maybe a woman in her age and stage of life should remain put, take the safe route, not rock the boat. Finally, she'd laid it all out to God again, asking him to lead her and to close or open doors. Eventually she'd fallen asleep.

To think that right now, less than twelve hours later, a prospective home buyer was coming to tour her house was encouraging. She'd done her own internet research and had a pretty good idea of the value for a home like hers in a neighborhood like this.

She also knew that hitting the right price was crucial in selling a home if you were listing it to the general public. A low price could ignite a bidding war and a high price could be dead in the water. But today didn't involve the general public.

Mallory had never liked game playing and, after sincerely praying, decided to simply name what she believed was a fair market price. They could take it or leave it. If they low-balled her, she would politely offer to keep their information, but then she'd list it herself online, and see what happened.

Jenna as well as her mother and Kara and her mother showed up at eleven o'clock sharp to tour the house. All the women were in good spirits and the general energy was upbeat and positive. After meeting and greeting and visiting a bit, Mallory stepped out of the picture, inviting them to explore as much as they liked while she remained on the back terrace where she had snacks and beverages waiting.

She poured herself an iced tea, dropped in a fresh sprig of mint, then sat down in a comfy patio chair. Looking out over her roses, which were in bloom, Mallory replayed her first impression of Jenna and her mom. She'd instantly liked them both. And not just because they were already gushing about her home. But for some reason, like Kara and her mom, the two women felt familiar, almost like family.

Jenna had three daughters between the ages of eight and thirteen. Like Mallory, Jenna worked from home, but her husband's job had transferred him here, where he was temporarily living in Jenna's mom's den. Their goal was to get moved and settled as soon as possible to help their girls get acclimated to their new life. Fortunately, all three girls were delighted to live near their grandmother.

Mallory sipped her tea, imagining how the three girls would like living in this old house. There were enough bedrooms for everyone, but the girls would probably have to share a bath. Louisa had used Mallory's bath while the boys controlled the one on their floor. A bathroom that got a makeover to accommodate Louisa after the boys left. But Mallory had always tried to make this house a place where her kids felt at home.

After more than an hour, the four women came outside. She suspected by their pleased expressions that her house hadn't disappointed them. She welcomed them outside and, after a quick tour of the pretty yard that her landscaper kept pristine, she invited them to join her for tea and snacks.

"Well, I probably shouldn't admit that I love it," Jenna said. "My husband would not approve of my technique, but he's on a business trip in LA, so I don't even care." She beamed at Mallory. "I adore your home."

Mallory smiled back. "So do I."

"How can you leave it?" Jenna asked.

Mallory sighed. "Well, my children are grown now and have lives of their own, so I thought it was time for a change."

"Well, we do have a budget," Jenna said. "Perhaps we should talk about price. I have no idea what you want, but I've been looking for a couple of months, so I do know what homes are going for around here. Although I haven't seen anything I love as much as this." She covered her mouth. "See there I go again. Jonathan would be kicking me under the table about now."

"Don't worry about it," Mallory said. "I'm not good at wheeling and dealing either. I did my research and have a figure already in my head." She pulled out her Day-Timer. "In fact, I've written it down here."

"Can you show me?" Jenna asked with a look of trepidation. "That way if it's too much, I can just slink away and try to forget about it."

Mallory opened her Day-Timer and slid it over, watching Jenna's face brighten as she read the number. "Yes," Jenna said in a slightly shaky voice. "That works for our budget."

Jenna's mother leaned over to look at the number, then nodded.

"This is so exciting." Jenna was beaming now. "Can I make you an offer?"

"Of course." Mallory waited, hoping Jenna wouldn't start beneath the figure she'd written down. That would be awkward.

Jenna bit her lip. "I do have a question though. Would you consider leaving any of the furnishings?"

Mallory considered this. "Well, I plan to take a lot of things to Portside with me. I've actually marked the items I want, but I've hidden their tags. Of course, all things are negotiable. Why don't you tell me what you're interested in and we can talk about it?"

"Okay." Jenna began to list furnishings she wanted to keep, while Mallory jotted them down in her notebook. Jenna was most interested in bigger items, like the dining room furniture and the guest bedrooms' larger pieces. "They go so perfectly in this house and we sold our home partially furnished, which will be nice when it comes to moving, but I will have some shopping to do."

Mallory looked over the list. "I'm happy to sell the pieces you want."

"Really?" Jenna's eyes lit up. "Okay, here's what I can offer you, for your house and those pieces of furniture." She said the figure and Mallory had to control herself from clapping her hands.

"It's a deal," Mallory told her.

"Seriously? Just like that?" Jenna looked stunned.

"Just like that. Although you might want to talk to your husband first."

"He'll be fine. I sent him a lot of photos on my phone and he liked it. As long as I stayed in the budget, he said the house decision was totally up to me."

"And the girls?" Mallory questioned.

"They're with their grandpa," Jenna's mom said. "I already sent them pictures and all three girls were over the moon. They've always wanted to live in an old house."

"Do we have a deal?" Jenna stuck out her hand.

"Absolutely." Mallory met it. "And honestly, I couldn't be more pleased. I'd hoped and prayed this house would go to someone just like you. It might sound silly, but I wanted the house to be happy too."

Jenna laughed. "It doesn't sound silly at all. I will do everything I can to make this house happy." She pointed to her mom. "And Mom works in an escrow office so she'll do everything to make the sale official and legal."

Jenna's mom promised to call Mallory the next day, and then she and Jenna did another quick look around, snapped more photos, took more measurements, and finally all four of them left. With the house to herself, Mallory slowly strolled through each room, going from her workspace in the basement all the way to the attic, where she still needed to box up some things for Louisa. Although she was relieved to have gotten a buyer so effortlessly, and Jenna couldn't have been more perfect, Mallory still had tears streaming down her cheeks. Oh, she would miss this place!

8

After another week and a half of packing, organizing, making phone calls, and tending to a zillion loose ends, Mallory was finally ready to return to Portside. She hadn't managed to fit everything into her two-week window like she'd planned, but she'd left a message with Thomas letting him know she would be a few days late. She'd also made a reservation at the hotel, asking for their weekly rate.

On the morning she was preparing to leave, with the moving van scheduled to follow her over there the next day, Thomas returned her call. "We're not as far along in the apartment as I'd hoped so you won't be able to move anything up there yet, but the downstairs looks pretty good."

Although she was disappointed to hear she couldn't start moving in upstairs, she told him she'd use the shop as a holding area until the apartment became habitable. And to be fair, despite Thomas's assurances, she hadn't honestly expected it to be ready this soon.

The drive to Portside, with every inch of her car packed full of her clothes and personal items, felt exhilarating. Like a pioneer heading West on the Oregon Trail — similar to what Grandma Bess used to describe about the way their ancestors had arrived in Oregon back in the 1850s. Had they felt a bit like this?

Because it was too early to check in at the hotel, she headed directly into town. To her pleasant surprise, the front of her shop looked much improved. The stucco was painted a clean milky white. The trim was the charcoal black she'd chosen, and the door had been completely stripped, stained, and sealed. The old wood gleamed with the red maple stain she'd chosen. Perfect.

With eager expectation, she unlocked the door and let herself in. The wood floors, also stained and sealed, looked better than ever. The walls were painted in a color similar to the exterior and perfect to set off the displays she had in mind, and even the trim had been refinished, stained, and sealed. She looked up to see the light fixtures she'd chosen in place, and the high ceiling, also freshly painted, didn't even show signs of where the old ugly florescent lights had once been.

She continued forward, looking at the back room where she'd stored a few things under a tarp. She hadn't asked for its floor to be refinished since she knew it would be used mostly for storage, but it too had been painted, making it much brighter and fresher than before. Even the wooden built-in storage shelves looked nicer now. She poked her head into the small bathroom, which, although it still had its old fixtures, looked clean and bright with its new paint. And, although she hadn't asked, Thomas had peeled off the old linoleum and refinished the floor. Not bad! But it would've been nice if he'd talked to her first.

Excited to see the apartment, and not hearing any noises up there, she hurried up to check on its progress.

The door was locked but she had her key. She unlocked the door, stepped inside, and — her heart sank. The main living area walls hadn't been touched by a paintbrush, but at least the carpet and linoleum were gone. The bare wood floors beneath looked solid but were stained and in need of attention. The partially gutted kitchen was a mess. She'd asked Thomas to leave the sink, but the ugly fridge and stove were still in place too. And worst of all — the places where some of the cabinets had been removed had left gaping holes in the plastered walls that she'd hoped to reuse. Now they would all have to be removed and replaced with drywall. She hadn't counted on that.

She went to the bathroom to discover that nothing had been done here. Her heart was beating even faster now. Although the shop down below was in great shape, she knew it hadn't taken that much effort. She'd left it in almost useable condition. She'd mostly wanted paint and floor refinishing and for him to check on a few things.

She walked around, reevaluating everything with growing dismay. What had been done up here could've happened in just a day. For that matter, she could have done it herself — and more carefully too! Something was wrong.

She pulled out her phone to call Thomas but was sent to his voice mail. Trying not to sound overly terse, she started by praising the shop downstairs and then expressed her disappointment over the apartment. "I hope you haven't been hurt and gotten sick," she finally said, "but it really looks like you have not spent much time up here."

She hung up and went over to the kitchen sink, testing to see if the water was still on and then, for no real reason, she reached for the old bottle of dish soap and an ancient-looking sponge and attempted to clean the stained sink. Of course, it was pointless. She went into the untouched bathroom and just shook her head. This was going to take much longer than she'd imagined.

Feeling deflated and concerned, she went downstairs and unloaded a few plastic bins in the storage room. Then, just as she went outside where the weather was as gray and dismal as she felt, she saw Grayson approaching. For a moment his sunny smile almost seemed to warm her, but then she remembered how she'd snubbed him at their last encounter.

"Welcome back," he said, his tone friendly.

"Thank you." She hurriedly locked the front door behind her.

He stuck his hands in his pockets. "I thought about what you said about giving this shop a second chance . . ." His expression was sincere. "I'd like to wish you the best of luck."

"Thanks." Her silk scarf whipped in the sea breeze and, trying to tame it, she studied his expression. "I think we all need a second chance sometimes."

"That's for sure." He tipped his head

toward her shop. "So how's your renovation coming?"

She concealed her disappointment with an overly bright smile. "Okay . . . I guess."

Suddenly the lead-colored sky burst into fat raindrops. "I better let you get out of this," Grayson told her. "I think we're about to get a real deluge."

They parted ways and Mallory headed to her SUV. The rain continued to pelt the streets as she drove over to the hotel. Her hope was to get to her room before the official check-in time, but the middle-aged desk clerk stubbornly refused. "Can't check you in until three o'clock," she said with a stony expression. Mallory, feeling equally stubborn, planted herself on the faded blue sofa and waited, suddenly wondering what she had gotten herself into.

When Thomas still hadn't returned her call the next day, Mallory paid Sandi a visit at the ice-cream shop. Since no customers were there, Mallory tactfully explained the situation. "Anyway, I'm worried something might be wrong. Did he get hurt or anything?"

"I've seen his truck come and go," Sandi told her. "But I haven't actually talked to him. Not in more than a week or so."

Mallory pulled out his dog-eared business card. "This only has his phone number on it, but if you told me where he lives, I could pay him a visit." She studied the card with bullet descriptions of his "expertise" listed more closely and suddenly she felt a jolt of panic. "Oh my goodness! He doesn't even have his CCB number on here."

"What's CCB?" Sandi rinsed her scoop in the water.

"Construction Contractors Board." Mallory's insides were twisting. "License, bond, and insurance information."

"Uh-oh." Sandi looked grim. "Kind of like the state health board? We'd be in trouble if we weren't licensed by them."

"Yeah, the CCB is supposed to protect consumers from fraud, but it's up to consumers to check on it. I can't believe I didn't." Mallory thought to the contractors she worked with in the city. Some were good, some not so much, but they all were licensed!

"I'm sorry, Mallory, I guess I never thought to ask about that when he worked for me, but he was only doing odd jobs. He retiled my powder room and did a great job."

"Right." Mallory felt incredibly stupid now. Why hadn't she asked about his licensing right off the bat? Or gotten more references? Instead, she'd stupidly handed over most of what was in her bank account without thinking twice.

"Is this going to be a big problem?" Sandi asked with a furrowed brow.

"Uh, well, yeah. For me, anyway." Mallory took in a stabilizing breath. "It's not your fault, Sandi. I was just incredibly stupid." She looked at the card again. "Or hopefully not. Maybe he does have a CCB license but didn't put it on here." She forced a raggedy smile. "Anyway, I'll figure it out."

"Want an ice cream?" Sandi offered meekly. "On the house?"

"No thanks." She shoved the card into her bag. "Maybe later."

Outside the ice-cream shop, she tried Thomas's phone again. But only getting voice mail, she left a message. This time she didn't care if it was terse or not. "I need to speak to you, Thomas. If you get this message, please, call me back ASAP. And if by some chance I don't answer, please leave me your CCB numbers and information. Thank you." She ended the call and shoved her phone into her bag and walked quickly down the street toward her shop.

But instead of going into her shop, she went to Portside Brew and ordered a triple latte. Not that she needed the caffeine, but for some reason it felt good just saying it. She sat at a table facing the street so she could keep an eye on her shop. The moving van was scheduled to arrive this afternoon and, although they were supposed to text her when they were in town, she didn't fully trust them. She didn't fully trust anyone at the moment.

"Can I join you?"

She looked up in surprise to see Grayson, with a coffee mug in hand.

Caught off guard, she didn't know what to say so she simply shrugged.

"You seem unsettled," he said as he sat down. "Anything wrong?"

She blew out a sigh, trying to gauge how much to say. "I'm waiting for my moving van to arrive," she finally admitted. "I suppose I'm a bit on edge."

"That's exciting. Already setting up shop. Once again, I'm impressed."

Still clutching her coffee mug with both hands, she boldly nodded. "Yes, that's exactly what I'm going to do. Set up shop." Of course, it seemed ridiculous to arrange her decor shop with her living quarters in such shambles. But for some reason — probably her stupid pride — she wanted him to think all was well in her messy little world.

He smiled. "Well, I'm happy for you, Mallory. I really wish you the best success."

She suddenly questioned his sincerity. Was he just toying with her? She narrowed her eyes at him. "Seriously? After you originally predicted my disaster."

He sat back in his chair, eyebrows raising. "I predicted your disaster?"

"Well, that's probably overstating it. But you did mention that businesses like what I want to set up usually fail within the first year."

His eyes crinkled at the edges. "I'm sorry about that. To be honest, I was probably just miffed over not being able to buy your property."

She perked up. "But you're not miffed now?"

He shrugged. "I'm exploring some new possibilities."

"For your *mall*?" She knew she probably sounded like a curmudgeon.

"First of all, it's not *my* mall. It's for the city. And if you'd ever let me show you the drawings, you might discover that it's not a bad plan."

She saw the moving van coming down the street and stood. "I'm sorry, but I have to go. My movers are here." She hurried out the door. The afternoon breeze felt cool and refreshing on her flushed face. And, before long, she was directing the movers as to where to put things.

Although she'd originally meant to leave her own things downstairs in the back room, she was so perplexed at Thomas's work, or lack of, that she started to direct the men to take certain items up, including the queen bed she'd saved from one of her guest rooms for herself.

"I know it looks awful up here right now, but just put everything in the center of the living room," she instructed them. "I'll get things into place after the painting is done."

The men looked somewhat doubtful but didn't question her and after a couple of hours, they were done. Thanking them for their patience, she tipped them and wished them a good trip back. As soon as they left, she tried Thomas's phone again, leaving another urgent message, begging him to return her call. Then, collapsing onto the short section of the small sectional with the pullout bed, she tried to keep herself from bawling like a baby. What had she gotten herself into?

The next morning, after getting the address

from Sandi, Mallory rose early, drove into town, and parked herself in Thomas's driveway. She knew it was his house because she recognized his red pickup. The house didn't seem to be in the greatest shape, but maybe he'd been too busy. She didn't know that much about Thomas. According to Sandi he was "available," but whether he was divorced or had kids or even a roommate was uncertain. She didn't want to offend anyone else living here but knew she needed to speak to him in person.

While waiting for him to emerge, she shot up a silent prayer, asking God to help her remain controlled and gracious. She knew that people were more important than things, but she still felt slightly outraged for having been taken in by this man. However, she realized she was partly to blame. She'd never asked for his CCB information. She should've known better.

Her nerves started rising as he came out the front door. He frowned when he noticed a car blocking his truck. Then as he came closer, he must've realized it was her, because he waved unenthusiastically as she got out of her car.

"Thomas," she said, "why haven't you returned my calls?"

"I'm sorry, Mallory." He looked down at

his dusty work boots. "I got super busy this past week. Got a big job."

"What about *my* job?" she asked. "It looks like you started, then abandoned it."

"I'll get to it." He rubbed his chin. "In time."

"Tell me something." She locked eyes with him. "Are you a licensed contractor?"

"Well, I, uh, I've *been* licensed."

Her hands felt clammy. "Are you licensed right now? Bonded and insured?"

"No . . . but I've been in construction for twenty-four years. I know what I'm doing. And your project doesn't require a —"

She raised a hand, cutting him off. "I know I should've asked you this before signing a contract, and I blame myself for that. But I also feel you misrepresented yourself to me."

"Did I ever tell you I was licensed?" He looked her in the eye.

"I honestly can't recall what you said, but I did get the impression that —"

"Did you like what I got done downstairs? In your shop?"

"Yes. That looks wonderful. But the apartment is a wreck."

"I'll get to it," he said. "Just not for two weeks. Three tops."

She shook her head. "No. You won't *get*

to it. Because I'm canceling your contract right now."

"Aw, you don't want to do that."

"I never work with unlicensed contractors."

"You're used to big city ways. We're laidback here in Portside. It's not like you needed anything structural done in the apartment, not tearing out any walls. We were mostly just doing cosmetic stuff. You don't need a license for that."

"I only used licensed subs," she told him.

"Even for painting or refinishing?"

"I also need plumbers and electricians, Thomas, and they *must* be licensed."

He shrugged.

"And what about permits? Did you even check into that?"

He shook his head. "You don't need permits for what you're doing, Mallory. This isn't the big city."

"I'm sorry, but I'm canceling your contract. I expect part of that advance back —"

"Wait a minute. I did a lot of work in there."

Her jaw dropped. "It isn't even half done."

"But I can finish it in —"

"No, I mean it, consider your contract canceled. I estimate the work is about one-fourth done, and that's generous. I expect half of what I gave you returned to me, Thomas. I'd like it now."

"That's not going to happen."

She crossed her arms. "Why not?"

He blew out an exasperated sigh. "Because you're going to have to wait for it."

"Wait?" She felt her blood pressure rising. "I don't have it right now."

She closed her eyes and pursed her lips, trying to maintain control.

"Look, Mallory, if you could just let me finish your job for you, I'll get to —"

"No." She opened her eyes to stare at him. "The contract is canceled. I need my money back today."

"I'm sorry. I honestly don't have it. But when I finish this job, I'll pay you back." He watched a car pull out of the driveway across the street.

"How can I be sure of that?"

"You'll have to trust me." He shoved his hands into his pockets.

"When do you think you'll be done with the other job?"

"Two weeks. Maybe three."

"Two or three weeks?" She frowned. "You said it was a *big* job."

"Well, it's not exactly big, but it's good money. Can you wait a couple weeks?"

She considered this. What other option

119

did she have? Even if she reported him to the state, they could fine him and ban him from ever getting licensed, but it wouldn't get her money back. "Fine," she said. "I'll trust you."

"And you won't report me?"

"To be honest, I've considered doing that."

He scowled.

"But I'm going to trust you to pay me back in two weeks." She wanted to add that if he didn't pay her back, she might report him after all, but that seemed pretty harsh. And she did want her money back. She needed it.

He thanked her, then stuck out his hand. Reluctantly, she shook it. She hoped she wasn't being a fool . . . again. Although she had serious doubts about whether she'd see her money returned, she knew she needed to let it go for now. She'd give him his promised two weeks. In the meantime, she'd need to rearrange the delivery of her appliances and cabinets to the storage unit she'd rented on the edge of town. For now, she would focus all her energy on her shop. The sooner she got that up and running and making a profit, the better off she'd be.

9

When Sandi called to invite Mallory to meet her for lunch, Mallory made the excuse that she was busy. Mostly because she didn't want the topic of Thomas to come up. She knew Sandi wanted to get to know him better, and Mallory didn't want to rain on her parade.

"Oh, come on," Sandi urged. "Everyone is busy, but you still have to eat. Meet me at Darma's Deli at noon or I'll get you something and bring it to you."

Mallory glanced around the shop crowded with boxes and furniture that all needed sorting out and knew she didn't want to try to have lunch here. "Okay, I'll meet you there."

"Great. See ya at high noon."

As Mallory opened a box, she wondered if Sandi had witnessed the showdown next door this morning. What if she asked about Thomas? Mallory decided she'd tell the truth. But kindly and graciously. Then she'd let Sandi figure it out.

By the time Mallory's phone alarm began to chime, she'd managed to move several large pieces about the room and opened at least a dozen boxes, but as she looked around the shop, she realized she had barely made a dent in getting things into place. This was going to take time. Especially since she'd let Kara help her pack and Kara had neglected to mark any of her boxes. Hopefully she'd be more organized when it came to running the design firm. Note to self: Check on Kara early next week.

As Mallory walked down to Darma's Deli, she looked around town, taking in the businesses along the street. She would never dream of telling any of the shop owners, but most of the shops could use a facelift. And it wouldn't even take much. Paint a door here, put a big planter there, remove some clutter from a window.

She looked at the boring lampposts and imagined how the street would look with old-fashioned iron ones with hanging planters. And what about city-owned benches here and there? Oh, she was full of ideas, but she also knew it was good to move slowly in a small town like this. She didn't want to overwhelm or alienate anyone.

Especially before her own business was completely ready. Even then, she would need to go carefully.

"Hello," Sandi exclaimed as they met in front of the deli. "Aren't you glad you came?"

Mallory adjusted her purse on her shoulder. "Yes, it's a gorgeous day. Thanks for prodding me out."

They placed their orders then got a table by the window. "I've never been here," Mallory told Sandi, "but everything on the menu sounded good."

"Yeah, it's probably the most popular lunch spot in town. At least with locals. Tourists still go for The Chowder House, which is fine with me since I hardly ever go there myself."

"I haven't been there since I was a kid." Mallory stirred cream into her coffee. "My grandma liked their chowder, but that was when I still hated seafood, so I always got a cheeseburger."

"That's one thing they actually do a good job on," Sandi said. "When I get the urge for one, I go there. Okay" — she lowered her voice — "tell me what was going on with you and Thomas this morning."

"This morning?" Mallory tried to play dumb.

123

"You know, in his driveway. I saw you guys having a serious talk. Is this about him not having his contractor's license?"

"We were just having a conversation," Mallory said lightly.

"Really?" Sandi frowned. "It looked like something more. Like a lovers' quarrel. Are you sure you're not getting involved with him?"

"No, of course not." She firmly shook her head.

"Of course not? Meaning Thomas isn't worthy of dating?" Sandi looked offended.

"No, I mean it was nothing like that. We were just talking about work. No big deal." Mallory forced a smile.

Sandi sat back, clearly relieved. "Good to know. I was worried you'd made more progress with him than me."

"No worries there. He's all yours."

"So you were just talking about work? I mean, you both looked kind of upset."

Mallory folded a paper napkin into a triangle, creasing it with her thumbnail, trying to decide how to resolve this. Maybe it was better to just tell it like it was. "Well, I sort of had to fire him."

"Fire him?" Sandi's loud voice garnered attention from the nearby tables.

"Yes," Mallory said quietly. "He admitted

that he didn't have a contractor's license. And like I told you, that matters to me. I never work with unlicensed contractors."

Sandi nodded. "Okay, I get that. It's probably partly my fault for recommending him to you. But honestly, he did good work for me."

"I'm sure he did." Mallory's smile was genuine now. "He did a great job downstairs in the shop." She didn't need to tell Sandi there wasn't much that needed doing. "I couldn't have been more pleased."

"But you still don't want him to do your apartment?" Sandi frowned.

"That's more involved. It'll take plumbers and electricians and a lot more." She didn't even want to think about it.

"Weren't you planning to live up there?"

Mallory nodded. "And I will. Just not as soon as I'd hoped."

"You're not holding this against Thomas personally?"

"No, not at all. We arrived at an agreement to settle this. I'm sure he feels working without a license is no big deal. After all, he does know construction. But maybe he should consider calling himself a handyman instead of a contractor."

"Well, I don't know about all that, but I'm glad there's not a serious rift. Because I

125

want to get to know him better, and I want my friends to like him. I was even toying with the idea of inviting him to dinner at my house, just to be neighborly, you know." Sandi folded her hands on the table. "But I was hoping you'd help me to romanticize it first. Sort of set the mood. So, when will Romancing the Home be open for business?"

Mallory couldn't help but chuckle. "Hopefully it's not too far out. If I could wave my magic wand, it'd be done today. But I'll be happy to help you romance your home, just as soon as I'm better set up. Right now, I can't find anything I'm looking for."

Their food came and they continued to visit. Mallory told her about her idea for lampposts and how she hoped the whole town would start to improve. Sandi suggested Mallory join the chamber of commerce.

"Maybe once I'm opened for business." Mallory paused when she saw Grayson and an attractive redhead enter the deli. She watched them go to the counter together and Sandi turned to look.

"Grayson and Corrina," Sandi said casually. "They eat here a lot too."

"Of course." Mallory turned her attention back to Sandi. "Anyway, I'd like to join the chamber. It'll be a good way to network and get to know people."

"Yeah, and a good way to promote your store. Plus, there are bound to be business owners who'd love some suggestions for improving their shops. In fact, I'd like some help with the ice-cream shop. I asked my mom if we could budget something, and she's a little cautious but agrees we're due for some improvements. As long as I don't go overboard."

"That's great." Mallory's attention switched as Grayson and Corrina turned around with their beverages in hand. Corrina was strikingly pretty. She waved to a couple sitting near the counter and stopped to visit with them.

"Hey there," Grayson called out when he noticed Mallory and Sandi. "How are you ladies doing?" He came over and they exchanged greetings. "How's the shop going?" he asked Mallory. "All set up?"

"I'm working on it." She placed her napkin on the table. "It's quite a task."

"Can't wait to see the end results." He glanced back to see that Corrina was already seating herself at a table near the other couple, still visiting with them.

"Hopefully I'll be open for business in a week or two," Mallory said.

127

"That soon?" He looked surprised. "I know I've said it before, Mallory, but you really are impressive." Mallory tried not to grimace at his praise as Grayson excused himself to rejoin Corrina.

"So that's Corrina," Mallory said and instantly wished she hadn't.

"Yeah." Sandi nodded. "Pretty, huh?"

"Very. I assume that's not his wife?"

"No. His wife died. I'm not sure when. It was before I moved back here."

"Oh. Is Corrina a girlfriend? Fiancé?" Mallory knew she was fishing for information but didn't really care. She wanted to know.

"I'm not sure what their personal relationship is, but I do know Corrina works for his construction company. In the office. She told me once that she's like a jill-of-all-trades — receptionist, secretary, bookkeeper — and she told me she even helps out on a jobsite sometimes."

Mallory had difficulty imagining the stylish woman running a power saw, but stranger things have happened. "So is Grayson's construction company pretty big?"

"Biggest one in town. If you see a building going up, you usually see his signs out in front."

"Are there other companies? Or contractors?"

"A few. But building has been in a slump the past couple of years. My mom keeps predicting it'll pick up any day based on what we've seen along the coastline north of us, but we're just a little more out of the way."

"Out of the way could be in this town's benefit someday."

"I hope so. I'd love to see Portside businesses become more successful."

Mallory glanced over to where both Grayson and Corrina were engaged in a lively conversation with the other couple. It was obvious the man respected Grayson, which contrasted with Thomas's disparaging opinion of him. She suddenly wondered how she could come up with names of other contractors. Not that she could afford to pay any of them before the money from the sale of her house came through. But it wouldn't hurt to gather some names and get some bids. She pushed her empty soup bowl away and pulled out her Day-Timer to make a note.

"You're super-organized, aren't you?" Sandi asked.

"I learned long ago to write everything down." She closed her Day-Timer and slid it into her canvas bag. "My partner, Kara, still teases me for using a Day-Timer instead of electronics, but old habits die hard." She glanced at her watch. "I should get back to the shop. I've got a lot to do."

"Well, I'm glad you could join me. And even more glad you're still on speaking terms with Thomas."

"And I am serious about wanting to help you with your house," Mallory assured her as she stood. "As soon as I can."

"I'll hold you to it."

Mallory glanced toward Grayson's table and caught him staring in her direction with what seemed like genuine interest. Feeling slightly awkward, she finger-waved, then quickly exited. Was it her imagination that he was seeking more than just a casual friendship? Or was he still hoping to get his hands on her property? Would she ever know?

Back in her shop, Mallory pulled out her phone and did an online search for Portside contractors. The list was small, but she decided to start at the top. Well, not the tip-top since that was Grayson's company, Matthews Construction. But every number she called had an excuse. One was busy until autumn. The next was not taking on small jobs. The third didn't do remodels on anything built before 1960. And the last didn't even connect.

She dropped her phone into her bag and sighed. What was she going to do about that silly apartment? She looked around her chaotic shop. Well, the apartment would just have to wait. Right now, she needed to get this place in order. Not only for her peace of mind, which was feeling seriously rattled, but for her bottom line. She needed the cash to start flowing.

After a full week of very long days and a lot of hard labor, Mallory's shop was nearly ready for business. Not that anyone outside would know since she'd covered all the windows with craft paper. Tempted to tear the paper down just to see how the shop looked in natural light, Mallory controlled herself. She wanted to wait until all was perfection . . . or very close.

She'd received notification that her metal awning would arrive next week. She'd already set her iron planters outside, flanking the door. Of course, they looked rather sad and empty, but they were so heavy no one would try to run off with one. Her iron bench was in place, too, and she'd already noticed walkers taking advantage of it, which was fine. She wanted people to feel welcomed here. Once she was open, she planned to set out an attractive water dish for dogs.

Sandi had given Mallory the name of a good sign painter named Laurie Wallace and, after swearing the young woman to secrecy in regard to the name of the shop, Mallory showed her the sketches she'd designed for the signs. Very Parisian. One would hang above the door, and the other stencil-painted on the big front window.

As Mallory did an umpteenth critique of her shop, she couldn't deny it was beautiful. But was it truly shopper friendly or had she simply arranged everything to appeal to her own aesthetics? There was a difference between admiring something and wanting to purchase it. As much as she enjoyed admiration, she needed to move merchandise.

Pretending to be a tourist casually strolling through town, she started just inside the door. Taking a deep breath of the pleasant but not overwhelming aroma, she paused to listen to the Chopin piano piece playing softly. Not everyone's cup of tea, but it worked for her. Already, she felt welcomed and relaxed, ready to snuggle into a comfy chair and — wait, she reminded herself, this was about critiquing.

She ran her hand over the handsome

antique glass-front credenza outfitted with handsomely packaged French soaps, lotions, atomizers, candles, and other aromatic items. She hoped the fragrant scents, as well as a luscious floral bouquet, would greet the shopper, enticing them deeper into the shop to experience more delights.

She'd staged various settings, including a "living room" area toward the front. A cream-colored sofa was the centerpiece, with a mix of antiques and new pieces complimented by delicious accessories.

The next display was focused on dining. She'd arranged two handsome place settings with candles and decor on a small vintage table. An oversized classic buffet was filled with fabulous table linens and other dining accessories. She even had a kitchen corner — wasn't that where true romance began?

In the bedding section, she'd splurged on a real mattress that was incredibly soft. She'd draped it in her finest linen duvet, with lovely layers of throws and pillows.

Mallory tested the mattress and, not for the first time, felt tempted to vacate her hotel room, with its overly firm mattress and smelly carpeted floor, and take up residence right here. She glanced over to where her windows were still covered in brown craft paper. At least it would be private . . . for now. But if she got caught sleeping in her shop, well, it might be more than just embarrassing. It might be illegal. Not exactly the way she wanted to start out her new business in this town.

She picked up the silver picture frame she'd set on the pretty bedside table, next to a charming glass lamp. Years ago, she'd found an interesting definition for the word *romance* and using her old calligraphy skills had penned it onto parchment and framed it. She read it again.

Romance:
A quality or feeling of
mystery, excitement.
Remoteness from everyday life.

She loved that line "remoteness from everyday life." And that was exactly why she had named her shop Romancing the Home. Because she believed a house should be more than just walls and a roof. It should be a home, a soft place to land, a getaway from the troubles and humdrum of everyday life.

Still holding the frame, she sat on the edge of the bed . . . remembering how the idea of a lovely home had become so important to her. There had been a time, a very brief time, when her childhood home had felt like a *real* home. Mallory was convinced her mother had been a natural homemaker. She'd baked cookies, kept a garden, picked and arranged wildflowers, dried sheets on a clothesline just to make them smell nice.

Those were Mallory's favorite memories from early childhood. Then, shortly after she started first grade, her mother became "sick." Mallory hadn't understood what that had meant at first. She'd thought, like a cold or flu or chickenpox, her mother would be in bed awhile and then get up and be herself again.

But instead of getting better, her mother got worse. Their home began to resemble a hospital, with a special bed and medical things all around, and a need to keep things "quiet." When her mother went to doctors or to get treatments, Mallory was cared for by a neighbor or sent to visit Grandma Bess. Mallory had just turned seven when her mother died of pancreatic cancer. It seemed like part of her dad died at the same time. To make up for his loss, as well as pay medical bills, he worked, it seemed, night and day.

Mallory remembered the efforts she'd made as a child, hoping to make their house more inviting . . . hoping it would make her dad want to be home more. Whether it was an attempt at cooking or putting a hand-picked flower arrangement on the kitchen table, it seemed her father never noticed. Finally she gave up, focusing her attention on friends and studies and activities and looking forward to summer and holidays with Grandma Bess. Her grandmother might've had offbeat taste when it came to her home's decor, like pink flamingos, plastic flowers, and lava lamps, but it was always cozy and welcoming and fun. Even going to Grandma's funky little church had been fun. Mallory made a mental note to herself: pay a visit to them next Sunday!

Mallory set the silver picture frame back in place then smoothed out the duvet, fluffed a pillow, and straightened a throw. Satisfied, she stepped back to admire the inviting bed, wishing again that she could flee her hotel room and spend the night right here.

She glanced upward and sighed. She hadn't been in the apartment since the day she'd directed the movers to stow her personal furnishings up there. But suddenly she wondered . . . couldn't she transform that sad space into something more comfortable than her hotel room? Seriously, how hard would it be to make it habitable? Her comfortable pillow-top bed alone would be a huge upgrade. And even if it was as ugly as sin up there, she would have all this loveliness down here to satisfy her cravings for beauty. Yes, she decided as she locked up the shop, she was moving on up!

10

After checking out of the hotel, Mallory's
top priority was getting the apartment
cleaned and somewhat livable. But after lugging two loads of clothing and personal
items upstairs and changing into some
grungy cleaning clothes, she felt like she
had set herself up for severe disappointment. The place was a disaster area. Still,
she reminded herself that she was an innovative designer who loved challenges. And
she'd probably never had a bigger one than
this. No contractors, very little budget, and
— once her shop opened — very little time.

She walked from the living room, which
was packed with her furnishings, to the
bedroom, which, although vacant, wasn't
what she'd call habitable. For starters, the
walls were a lime green that the ugly overhead fixture illuminated even more brightly.
Not exactly restful, although she wouldn't
see any of this while sleeping. In a way, this

room had more potential than the rest of the apartment because other than the garish walls, it was a blank slate. Even the unfinished wood floors, with a good scrubbing, wouldn't be half bad. She would make it work.

Next she went to the bathroom, which was totally disgusting. Even a deep clean wouldn't eradicate the musty smell of dry rot beneath the ugly yellow-and-green linoleum floor. The stained fixtures, cheap and rusted medicine cabinet, and light strip did nothing to improve the space. She tested the chrome shower fixture and was surprised to see that it actually worked. She'd need to get a shower curtain before using it though. Hopefully an attractive one that could hide the ugly tub.

She went back out to stare at the kitchen. This was the real eyesore of the apartment. Since it was visible from the living room, it would be hard to ignore. But could she cover it somehow? A screen wouldn't be big enough to hide the torn-up walls where cabinets had been carelessly removed. Perhaps she could place a dresser by the sink to use as counter space. She had no plans to actually cook in here, but she could bring in a small microwave to heat water for tea. And maybe she'd hang some pictures over the holes where the upper cabinets had been recklessly ripped out. It might look a bit odd, but it would be an improvement.

Mallory started making a list of supplies she'd need. Mostly cleaning and repair tools, a closet rod, and a few other miscellaneous items. Next she went to the hardware store. It wasn't until she was going inside that she remembered her appearance was that of a scullery maid. Well, wasn't that what she was today? She pulled her ball cap lower on her head, as if to conceal her identity, then wondered why she bothered. She'd rush through to get this done quickly.

She was just wheeling her cart to the checkout stand when she saw Grayson enter the store. Hoping he wouldn't see or recognize her, she started to unload her items.

No such luck.

"Hey, Mallory." He came over to her. "I thought that was you."

She forced a smile. "Yep. Just getting some cleaning supplies."

"I see." He glanced at her cart with a curious expression.

"Just getting a few things, setting up housekeeping upstairs," she muttered as she awkwardly set the mop on the counter.

"So your remodel is finished?"

She glanced at him, noticing his arched

brows. Did he know something? "Well, it's finished for now." And it wasn't untrue, because her remodel was finished *for now.* What would come later would have to come, well, later.

"And your shop?" he asked. "How's that coming?"

"Great." Her smile was genuine now. "I'm almost ready to open."

"Really?" He looked surprised. "That's great."

"I've still got a few small details to take care of, but I hope to be open soon." She set a plastic shower curtain and rings on the counter. Not very stylish, but it was only temporary.

"In time to get most of the summer season. That's good."

"I hope so. I plan to have a grand opening celebration in a week or so. I'll put something in the newspaper." She set a bottle of bleach on the counter with a thunk, hoping this conversation was about to end.

His eyes twinkled. "I'll be sure to watch for it. Nice to see you again, Mallory. You take care now."

Her cheeks flushed with warmth as she thanked him. Feeling conspicuous, she turned her attention to the clerk, who seemed to have been listening intently.

141

"What kind of business are you starting?" the balding man asked.

"A home decor shop." Mallory fished her wallet from her bag.

"Oh, good luck with that." He grinned, but his tone was sarcastic.

"Meaning?" she asked a bit sharply.

"Well, you know, shops like that . . . they come and go." He put her smaller items in a bag as she slid her debit card into the reader.

"So I've heard," she said stiffly. "But hopefully my shop will be different. Hopefully it won't just *come and go.*"

He looked slightly apologetic as he handed her a receipt. "Well, good luck to you." This time with more enthusiasm. "I hope your shop is a success."

"Thank you." She loaded the mop and broom and things back in the cart. "I hope you'll come to my grand opening." She smiled brightly.

His eyes lit up. "Well, thank you. I'll be sure to watch for it in the newspaper."

As she left she remembered something her grandma used to tell her when she was helping out in the shop: "Grumpy people beget grumpy people, whereas a smile invites a smile." Maybe she should frame that pithy saying and keep it in the upstairs apartment

— just to remind herself not to complain too much.

With her cleaning tools in hand, Mallory attacked the apartment. She knew if the situation were different, she would hire someone to do this deep clean for her, and perhaps even get a painter to tone down the *Rainbow Brite* paint job, but she honestly did not want anyone to see this place. Or to know she was living in such squalor. She wasn't too worried about Thomas. It seemed unlikely he'd want to rock her boat since he might sink his own in the process.

Finally, she got the lime green bedroom clean enough to move her bedroom furnishings in. She already knew exactly where everything would go since she'd drawn it all out weeks ago. First she laid out an old oriental carpet in subdued tones of gray and beige. Then she used her favorite moving tools — smooth sliders for carpets and fluffy ones for hard floors and dollies when needed. She'd mastered the art of rearranging spaces without help years ago. People still marveled that she was able to move heavy pieces of furniture by herself, but she kept these trade secrets to herself.

She had just gotten her bedroom set up and was about to put linens on her bed when her phone buzzed. Hoping it wasn't Kara again — she'd already called twice today — she was surprised to see it was her aunt Cindy.

"Hello?"

"Mallory, this is Aunt Cindy. The girls and I just arrived in Portside. We're taking a trip down memory lane." She chuckled. "Anyway, we'd like to get into mother's little shop to look around. Just for old times' sake."

"Oh?" Mallory didn't know what to say.

"I still have a key, so I can just let myself in."

Mallory wanted to kick herself for not getting the locks changed. "Well, I'm here in Portside too," she said.

You are? Aunt Cindy sounded shocked. "What on earth are you doing here?"

"I actually live here now," Mallory said, taking a deep breath to remain calm.

"You live in Portside?"

Mallory paced in her bedroom. "Yes. In fact, I'm at the shop."

"Oh." Aunt Cindy relayed this information, Mallory assumed, to her daughters. "Well, we just turned onto Main Street and — Oh, I see the shop. At least, I think it's the shop. It looks different. Are you in there *right now*?"

Mallory confirmed she was as she ran down the stairs. She knew she looked a mess, but there wasn't much she could do about that. Mostly she wanted to get out the door and head off her family before they insisted on coming inside. She knew Aunt Cindy could be bossy. She still remembered the torturous week she'd spent at her house as a child. Grandma Bess had thought it would be fun for Mallory, but her older cousins, Val and Marie, had seemed spoiled and selfish and mean. After that awful week, Grandma never made her go again.

Mallory was breathlessly unlocking the door and stepping outside when she saw Aunt Cindy and Val and Marie coming toward her. Were they marching or was that just her imagination? Remembering Grandma's *beget* saying, Mallory pasted a big smile on her face as she greeted them. Her smile was not returned.

"Why are the windows covered?" Marie demanded. She was the older sister and very much like her outspoken mother.

"Because I'm working on creating a new shop in there." Mallory pulled the door closed behind her, then leaned against it. "And I'm not ready to open it to the public."

"A tourist shop?" Val asked.

"Not exactly. But I hope tourists will shop here." Mallory continued to smile. "It's a home decor shop."

"Oh, that's right, you're an interior *decorator.*" Aunt Cindy studied Mallory as if she questioned her ensemble choice of torn faded jeans, stained sweatshirt, and ball cap.

"That's right, I'm an interior designer." Mallory stood taller.

"So, what happened to Grandma's shop?" Val asked, a tinge of a whine in her voice. "All her stuff? What did you do with it?"

"Yes, I'd like to know too," Aunt Cindy said. "We had always thought that Val would run the shop someday . . . after my mother passed away."

"Oh?" Mallory looked at Val. She was only two years older than Mallory but could've easily passed for seventy with her permed hair and pink polyester pantsuit. And, really, she probably would've been completely at home in the tourist shop. It almost made Mallory feel guilty. Except that Grandma Bess had made the choice.

"We always hoped Val could live in the apartment upstairs." Marie scowled at Mallory. "You know, Val hasn't had the opportunities *others* have had."

"Yes, Val never had a husband to take care of her." Aunt Cindy's tone seemed to insinuate that Mallory had.

"I know how it feels to be on your own." Mallory turned to Val, trying to be empathetic. "My three children were still young when Vince walked out on me."

For a moment no one said anything, and Mallory hoped her relatives were going to be understanding and let her be. "It is good to see you all." Mallory tried to sound more sincere than she felt. "I wish I weren't so busy, but as you can see, I'm in the middle of cleaning and I just can't —"

"I *want* to see Grandma's shop." Val insisted in a loud voice. "I need to see it."

Mallory didn't know what to do. Across the street, an older couple stopped to stare at the scene. As if enjoying the attention, Val's voice grew even shriller.

"She was my grandmother too!" she declared. "I have a right to go inside her shop. I want to see it now."

"Good grief, Mallory," Marie growled. "You could at least let us inside. Is that too much to ask?"

Mallory noticed a pair of young women coming their way, looking on with curiosity. "No, of course not. Come in." She opened the door, then stepped aside so the three could enter.

"What on earth?" Aunt Cindy sounded as

if she'd just stumbled into a steaming pile of cow manure.

"What have you done with this place?" Val demanded. "Where's Grandma's stuff?"

"It's been moved to another tourist shop in a different town," Mallory calmly explained. She knew nothing she could say would appease these women, so she just stepped back and watched as they walked through her shop, making thoughtless comments and talking as if she weren't there.

"Who in the world would want something like this?" Aunt Cindy picked up a soft faux fur pillow by its corner, holding it at arm's length as if it were a dead rat.

"Who would want any of these fancy things?" Marie asked. "It all looks too ritzy and totally useless."

"Look at the price of this lamp!" Val exclaimed. "I'm sure I've seen the exact same one at Value Mart for $9.99."

"This is highway robbery," Aunt Cindy said.

Mallory had had enough. "Look, I understand this shop isn't your personal style, and that's fine. Different people like different things. But I have a lot to get done today, so if you're finished looking around, I'd like to lock the place up and —"

Val crossed her arms and leaned on one

of the shelves. "I want to see the apartment."

Mallory shook her head. "I'm sorry, that's not going to happen."

"But I need to see it."

"Why do you *need* to see it?" Mallory asked. "You couldn't possibly have any sentimental attachment to it. Grandma never let us kids go up there."

"But Val always dreamed of moving in up there," Marie argued. "Let her see it."

"I'm sorry. But it's my private living quarters and I'm not ready for anyone to see it." Mallory was trying to guide the women toward the front door, which felt a bit like herding cats.

"You know that we're contesting the will, don't you?" Aunt Cindy narrowed her eyes at Mallory. "I already informed Lloyd Henley that I'm hiring an attorney to represent us in our claim."

"I'm sorry you feel that way, but I've been assured by Mr. Henley that the will is solid. Grandma Bess left this property to me."

"But it's not fair," Val said. "She was supposed to leave it to me."

"I'm curious where you got that idea." Mallory tried to keep her voice even. "Did Grandma Bess tell you she would do that?"

Val's expression was blank.

149

"It was *insinuated*," Aunt Cindy told her. "We all assumed —"

"Look, I was as surprised as anyone that Grandma left it to me. But I got to thinking about how much time I spent here with her. After Mom died, I was here every summer, every holiday, and every school break. Grandma Bess was like a second mom to me. We were very close." She pointed to Val and Marie. "How much time did you guys spend here with her?"

They didn't answer because, as they all knew, Val and Marie rarely made it to Portside.

"So, of course, you can contest the will if you want to pay a lot of attorney fees for nothing. Grandma Bess chose to leave her property to me, and I'm very happy to have it. I plan to live here and run my shop. I'm sorry it's offensive to you, but perhaps in time you'll get beyond it." Mallory placed her hand under Val's elbow, guiding her toward the front door. "When my apartment is finished and the shop is open, you are welcome to come back and look around for old time's sake. Although I suspect with all the changes I've made, you probably won't want to."

"Well, I —"

"I hope you'll enjoy your visit in Portside."

Mallory opened the door, thrusting a speechless Val outside. "Thank you for stopping by." To her relief, Aunt Cindy and Marie trickled out after her. Mallory waved goodbye, then closed and locked the door before she started to cry. She wasn't even sure why the tears came. Was it because of the mean things they said or because they hated her shop or because they were her relatives? Maybe even due to the sad state of her living quarters upstairs? She wondered what Grandma Bess would say about what had just transpired. Knowing Grandma, she would probably just laugh and say that "grumpy begets grumpy."

Even so, Mallory decided to call Lloyd Henley again. Thinking she'd need to leave a message, she was surprised when he picked up.

"I know why you're calling," he said. "Your relatives were here earlier."

"Yes, they were here too."

"I assured them the will was legally written and witnessed. Bess was in her right mind when she made it, and no self-respecting attorney would contest it." He cleared his throat. "But there are always a number of unscrupulous lawyers who'd gladly accept fees up front, but very few would take it on contingency, especially

151

after discovery."

"What does that mean?"

"It means you shouldn't be concerned. Once their unscrupulous lawyer saw the will, he or she would require more money than the property's real value. No matter how the lawsuit went, it would be a lose-lose for your relatives."

"Meaning they would be crazy to proceed?"

"Unless they are just extremely wealthy and horribly vengeful, I venture to say even the stubbornest people would not attempt to contest this will."

"So you do believe it's solid?"

"Rock-solid."

"I wouldn't be this worried except that I've made improvements and ordered inventory and spent money I can barely afford. I even sold my house to invest into the property. I just hope I didn't move too fast."

"I understand your concern, but I assure you, if your relatives contest the will, I will stand behind it at no cost to you. I would do it just for entertainment's sake. Their attorney would have to cover all the court fees, as well as my expenses, when he or she lost." He laughed.

"Thank you. I feel better now." They chatted for a bit more and she invited him to her grand opening. He promised to bring his wife and daughter. She did feel better when she hung up, but her heart still ached about her relatives. Why did they have to be so mean-spirited?

11

11

Despite having set up her bedroom the best
she could, it was a disheartening first night.
At first she blamed it on the ugly confrontation with Aunt Cindy and her girls because
it had sapped her energy and enthusiasm
for cleaning yesterday. But when she woke
up this morning, she knew it was more than
just her disagreeable relatives. She couldn't
decide if it was the pervasive musty smell
that she guessed would be eradicated only
with a gutted bathroom or the general
disgusting aura of the whole apartment.

She walked around the dysfunctional
rooms, considering whether the place
needed an exorcism. Maybe that was over-
kill, but something about this dreadful
apartment — besides the obvious problems
— was creeping her out.

She dressed in yesterday's housecleaning
clothes, then slipped downstairs to where
she was happily greeted by her picture-

perfect shop. It was all so lovely and welcoming — such a contrast to what lurked upstairs — it felt like walking out into a bright day after being shut up in a dark room.

Once again, she wished she could live down here. Just to give her senses the full treatment, she went around turning on table lamps and putting on music. She even lit the hurricane candle by the door. Ahh. She was tempted to snuggle into the comfy sofa and absorb the loveliness, but her stomach was growling and she wanted to grab a bite while town was still quiet.

She hurried down to the Red Hen Café and ordered breakfast to go, hoping she wouldn't run into anyone. To her relief only a few customers were there and no one seemed to notice her. She knew it was silly to be concerned about how she looked, but years of presenting herself as a professional interior designer had taught her to take her appearance seriously. She knew people *did* judge books by their covers — especially in her line of work — and she'd always tried to put her best foot forward. She frowned down at her dirty tennis shoes. Just not today.

Finally, with her to-go bag in one hand and hot coffee in the other, she was fumbling to balance her breakfast and unlock her front door when she heard footsteps behind her. For a moment she imagined her rude relatives returning to demand an upstairs tour. But she glanced over her shoulder to see Grayson grinning at her. She honestly wasn't sure she wouldn't have preferred Aunt Cindy.

"Here." He reached for her coffee cup. "Let me give you a hand before you lose that."

"I'm okay." But she didn't stop him from taking her bag as well so she could get the right key into the door. "Thanks," she nervously told him as she pushed inside.

Without being asked, he carried her food right into the shop.

"Wow!" He paused in front of the glass front credenza, looking all around. "Wow, wow, wow!"

Mallory closed the door then crossed the room to remove her to-go bag and coffee from him. Despite her resolve to keep her shop out of the public eye, she didn't mind as he slowly walked around. "This is incredible, Mallory. Very beautiful."

She made room to set the breakfast bag on the small dining table, then popped the lid off of her latte. "Thanks."

"You're *really* good at this," he said as he

came over to the table. "I'm totally blown away. Well done!"

"Thank you." She smiled meekly. "I hadn't really wanted anyone to see it yet. Kind of wanted to keep it all under wraps until my grand opening."

"Sorry." He sighed. "Sort of bullied my way in, didn't I?"

She shrugged as she sipped her coffee. Truthfully, she didn't mind. His praise felt like a soothing salve to the wound created by her relatives yesterday.

"Well, I don't want to wear out my welcome or let your breakfast get cold." He grinned. "I'm glad I got to see this though. And if it makes you feel better, I won't mention how wonderful it is to anyone."

She laughed. "I guess I wouldn't mind if you mentioned it was *wonderful.*"

"They say word-of-mouth advertising's the best."

She nodded. "I've found that to be true."

She followed him to the front of the store, where he paused with his hand on the doorknob. "You know when I saw you yesterday, I was worried that you were in over your head."

"I probably looked like it."

"But this is fantastic, Mallory. Honestly, it's beyond any home decor shop that's ever

157

been in Portside. Elegant yet very inviting."

"I appreciate hearing that." She waved her hand down her grungy work clothes. "I look like this because I'm still working on my apartment upstairs."

"I see." His brow creased. "Thomas Norton still doing work for you?"

"No, not exactly."

"So it's all done then?"

"Done enough."

"Okay then." He opened the door. "I'll let you get back to your breakfast."

"Thanks for dropping in." Oops. Did he hear that tinge of sarcasm in her voice?

But he just laughed. "You mean for forcing my way in?" She grinned. "Yeah, whatever."

"Well, I'll start spreading the rumor that amazing things are going on behind those covered windows."

She closed the door behind him, securely locking it. She didn't even mind that he'd seen her shop, because he was right — nothing beat word-of-mouth advertising. And as the most popular contractor in town, he probably had lots of connections. As she sat down to eat, she wondered about his questioning her about Thomas Norton. He probably knew that Thomas wasn't licensed. As a licensed contractor that probably didn't sit well with him. But she hadn't said anything one way or another. Not because she wanted to protect Thomas, but at the same time she wasn't ready to throw him under the bus. Not yet anyway. If he didn't give her back her money . . . well, she would think about that later.

Even after two days of cleaning everything that was cleanable in the apartment, the unpleasant odor remained. She put scent sticks and candles on every surface, but it still didn't mask that stinky smell. Realizing there was nothing she could do to make the place any cleaner, she spent the third day setting up house. Which was sort of a joke.

But she did move her living room furnishings into place. She rolled out a sisal carpet over the unfinished wood floor and even hung a few things on the magenta wall. Of course, everything looked all wrong against the garishly bright walls, but at least she had a place to sit and a place to sleep. Not that she planned to spend any more time than necessary up here.

The kitchen was still a hot mess where little could be done. The refrigerator worked, but even after she cleaned it twice with a bleach solution, it felt dodgy. Other than sealed-up items, she wouldn't be using it much. She hung a beloved painting over a gaping hole above the sink, but the seascape looked silly against the fire engine–red wall. She was tempted to get some white paint and slap it on, but it would take at least two coats to hide these walls, and until she got a real contractor in here, it would just be a waste of time and money.

The bathroom, though functional, was still the most disgusting room in the apartment. Despite her fluffy white towels and luxurious bath amenities, it was foul. And the cheap plastic shower curtain only served to remind her of that horror movie scene in *Psycho.* She would have to shower quickly — with her eyes tightly closed.

All in all, the apartment was a dismal disappointment. It was not the sort of place she would ever willingly inhabit. Not in this condition, anyway. She could still see the potential with a major overhaul. And hopefully, after the money from the sale of her house was deposited into her account, she could hire a real contractor to do things right. Maybe she could even swallow her pride and hire Grayson Matthews. Unless, like everyone else, he was too busy.

There wasn't anything she could do about that now, she told herself as she dressed in normal clothes. Today she had the challenging task of asking Thomas to hang the awning that was supposed to be delivered that morning. And since he'd ignored her calls and texts yesterday, she'd gotten up extra early with the plan to meet him in his driveway again. In an effort to sweeten him up before she brought out the big guns, she was bringing coffee and donuts.

"Hello," she called out cheerfully as he exited his house. She held up the coffee cup and donut bag. "I'd like a word with you."

His brow creased as he approached.

"Don't worry, they're not laced with arsenic," she teased. "I just need to talk to you."

"Well, I don't have your money yet," he told her.

"I'm not here for money. I just really need your help today."

"For what?" He took the coffee, sniffing it as if he honestly thought it might've been tampered with, then took a cautious sip.

She explained about the awning. "I want to open my doors on Friday so I really need it up."

"I'm pretty busy —"

She frowned. "I don't want to pressure you, Thomas, but I do need your help. And I'll take a good chunk of change off what you owe me if you do it today." She held

161

the opened donut bag toward him.

"Today?" He selected a maple bar and took a bite, slowly chewing. "Okay, I guess I can make time to do that for you. You sure the awning will be here today?"

"It's scheduled to arrive this morning."

"Okay. I'll be there around five. Probably a two-man job. I'll bring someone with me."

She handed him the bag of donuts and smiled. "Thanks, Thomas. I appreciate it."

He nodded. "Okay. See ya later."

Surprised that it had been that easy, Mallory got into her car. Maybe Thomas wasn't such a bad guy. She knew there were others in the trades without licenses, and she realized it could be a challenge to keep up with all the fees, bonds, insurance, and all that, but in her business of serving clients who trusted her, she had to deal with true contractors. As far as hanging her awning, since it was her shop and she planned to supervise the hanging, she didn't feel too concerned.

She'd just gotten back to her shop when she received a text from her sign artist. Laurie sent photos of the wooden sign to go above the door and the stencil for the window. Both looked great. Hopefully Mallory could get Thomas's help with hanging the sign too. Again, she'd make it worth his while. She felt a surge of hope. Everything seemed to be coming together.

She called the newspaper office and made an appointment to meet with their ad designer. Since it was a weekly newspaper that came out on Wednesday, she decided to just go for it. She'd host her grand opening on the upcoming Friday, only five days away. As she walked down to the newspaper office later that afternoon, she felt a nervous excitement at the thought of opening her shop. It was becoming real.

The advertising designer, Libby, was enthused about the possibility of a new design shop. "You know I've been looking for someone to help me with a condo," she told Mallory as they sat down. "I just got it last winter and I don't know what to do with it. It's got this gorgeous ocean view and I got a couple pieces of furniture, but I'm not even sure they look right in there."

"I'd be happy to do a free consultation," Mallory said as she pulled the sign pictures up on her phone.

"Fabulous."

Mallory found the photos from Laurie and angled her phone toward Libby. "Romancing the Home might not make sense to everyone, but I have this theory that romance is more than most people imagine." She handed Libby one of the business cards she'd ordered a few weeks back, pointing to the definition of romance. "A quality or feeling of mystery, excitement. Remoteness from everyday life," she read aloud.

"Ooh, that's nice."

"Great. I want that quote to be part of the ad." She swiped at her phone to show Libby the stenciled window sign Laurie had drawn up. "And something like this on top."

They played with the design on Libby's computer for a while until they both liked the outcome. "I want this week's ad to be focused on the grand opening," Mallory explained. "And then in the following weeks, just a regular ad. Then, depending on how things go, I might want something bigger with photos. I'll just have to play it by ear."

"Perfect." Libby leaned back in her chair. "And if you have any special promotions, we can always tweak it."

"Just one thing" — Mallory held up a finger — "I'd appreciate it if you didn't let the name of my shop out until the newspaper ad is published. I want it to be kind of a surprise."

Libby winked. "You got it."

"And I hope you'll come to my grand opening," Mallory said as they shook hands.

"Feel free to bring friends. My shop will give you an idea of what I can do, but keep in mind that it's a limited space with a specific theme. I've done all kinds of design — everything from modern classic to rustic ranch to shabby chic."

"I'll be there."

As Mallory strolled back to her shop, she felt a lightness in her step. Not only was she dressed in clean clothes again, she was also about to become a bona fide business-woman in this darling small town. Life was good!

She turned onto her street and was surprised to see Thomas's pickup parked in front. It wasn't even four o'clock and he was already removing the packaging from the awning that had been delivered shortly before noon. Life was really good. She greeted him and watched as he used his pocket knife to slit open the box.

"Careful," she warned. "You don't want to scratch the metal."

He just nodded. "Yeah, yeah."

"I know it's super heavy because it took two people to unload it from the truck." She glanced around. "I thought you were bringing someone to help."

"Eric couldn't make it. But that's okay. I can handle it." He went over to remove a ladder from his pickup.

"I don't know." She frowned. "I don't see how one person can possibly get it up there."

"It's probably not as heavy as you think. I doubt it will all be in one piece." He leaned the ladder against her building.

"Might help if we got this out of the way." She started to move the metal bench and he grabbed the other end.

"And these planters too." He lifted one, then grunted. "Man, this is heavy."

"Be glad I didn't plant them yet," she said as she helped him lug it to the other end of the building and then the other one too. When she looked up, she noticed another familiar pickup across the street. Of course, Grayson was here. It figured he'd happen by just as they were attempting this. She pretended not to notice, turning her attention back to Thomas who was halfway up his ladder.

"So first I need to find and mark the studs," he told her.

She stepped back to watch as he ran his electronic stud finder across the stucco. He went back and forth a few times without success. "Guess I'll do it the old-fashioned way." He pulled a hammer and a large nail from his tool belt and started tapping holes into the stucco.

Not liking the mess he was making, both on the recently painted stucco as well as on the sidewalk, she was tempted to protest, then realized it was likely the awning would conceal it. And if not, she wasn't afraid to get on a ladder and fix it on her own. To distract herself, she checked the delivery package and pulled out instructions for the awning. All the years of working on her old Victorian house, as well as designing, had taught her the value of carefully studying instructions.

"Found one," Thomas declared. "The rest should be easy."

As he climbed down, she held up the instructions. "It says here this is a two-person job, Thomas."

"You wanna help?" he asked in a teasing tone.

"Well, I'm good at some things, but this might be more than —"

"You want this done or not, Mallory? I don't have all day to stand out here yapping."

Mallory was torn. Sure, she wanted it done. But she wanted it done right. What if Thomas wasn't capable of doing it right? What if he ruined the awning? Or what if he ruined her building? She imagined

167

broken stucco all over the sidewalk. Or what if he crashed the heavy metal through the big window? Or worse, what if he hurt himself, then sued her? What had seemed a relatively simple task and even an inspired idea this morning suddenly felt like a nightmare. But how to get out of it now?

12

Still trying to find a graceful escape from having Thomas incorrectly hang and possibly ruin her awning, Mallory heard someone coming up behind her.

"Hello there." Grayson had walked across the street to join them. He paused in front of her and surveyed the mess they'd created in front of her shop with curiosity.

"Hi," she said meekly. Grayson had already questioned her regarding Thomas's standing as a contractor. Hopefully he wasn't going to turn this into a scene.

Grayson greeted Thomas, then pointed to the big box. "What's that?"

"An awning," she told him.

"Yeah, Mallory needs some help getting it up." Thomas used a slightly sharp tone. "Got a problem with that?"

"No, I actually think an awning would look great up there." Grayson rubbed his chin. "But are you two putting it up there by yourselves?"

"Thomas was going to bring someone," she said, "but his friend was busy and I just want to get this up. My grand opening is Friday and I hoped —"

"How about I give a hand?" Grayson cut her off.

"We don't need your help." Thomas bent his knees and reached into the box. He wrapped his arms around the metal but was clearly struggling to remove an awkwardly large piece. Before he got it out, Grayson stepped in to help and both men pulled it out and set it on the sidewalk.

Mallory looked at Thomas. "I think we could use some help."

"Whatever." Thomas wouldn't meet her eyes.

"Look, Thomas," Grayson began a bit tersely. "It's no secret you're not licensed and bonded. All you need is for someone to turn you in and —"

"I don't give a rip about that."

"You don't care that you could be dragged into court and hit with some pretty stiff fines?" Grayson asked.

"I'm sick of the government in my back pocket, regulating every move I make." Thomas sounded belligerent.

Grayson nodded. "I hear you, man. But

they've got us over a barrel. Do it their way or the highway. Or worse. Trust me, I know."

Thomas pulled off his cap and ran his fingers through his hair. "Yeah, man, you're probably right. But it just ticks me off, ya know?"

"I do know. I've been getting pretty ticked with some of the recent code changes. Sometimes I even question them on it. Not that it does any good. But if I want to stay in business, I have to play by their rules." He tipped his head down the street. "Not sure if you noticed it or not, but there's an inspector down there right now. He's taking a look at the new deck The Chowder House had installed in back."

"No kidding?" Thomas peered down the street, then frowned. "Hey, thanks for tipping me off."

"No problem. Now how about letting me help? If the inspector happens along, it'll look like this is my job. Like you're working for me."

Thomas didn't argue this and before long, the two men, with Mallory reading the instructions, started to get the awning into place. It took longer than expected, but when it was done, it looked great and Mallory knew it had been done right. Thomas reloaded his ladder then told them both goodbye and took off.

"I don't know how to thank you," Mallory told Grayson. "What do I owe you for your time?"

He held up his hand. "Just being neighborly."

"But you can't —"

"You want to repay me?" he asked. "Invite me up there for dinner." He nodded up to her apartment. "I'd like to see how your reno looks."

Her nerves shot up. "Well, I'm not set up for cooking yet. My appliances haven't arrived." That was only partly true. Some were in her storage unit. She'd just received an email saying the others were still a couple weeks out. "But I could take you out for dinner. Would that work?"

He grinned. "You bet."

She checked her watch. It was nearly seven and, after having only an apple and some cheese for lunch, she was hungry. "Does tonight work?"

"Sure."

"Did you want something fancy?" she asked.

"You know, all day long I've been craving just a really good burger."

She laughed. "Works for me."

"What do you say we try out that new

deck at The Chowder House? It's a nice balmy night for eating outdoors."

"That sounds great." She nodded eagerly. "I've always loved Chowder House cheeseburgers."

Grayson pointed to the clouds on the western horizon. "Might even be a good night for a sunset. Want to walk over there now?"

"How about if I meet you there in a few minutes," she suggested. "I need to check on a couple things."

He agreed and she hurried into the shop. She really just wanted to clean up some after their awning installation but felt it would be rude not to invite Grayson to do the same. But she wasn't ready for anyone to use the restroom in the shop's back room yet, and there was no way she was letting him upstairs.

Mallory quickly cleaned herself up, grabbed a light jacket, and hurried over to The Chowder House to find Grayson comfortably seated on the back deck.

"Good-looking deck." She sat down in the plastic patio chair and picked up the menu. "Quite the improvement."

She glanced around. "All they need are better tables and chairs, some attractive planters, and a few other touches and this could be a pretty swanky dinner place."

He laughed. "Well, I doubt they'll put much more into it. After all, this is The Chowder House."

"Yes, you're right. And to be honest, I like it like this. The view is spectacular." She looked out over the ocean. "I think you're right, looks like we're in for a good sunset."

They ordered their burgers then Mallory leaned back in her chair, taking a deep breath and letting it out. "It feels good to relax."

"Busy day?"

She told him about some of the things that had been keeping her moving. "But I got almost everything on my list done."

"Good for you. What didn't get done?"

"Oh, I was going to ask Thomas to hang my store sign above my door after the awning got hung. But I can probably do that myself."

"I can do it for you."

She waved a hand. "You've already done more than enough. Besides, I think I'd like to wait until the day before my grand opening."

"You're excited about that, aren't you?"

Mallory couldn't hold back her smile. "I feel like a kid at Christmastime."

"Have you had any regrets? I mean about

giving up your house and design business in the city?"

She considered this. "To be honest, I've had some doubts as to whether this was a smart thing to do, you know, at this stage of the game. But I haven't had any serious regrets." Her mind wandered to the state of her living quarters, and she realized it was more of an irritation than a regret.

Grayson folded his hands in front of him. "Well, as much as I like what you said about second chances, I realize it wasn't easy to take that big leap. I admire you for it. I'm not sure I'd be that brave about making such a big life change."

"I'll admit there have been some difficult moments." Now she told him about her aggravating relatives' visit.

"You're kidding — they threatened to challenge Bess's will?"

She was surprised to hear him call her grandmother by her first name. "Did you know my grandma?"

"Oh, sure. Everyone in town knew Bess. She was quite a gal. She might've been old, but she was sharp as a tack right up to the day she died. So if your aunt wants to contest her sanity, I'd be happy to testify on your behalf. Bess was at a chamber meeting the week before she passed, urging the local businesses to support a summer street fair in late August."

"Really?"

"Yeah. We always have one on the Fourth, but that's one of our good tourist times anyway. Bess's point was that having a second fair in August would give us another opportunity to capitalize on summer vacationers."

"That makes sense." She caught a whiff of something delicious — hopefully their burgers — and realized she was really hungry.

He nodded. "She was a sensible woman."

"With a sense of humor."

He chuckled. "That's for sure. Seriously, if your aunt and cousins claim she wasn't in her right mind, I could get a whole lot of folks to sign a statement saying she was as sane as anyone."

"Thanks. I'll keep that in mind. Her lawyer has pretty much guaranteed me that he'll handle my relatives." She shook her head. "But it was stressful. They insisted on coming into my shop and then walked around making all these derogatory comments. I thought I was pretty tough, but their words hurt."

"Derogatory comments? About your beautiful shop? What kind of women are they?"

She kind of laughed. "Not very nice ones, I hate to say. They're angry that Grandma left everything to me." She told him about how she'd spent so much time with her grandmother, and how they rarely visited.

"Then of course she'd leave it to you. I bet she'd be proud to see what you've done with the place too."

"I hope so." Mallory didn't care to think about what Grandma would say if she saw her living upstairs amid the chaotic mess.

Grayson's voice broke through her thoughts. "I hate to admit this, but I was pleasantly surprised Thomas did such a good job with the shop . . ." His voice trailed off as if he had more to say but was holding back.

"Didn't he do a nice job on the woodwork?" She sipped her ice water. "I was so pleased to see how it came back to life."

"I think his strength as a craftsman is in restorations. Not everyone likes to work on old houses."

"Believe me, I know about that. Vince, my ex, was all in when we first bought our old Victorian, but he got tired of it after a couple of years. I guess I can't blame him. I was tired of it too, but that didn't mean I wanted to just give it up and quit."

"But he did?"

"Yeah. He gave up and quit on every-thing." She sighed, trying to think of a way to change the topic. "So I'm going to guess that you prefer new construction to restora-tions."

He shrugged. "Well, it's simpler, that's for sure. I like the smell of new lumber and controlling the bones of a home, making sure it's all done right and will stand the test of time. I like thinking that the houses I build will still be around for my great-great grandchildren. But I can respect a well-done renovation. *If* it's well done."

"My Victorian was well done." She was relieved to see their waiter approaching with food. "Even in the years when I had to do things on a shoestring with more elbow grease than money, I made sure it was done right." Mallory paused as their plates were set on the table.

"I'm starved." Grayson picked up his burger and for a bit they were too focused on eating to talk.

"This hits the spot." Mallory dipped a fry in ketchup.

"So, I'm curious about your Victorian renovation. Did you have to upgrade your plumbing and electric?"

She nodded somberly as she reached for another fry. "It took me a while to pay off those bills."

"I can imagine." He reached for the ketchup. "One reason I don't like renovating anything that old."

"I eventually caught up. Once my design business got going."

"What about your shop? Did you upgrade plumbing and electric?"

Mallory pursed her lips. "Thomas thought it was okay." She remembered how he'd played with the light switches, not exactly a careful examination of the wiring.

"Just okay?"

"Well, I know my grandfather did some remodeling to the whole building. I think in the fifties. He was pretty handy. I remember Grandma saying he remodeled the apartment upstairs so they could rent it out. He died not long afterward, but she still had the apartment as a secondary source of income."

"Smart thinking on his part."

"Unfortunately, those upgrades included linoleum and some other things considered quite modern back then. To be honest, I'd have preferred the original fixtures. They might've been worth restoring. The newer ones just need to be tossed."

"So you think your grandfather upgraded the electric and plumbing *then*? In the fif-

179

ties?" he pressed.

"Thomas seemed to think so." She knew that sounded flimsy.

"Because I'm sure that building had knob and tube wiring to start with."

"Probably." She shifted uncomfortably in her seat. Mostly because he was on to something — something she didn't want to think about right now. She pointed to where the sky was turning amber and rose. "Oh, look at that. You were right, it is a good sunset. So beautiful."

"The sun is romancing the sky." His eyes twinkled.

"Are you making fun of me?" she teased.

"Not at all. I read that framed quote in your shop. The definition of the word *romance*. I liked the part about remoteness from everyday life."

"I do too. In fact, I've put that quote on my business cards and in the newspaper ad. I want people to understand that my shop's name isn't about hearts and flowers or me wanting to play cupid in people's houses."

"No, it's obviously much more."

She was glad that he got it, but speaking about romance and enjoying the gorgeous sunset with a man she liked reminded her of Corrina. She wanted to think of a discreet way to question him about his attractive assistant, but there wasn't one, so she just let it alone. Besides, if he was romantically involved with Corrina, would he be here having dinner with another woman? She didn't think so. Grayson wasn't that sort of guy. Still, she couldn't be certain. Time would tell.

13

The next morning, Mallory got out of bed
with a purpose. She needed to attack that
downstairs restroom — rather, she needed
to *romance* it. Just in case a guest needed to
use the facilities. She went down to do a
quick evaluation of the problem. Like the
rest of her shop, the restroom's old wood
floor was refinished and looked good. But
also like the downstairs, the walls were a
milky white, which worked in her shop but,
thanks to the cheap overhead light, looked
overly bright and stark in the restroom.
Plus, it drew unwanted attention to the
outdated plumbing fixtures.

She couldn't do anything about the old
toilet, but the wall-mounted sink could be
skirted with fabric to hide the pipes. Except
that would look more shabby than chic.
Maybe it was just a restroom, but she
wanted to continue the air of sophistication
she'd created in the shop. Even her back

storage room looked better than this. She'd cleaned and organized the tall wooden shelves, stocking them with items she would eventually put in the shop, but in such a way that it was rather attractive all by itself.

She needed to zhuzh that restroom up though. Finally, with a specific plan in mind, she headed to the hardware store for supplies. It took a while to choose a color for the walls, but she finally decided on a dark olive that would look good against the wood floor. She got a few other things, then headed back to her shop.

Mallory had painted a lot of the rooms in her old Victorian, but once her design career launched, she left painting to the professionals. Still, she knew some tricks of the trade, and it was a small room. How long could it take?

Five hours later, she was done. And exhausted. Crawling around the toilet to get corners and then under the sink where she'd also painted pipes and underparts of the sink to make them "disappear" hadn't been easy. By the time she cleared out the stepladder and paint things, it was nearly seven and she felt like the walking dead. She had to admit the room looked better.

She spent the next morning putting the restroom together. And now, standing in the doorway, she admired how the small cherry dresser she wedged next to the sink — topped with a fresh flower arrangement, large scented candle, and handsome brass table lamp — added a touch of class. On the other side of the sink, she'd mounted a small shelf, complete with neatly folded linen guest towels and a French decanter of liquid soap from her inventory. Above the sink, she'd hung an oversized mirror with an antique brass frame. She'd also placed a few carefully chosen paintings and changed the overhead light to a dimmer bulb, and the old restroom now looked like a real powder room. Too bad she forgot to take *before* pictures!

Knowing the newspaper ad would be out today, Mallory wanted to make sure the front of her shop was as picture-perfect as possible. The awning, fresh paint, and stained wooden door were already a great improvement to the exterior, but she needed to get those cast-iron pots planted with luscious greens and flowers. To that end, she drove to the nearby nursery and picked out some healthy-looking plants, as well as several bags of potting soil. How she'd missed gardening!

By the time she swept the sidewalk free of spilled potting soil, the front of her shop looked more inviting than ever. She still wanted to hang fairy lights for the grand opening, and Laurie would bring her signs tomorrow, but the pieces were falling into place even better than she'd imagined. Well, except for that apartment, but she didn't want to think about that. Although she knew one thing for sure — she wouldn't do any more painting herself. Not that she could hire anyone just yet. At the moment, she was too embarrassed to let anyone, not even hired help, up there.

By Thursday afternoon, after Laurie finished painting the sign on the window, Mallory was preparing to hang the other sign when a pair of women stopped by to admire the shop's exterior. "This reminds me of Paris," the older of the two commented.

"I can't wait to see inside," the other one said. "Judging from out here, I bet it's going to be amazing."

Nothing could've pleased Mallory more. She invited both to return the next evening for her grand opening. "It's from five until seven," she told them. "And I'll have refreshments." They assured her they would come.

Mallory had just set up her stepladder when she saw Grayson's pickup pull up in front. Grinning, he got out. "Looks like I'm just in time."

"Really?" She looked hopefully at him.

"Yeah, I told you I'd hang that for you." He took the heavy sign from her. "By the way, it looks great out here. I've heard lots of people commenting on it. You've made quite an impression."

She held up her hammer and nails, but he shook his head as he examined the back of the sign. "I think we should put a good layer of construction glue on the back and then just place one long screw through into a stud. We'll conceal that with a dab of paint and that sign won't be going anywhere."

"So you don't think I'll be out of business in a year?" she teased as she followed him back to his truck where he was opening a big toolbox.

"Did I honestly say that?" He rummaged around the various tools and things.

"That was your prediction."

"Well, that was before I saw what you were capable of." His brow creased as he pulled out a tube of glue. "Now you'll see how the market responds. That's the real test."

She knew he was right, but she didn't want to dwell on that. Before long, the sign was hung. "Thank you." She stepped back to admire his handiwork. "That looks perfect."

"The whole place looks perfect," he said.

"But now I'll make another prediction."

She frowned. "Uh-oh."

"No, this is a good one. I predict you'll be elbow to elbow with enthused guests at your grand opening tomorrow night."

"Oh, I hope there's room." She looked around the sidewalk. "I'd considered setting the refreshment table out here if weather cooperates. Sandi offered to manage it for me."

"Sounds like a good idea."

"Will you be coming?"

"You bet." He nodded. "Wouldn't miss it."

It was the big day and Mallory was a bundle of happy nerves. Sandi came over early to set up the food the caterers had delivered. To Mallory's relief, Sandi hadn't worn her usual garb of faded jeans and a sports hoodie. Instead, she had on an attractive knit dress and stylish ankle boots. "Don't you look pretty," Mallory told her.

"My mom's always giving me a hard time for dressing inappropriate for my age. She says I look like a teenager. She thought I'd dress like her and her friends once I turned forty." Sandi looked at Mallory's sleeveless black dress. "Don't you look chic in your LBD."

"I didn't want my outfit to distract or compete with the shop." Mallory fingered her string of silver beads and pearls.

"Well, you look very classy." Sandi waved her hand over the store. "Just like your gorgeous shop. I still cannot believe you put all this together so quickly."

"Quickly?"

"Less than a month. I'd call that pretty fast. I can't wait for you to give me a consultation at my house. I bet you'll have a lot of requests after tonight."

"That reminds me." Mallory handed Sandi the silver holder she'd filled with her business cards. "I want one of these on the refreshment table. Not in front, but just accessible." She returned to tweaking the large flower arrangement on the entryway credenza.

"Want me to plug in your fairy lights?" Sandi asked.

Mallory checked her watch. Half past four. "Sure, why not." She followed Sandi outside to where the refreshments were still protected by a white sheet. She'd also placed a pair of wicker chairs adjacent to the bench. For overflow or weary shoppers.

"Did I forget anything?" Mallory asked Sandi.

"I can't imagine what. Your music is

188

lovely. The candles you lit smell amazing. The wine table inside looks inviting. I just hope no one spills any red on that scrumptious white sofa. You know, I want that sofa in my house, but not with wine stains."

"I've got a quick clean-up kit in the back room. It's on the worktable, just in case we need to use it."

"You think of everything, don't you?"

"It's kind of a designer curse. We're very OCD with details."

"Not me." Sandi laughed. "When you see my house, you'll understand that."

"Speaking of obsessing over details, go check out my powder room," Mallory said. "It used to be the ugliest restroom imaginable. I couldn't change out the old fixtures, but I zhuzhed it up the other day."

"*Zhuzhed?*" Sandi tilted her head. "Is that some new designer word?"

"Sort of." Mallory laughed. "Anyway, go check it out."

When Sandi came back, she was nodding in approval. "I love it! I want you to help me do that to my second bathroom. My fixtures are almost exactly like those. And then we can redo the ice-cream shop bathroom."

"Two possible design jobs already." Mallory clapped her hands. "The night is a success."

And, for the most part, the night was a success. Everyone she'd invited, plus a whole lot more, had filled the shop. Grayson's prediction was right — the guests were elbow to elbow. Hopefully they'd still been able to get a feeling for the shop. Or maybe that didn't matter. Maybe it would simply motivate them to return for a more extensive visit during regular business hours when the place didn't feel like a packed sardine can.

It had been fun to greet various people that she'd met and befriended around town. From her sign artist, Laurie, to the hardware store clerk and his wife and everyone in between. By now Mallory knew a couple dozen people by first name, and that felt good. She'd even been pleased to see that Thomas came. Wearing a clean white shirt and khakis, he'd politely greeted her, complimented her shop, then spent the rest of his time hanging around Sandi.

Despite Sandi's worries about stains on the sofa, it didn't appear to have suffered. All in all, it had been a very good time. Before leaving, a number of women asked for her business card, suggesting the need for a good designer in Portside. So it had definitely been well worth the effort and money she'd invested. She was glad to have the opening behind her and eager to get down to the daily business of running her shop and scheduling casual consultations. Her goal hadn't been to plunge fully into design again, but it would be nice to keep her toe in the water.

By the time Mallory was turning off the lights, she had only two concerns over the entire evening. The first one actually had nothing to do with her grand opening and, she told herself, it was just plain silly to even think about it now.

She hated to admit it, but she'd been bothered to see Grayson arrive with Corrina. Because, unless Mallory was mistaken, Corrina was more than just his assistant. At least, from Corrina's perspective. The way that pretty redhead kept her eyes fixed on Grayson, even holding on to his arm as they navigated the crowded shop together . . . well, it seemed clear Corinna had more than a working relationship in mind. Mallory wondered if Grayson was aware of this, or if he perhaps returned the feeling. But she was determined not to obsess over it now. Why let it spoil what had been a nearly perfect night?

However, there was a second fly in the

ointment. In some ways it was almost disturbing, and it kept her awake half the night. Caroline Kempton, a fellow business-woman and owner of the Chic Boutique, had been fully impressed with everything. She'd oohed and aahed and gushed over the tiniest details.

Of course, nothing could've pleased Mallory more. But her joy unraveled when Caroline took her aside and begged to see the upstairs apartment. Mallory experienced a serious rush of anxiety but had maintained her smile and kept her voice light.

"Oh, it's such a mess up there right now," she said. "I've been so busy getting everything ready for the grand opening, well, my poor apartment's been totally neglected." Perhaps that was easy to misinterpret, to assume her apartment could be easily straightened up and made visitor worthy. Of course, that's not what she meant. It was true her apartment had been neglected, but she didn't know if it would ever be ready for viewing.

"I know what you mean," Caroline had said. "I'm sure your focus has been on your shop, but I'll bet your apartment is amazing and I'm just dying to see it."

"Well, someday when I get it all together, I'll invite you over," Mallory assured her.

"Just not tonight."

Caroline nodded. "The reason I'm so curious is because I've been thinking about selling my house. It's just outside of town and more room than I need after my husband passed. I've been dreaming of doing the same thing you did. I'm getting older, and it would be so handy to live above my shop."

"It is convenient."

"But I haven't rented out that apartment in years. I would've liked the extra income, but it's in horrible shape and needs a complete overhaul. Probably like yours did. I remember Bess saying she couldn't rent it out without feeling guilty."

Mallory just nodded.

"Oh, but the ocean view from my apartment is fabulous. It'd be even better if I added more windows. My house's only view is of the neighbors' Great Dane running back and forth across their backyard. And he barks."

"That would get old." Mallory glanced toward the entrance. The two women she'd met on the street were coming in, giving her an excuse to pop over and welcome them, but Caroline was still holding her arm.

"So, Mallory, as soon as you're ready to

show off your apartment, I want to be the first to see it."

"Yes. I'll be sure to let you know when it's ready." Mallory peeled herself away, relieved that she'd securely locked the upstairs door, just in case anyone wandered.

But now, as she tossed and turned in bed, her worries returned. How long could she hold off someone with Caroline's enthusiasm? Under the circumstances, it was only natural Caroline would be curious about Mallory's living quarters. Mallory could honestly claim it was still a work in process, but how long would that excuse last? And what good did it do to obsess over this silly conundrum when she should be sleeping?

Just enjoy the success of your grand opening, she told herself. *Shut down your brain and go to sleep! Tonight couldn't have gone much better. Just pat yourself on the back and sleep on it.* It had truly been more than she'd even hoped for.

Well, except for that part about Grayson and Corrina. And now she was replaying that all over again — unwillingly looping the movie of the happy pair, arm in arm, like a wedding processional, working their way through the crowded shop.

Knowing sleep was useless, Mallory climbed out of bed and turned on the lights.

194

Of course, this only reminded her of the awful condition of her habitat. What a startling contrast to where she'd been used to living. If someone had told her she'd be living like this just two months ago, she never would've believed it. As she heated water for tea, she wondered what her grand opening crowd would've thought if they could see her up here, living in such chaotic squalor. Hopefully that would never happen.

14

In the light of day and free from the intense rainbow walls of her raggedy apartment, Mallory could keep her focus on her shop, and the beauty she was creating there. This was her home and even after locking up each evening, she'd taken to sitting in the "bedroom" corner, a spot not visible from the front windows. There, she'd make herself comfortable in the cozy chair. She even kept her slippers tucked under the bed. She'd put her feet on the sheepskin ottoman and read, or work on social networking, or simply dream. When she finally grew sleepy, she'd creep up the stairs and, with mental blinders protecting her eyes, she'd prepare for bed, turn off the lights, jump into her comfy bed . . . and pretend her apartment wasn't a humiliating derelict eyesore.

She also took encouragement from the unbridled enthusiasm of new customers discovering her little shop. She delighted in her daily walks through the charming seaside town when she closed up between noon and one for her lunch break. Most of all, she derived pleasure from the newfound friends she seemed to be making daily. The first week passed peacefully and pleasantly, and she became less concerned with the condition of her sleeping quarters.

She even managed to keep Caroline from pressing too hard about visiting Mallory's apartment. This was accomplished by a free consultation of the run-down apartment above Caroline's shop. Mallory had probably overwhelmed Caroline with all her ideas of how to transform the grubby space into an attractive studio loft with a large span of windows overlooking the sea. "If money were no object, I'd recommend putting a terrace out there."

"Ooh." Caroline nodded eagerly. "I'd love that."

"It won't be cheap to remove this wall and put in a beam" — Mallory patted the wall that chopped the area into small rooms — "but it'll be worth it to have this all opened up. Your view will be visible from the kitchen area. You could have coffee at your breakfast bar and gaze out at the sea." She pointed upward. "And the ceilings vaulted clear to the rafters will make it all seem even bigger. It'll be gorgeous."

Caroline sighed happily. "I can almost picture it."

"Of course, I've given you the costliest version. If your budget can't handle it, there are less expensive routes. Or we could even create the space in stages."

"No, I want it just like you described, Mallory. Now all I need to do is sell my house," Caroline said.

"Then I should start drafting the design and line up a contractor." Mallory made notes in her Day-Timer. "I know they're all pretty busy right now, but maybe we can get you on a waiting list." And maybe Mallory would put her name right above Caroline's.

But when she called around later that day, her hopes were dashed. Instead of being backed up to September, some contractors were busy into October or even November. And one company mentioned next year. She supposed that was a fortuitous sign for the future of Portside. And she was glad for everyone.

The boom that had impacted all the beach towns north of them was finally trickling down. Good news for businesses that thrived on tourism, but bad news for people like Mallory and Caroline who needed an available contractor. Mallory felt almost desperate enough to swallow her pride and ask Grayson for help. Except she knew he didn't like renovations. Plus, she'd have to let him see how she was living upstairs.

With the Fourth of July, and the tourists it would bring, just days away, Mallory had no time to obsess over her *Rainbow Brite* apartment. And that was good! Sales had steadily moved her inventory. Even the back-room shelves were getting picked bare. She needed to restock her shop. With hopes of her house-sale money being deposited next week, she was already creating order lists for new merchandise, and had asked Kara to send a few things she'd left in storage.

In the meantime, she wanted to keep her local shoppers coming back to see what was "new." To that end, she cleverly rearranged things almost every day. It was actually a fun challenge to come up with new ideas for displays. Sometimes a customer wouldn't be able to find an item, and she would have to direct them. "I'm just playing house," she'd say as her excuse.

It'd been more than a week since her grand opening and Mallory was in the back room sorting through a box of French soaps when the jingle of the front door bell went off. She checked her watch and saw that it was already seven, closing time for a Saturday. It had been a long week and she was tired and looking forward to her shortened Sunday workday. Still, a customer was a customer so, pasting on a smile, she went out to welcome them. To her surprise, it was Grayson, standing just inside the door.

"That attractive sign by your door says you close at seven." He held out his wrist, pointing to his watch.

"I was just getting ready to lock up." She continued to smile.

"Want me to do that for you?" He reached for the dead bolt on the door, then paused. "Or would you rather lock me out on the other side?"

She chuckled. "Sure, go ahead and lock yourself in here with me if you'd like. But be warned — I might put you to work."

"Hey, I'm not afraid of some honest work." He clicked the dead bolt. "Haven't seen you since your big wingding. I wondered how you're doing."

"It's been a busy week." She crossed the room.

"Probably because your grand opening was such a hit."

"Yeah." She sank into the white sofa with

200

a tired sigh. "Care to sit?" She pointed her foot toward the overstuffed chair opposite her.

"Is it okay? I don't want to abuse the merchandise." Even as he spoke, he moved some of the throw pillows away to make room.

She waved a hand. "No worries, the owner is a friend of mine."

He grinned, then glanced at the window next to her. "But we can be seen here. Will that give the impression you're still open?"

She reached over to click off a table lamp. "How's that?"

"Better." He smiled and sat down. "This is comfortable."

"Of course." She leaned back. "So is this. Hopefully Sandi won't mind. She just put a down payment on this sofa, but I gave her a pretty good discount."

"Nice. So, business is good?"

"Better than good. It's great." She stretched her neck. "And I'm beat."

"Have you hired any help?"

"Not yet. Can't afford it. Besides, I'm still having too much fun."

"Well, that'll change."

"Huh?" She frowned.

He met her confused expression. "Not the fun part. Hopefully that won't change. I meant you not being able to afford help. I bet that'll change before long."

"Another prediction?"

He shrugged. "Seems like you're off to a good start."

"How's your business going?" she asked, still considering whether to ask for his help with her second-floor disaster area.

"Building is booming. I'm running a full crew and they can barely keep up. Besides that, I think I've ironed out a deal for my mall property."

"That doesn't involve shops right here in town?"

"Only a couple on the north edge of town. And they want to sell. Even though it's not in the center of town, not like this prime location." He waved his hand toward the street.

"Yes, I'm sorry I was the one to throw a wrench in your plans."

"Well, I'm pretty much over it now. Besides, I wound up with a great location. There's even more room for some fun outdoor things. Plus all the living spaces above the mall will now get an ocean view."

"Living spaces?"

"Yeah. Didn't I ever show you the plans?"

"No. I'd love to see them sometime."

"Great. Because that's one reason I

stopped by tonight. I wanted to talk to you about helping with some of the design work. My architect has his ideas, but I'd like to hire you for your feminine input."

"What's *that* supposed to mean?" She frowned, holding back from accusing him of being sexist.

"It means my architect is talented, but he's a modern young man in love with modern architecture. His designs can be somewhat stark and some women are put off by it."

She remembered Thomas saying something about how Grayson was into modern design. "Just women?" she asked.

"To be honest, I find it a little cool and clinical too."

"Ah, I see." That was a relief.

"My assistant, Corrina, actually said his latest interior elevations reminded her of a German hospital."

"Has she spent time in a German hospital?"

He smiled. "Not that I know of."

"Well, that doesn't sound very warm and inviting regardless." She shifted to a different position. "So did Corrina suggest you come here to talk to me about it?"

"Not exactly." His mouth twisted to one

side. "But she did think your shop was, uh, nice."

"Nice?" Too tired to censor her thoughts, Mallory couldn't help but ask, "Does that mean she didn't like it but was attempting to be polite?"

He looked sheepish. "Well, it was pretty crowded in here. I think Corrina felt claustrophobic. I suggested she come by again sometime when it wasn't so busy."

"Oh." She nodded. She suddenly noticed how dusky it was outside, which probably made her interior glow with light. A couple on the sidewalk was peering in the window right next to them. Mallory slowly slumped down below their sight level. "I guess you could be right about giving the impression my shop is open," she whispered, although the couple outside couldn't possibly hear her. "We are being watched."

Grayson struck a frozen pose. "I'll pretend to be a mannequin, part of your display," he said without moving his lips.

She struggled to hold back her laughter. "A mannequin or a dummy?"

"You calling me a dummy?" he mumbled, keeping his motionless position.

"You know, like a *Charlie McCarthy* dummy. Or maybe, I meant you were a ventriloquist. You know, because your lips aren't moving." She snickered at her own silliness, glad that she wasn't as visible as he was.

"Are they still out there?" he murmured, still not moving.

"Yep. I think they're trying to figure out whether you're a dummy or not." She giggled.

"What do I do?" he asked between his teeth.

"If only you had a pipe in one hand and a martini glass in the other, it would be picture-perfect." Still slumped down, she couldn't help but giggle at the image in her head. She could see him trying not to laugh, and it wasn't easy. Finally, his composure evaporated, and he exploded into laughter. She popped her head up in time to see the startled couple taken aback. But now they were laughing. She waggled her fingers at them, then smiled. They waved back and then, to her relief, continued on their way.

"Is there a less conspicuous place to sit?" Grayson stood.

"Nothing as comfortable as this arrangement." She got off the couch and looked around. "Maybe I should consider moving this display to the rear of the store."

"Or you could invite me upstairs," he said.

She grimaced but said nothing.

"Honestly, I don't mean to be pushy, but I'd love to see how you romance your own place."

"Huh?" She frowned.

"Okay, that didn't sound right. But you know what I mean." He stretched his back. "Your decor up there might inspire something for the living units above my mall."

"I know what you meant, but the truth is that my apartment is still in process. I'm not showing it to anyone yet. Kind of like how I kept the windows covered in here."

His brow furrowed. "Is Thomas still working on it?"

"Not exactly." She didn't care to admit that Thomas had called her just yesterday, hoping to continue with her project. It had actually been Sandi's idea. Anyway, Mallory had promised to think about it and already she'd started a list of projects she thought she could trust him with.

"What does *not exactly* mean?" Grayson asked.

"It means either Thomas pays me back what I advanced him, which he's not too keen to do, or else I get him to do the finish work that still needs doing."

"Did you get anyone here to check out your electrical or —"

"Honestly, I just haven't had the time."

She didn't care to admit that she didn't have the money either.

"So you feel safe with everything as is?" He rubbed his chin.

"I guess so. I mostly don't give it much thought."

"Want me to take a look? I could poke around and —"

"No." She firmly shook her head. She did not want him to see the *Rainbow Brite* apartment. Not right now anyway. Maybe if she had a chance to straighten things up some. But right now it was worse than ever. Her clothes were piled in the living room since her closet rod fell down that morning. "I am pretty sure my grandfather replaced everything." Okay, she wasn't as convinced as she sounded. But it's what she told herself when she said her prayers at night, after begging God to protect her from fires and other old building–related hazards.

"Okay, but you won't know for sure until you check it." He walked toward the back of the shop with purpose in his stride. Did he plan to ignore her, to go up there despite her refusal of help? And if so, what would she do?

"You know, I wouldn't mind if you took a look at it sometime, Grayson." She softened her tone. "Just not right now."

"There's no time like the present."

"It's just that it's a mess up there."

He shrugged. "Messes don't scare me."

"Well, it's late." She faked a yawn. "And it doesn't seem proper to entertain a gentleman up there right now." She couldn't help but grin at how silly that sounded. "I mean, what would people think?"

He looked amused. "I'm not worried about *my* reputation, but apparently you're worried about yours." His expression grew more serious. "You know, I actually respect that."

"Thanks." She pointed a finger his way, switching to a teasing mode. "But why aren't you worried about *your* reputation? Is it that bad?"

He laughed. "Have you heard something?"

"Well, some folks think you and your pretty assistant might be involved romantically. And then here you are, trying to get an invitation into *my* apartment." She shrugged with mock innocence. "Just saying."

"Seriously?" His eyes grew wide. "People actually think Corrina and I are involved like *that*?"

"I've heard something to that effect." She didn't care to admit Sandi was her source.

"Interesting. Well, maybe you're right.

Maybe I am acquiring a reputation." He glanced toward the front of the store. "Sorry to have barged in on you again. It is late, and I can tell you're tired."

She wanted to say she wasn't that tired and beg him to stay longer. She did enjoy his company and didn't want him to go, but he was already at the door.

"I do appreciate you being concerned for my safety," she said as he unlocked the dead bolt. "If you promise to stop bugging me about the wiring and all that, I promise to get someone to look into it."

"It's a deal." His smile looked forced as he opened the door. "Good night, Mallory."

She told him good night and locked the door behind him. Then, she went around methodically turning off all the lights in the shop like she did every night. Although not usually this early. She went upstairs and, instead of wearing her imaginary blinders, she looked around. Hoping to see beyond the ugliness, she tried to imagine what she could get Thomas to do. How could she make this place and these awful walls less embarrassing? But Grayson's concerns about what lay behind the walls ruined everything. What if he were right? Why waste a paint job on what would have to be torn out? It would be like putting a beautiful bedspread over a rotting mattress. What was the point?

15

Portside had been packed with tourists during the Fourth of July week. More so than usual, according to the other business owners. The small-town parade and street festival filled the place with life and color and music, and Mallory's shop reaped the reward of lots of customers, lots of sales, and lots of people wanting free consultations. In fact, things were going so well, Mallory was tempted to look into some part-time help, except that, thanks to all her inventory purchases, her bank account was getting low. And the house sale hadn't closed.

Kara and her mom had been trying to manage the closing details for Mallory, but it seemed like there was something new to slow down the works every few days. Another home inspection, an insurance snafu, the buyers' bank had missed some paperwork, an expired escrow document —

always something. Mallory just hoped and prayed the sale wouldn't unravel completely.

She'd felt bad telling her kids that it wasn't the most opportune time to visit her during the Fourth. "That is, if you want to stay with me," she'd explained to Seth over the phone. "The shop's doing great, but the apartment's still in process. I'm sort of just camping up there myself."

She'd suggested they get a hotel if they were determined to visit but warned them that could be difficult during the holiday week. As it turned out, everything was booked, and her kids decided to wait until after the Fourth so that some of them could stay with her. She tried to avoid admitting her place might not be ready for guests anytime this summer. She didn't even want to think about it.

On the Wednesday following the Fourth, she stood in her back room, gazing over her thinned-out shelves, and sighed. The orders she'd placed, which drained most of her shop's recent profits, should arrive this week. But at the moment, her shop looked a bit barren. So much so that she'd actually raided some items from upstairs to place down here — just to fill up some bare spots. It's not like those items did much for the sad apartment anyway. Anything she didn't want to sell, like some of her favorite original paintings and a few personal items, she would simply mark as sold.

The shop didn't open until ten. She'd hoped to have it all "fluffed" out by then, but it would be a challenge. She considered closing for a day or two until her new shipments arrived, but she worried about the message that might send. She hadn't even started to close on Tuesdays like other local businesses did, mostly because she hated the idea of missing out on any foot traffic. Maybe she would do that when they headed into winter. If she could stay in business that long.

She remembered again how Grayson had originally predicted she wouldn't last a year. She'd never guessed it would be due to a lack of merchandise. Mallory had only seen him once since the night they'd bickered over her electrical wiring, and that had been literally "in passing" on the Fourth of July. Standing outside her shop that day, she'd been sipping a latte and observing the parade when she spotted Grayson behind the wheel of a big red truck with his company's logo on the side.

He'd been pulling a long construction trailer with what looked like a partially built shed. Corrina, dressed in a yellow hard hat and a buffalo plaid shirt with denim short-shorts held up by red suspenders, was wielding a big hammer and an even bigger smile. "Helping" Corrina with the building project were several kids dressed like young carpenters. They wielded kid-size tools and eagerly hurled candy to children watching along the crowded sidewalk. The banner on the side of the wagon read: "Building a Better Portside for Tomorrow." Hopefully that was true. Who wouldn't want a better tomorrow?

Mallory had gone back inside after that, but it took a while to get the image of those short-shorts out of her mind. It'd probably put her into a sour mood for the rest of the morning.

Now most of the holiday crowd had dissipated and, as Mallory rearranged her shop, she prayed her orders would start arriving soon. Otherwise she'd have to give in and close shop until after the upcoming weekend. She could pretend she'd gone on vacation. Too bad she'd already emptied her old Victorian house, which must be looking sad just sitting there empty, waiting for its new family to arrive. She would've loved to get away for the weekend.

By ten, the shop looked better, but not anything like it had for the grand opening.

Still, she wouldn't be ashamed to open her doors. She had just unlocked the dead bolt when she got a text from Louisa. Mallory went outside to check on her flowerpots, which were still moist, then sat down on the bench, taking a break to enjoy Louisa's text.

She unlocked her phone, then jumped up as she read her daughter's words. "Oh, no." Despite her racing heart, Mallory tried to order her thoughts as well as she'd just organized her shop. Louisa's message said that she and Marshall planned to come to Portside for the upcoming weekend. Did that mean they wanted to stay with her? She continued to read quickly, seeing they'd rented a "fabulous Airbnb on the beach." Well, that was a relief. Louisa said the huge house was big enough to invite Seth and Micah too. All of them would arrive on Friday and couldn't wait to see their mom.

Mallory went inside to text Louisa back, saying she looked forward to seeing them too. She wondered if the beach house might have a spare room for her but didn't want to ask. After all, she was the mother. She'd always been the one to host her kids. Now she couldn't even do that. The jingle of the bell on the door brought her back to the present, and she knew she'd just have to let tomorrow take care of itself.

As luck would have it, Mallory's kids and her orders for the shop arrived within minutes of each other on Friday afternoon. She welcomed her kids in, then flipped the closed sign over. It was only five, but there was no point in having customers underfoot while delivery workers carried all sizes and shapes of boxes into the shop. The largest truck parked out front, and the smaller one was in the alley behind, right by the rear entrance Mallory rarely used. Once the movers got into a rhythm, the feeling inside the shop was that of a mini Grand Central Station.

"Everything looks great," Louisa said after they'd all hugged. "Marshall stayed at the beach house to relax. Oh, wait until you see it, Mom. It's fabulous. We came to town to grab some groceries and couldn't wait to see you."

"Yeah." Seth picked up a handblown vase from Mallory's personal collection, studying it with a quizzical brow. "Your shop looks good."

"Well, it's not at its best right now," Mallory said, "but I sent you kids pictures of how it looked before my grand opening."

She explained how she'd made so many sales that she'd gotten low on merchandise, and they all seemed impressed.

"I want to see the upstairs now," Louisa announced.

"Well, it's not —"

"I know, I know," she replied. "It's not finished yet. But I do have an imagination. I know it'll be perfect in time."

Mallory's nerves peaked. "But it's —"

"Come on, Mom." Seth tugged her arm to make way for two men lugging in a sofa to replace the one Sandi had taken home.

"Put that there," she told them, pointing to a space by the door.

"Come on, Mom," Louisa urged. "We're in their way. Let's go upstairs and check out your new digs."

"Yeah." Micah was leading the way. "Onward and upward."

Mallory hurried to catch up with him. "It's locked up there," she said.

"Then unlock it, Mom," Louisa commanded. "I need to use the restroom."

All four of them were trudging up the stairs, Mallory at the back. Her mind was blank. She tried desperately to think of an explanation as she unlocked the door, but she felt literally speechless. They all poured into the apartment, and the spirit of fun

217

and games and merriment instantly evaporated. No one said a thing as all three of
them looked around the room, shocked
expressions of disgust taking over their
faces.

"I know it looks awful right now," she said
in apology, "but I've been so busy with —"

"Mom!" Louisa's eyes were wide. "It's
ghastly."

"It's worse than ghastly." Seth nudged a
lopsided kitchen cabinet door with his toe.
"It's like something out of a horror flick."

"You *live* up here?" Micah asked.

"Oh, Mom." Louisa looked close to tears.

"Oh, you kids." Mallory forced a smile.
"Don't make a mountain out of a molehill.
This is just temporary. I haven't been able
to find a contractor to finish the work up
here." She nervously snatched clothes from
the drying rack she'd set in the kitchen after
discovering the dryer didn't work.

"Can't you rent another place until it's
done?" Micah asked.

"I suppose I could." She glanced around,
cringing at the thought of how horrible her
situation must look to her children.

Louisa hugged her. "I had no idea, Mom.
I'm so sorry."

"Don't cry, honey." Mallory felt emotional
too.

"It's just so unlike you." Seth was walking around, taking in the details. "It's so . . . so destitute, I can't believe it."

"This is just temporary," she repeated. Feeling too flustered to continue this conversation, she backed up toward the door. "I need to be downstairs to direct traffic with the deliveries. Otherwise, I'll just have to move everything again later. Excuse me."

As much as she hated to leave her children up there, she was glad to have a reason to escape. The movers didn't actually need her direction, especially since it was hard to tell what was in most of the boxes, but it proved a good distraction.

They were still unloading when her kids came downstairs a few moments later. "The guys are going to pick up some things in town," Louisa told her in a somber tone. "I'm going to stay here with you."

"Oh, you don't need to do —"

"No, we all decided, Mom." Seth was using his I'm-the-boss voice. "We're taking you back to the B&B with us. There are five bedrooms, and you're taking one of them."

"Oh, that sounds nice." She attempted a smile.

"Louisa will hang with you long enough to get this junk unloaded and for you to pack a bag," he said.

She nodded. Although she didn't appreciate him calling her merchandise "junk," she
wasn't opposed to a beach getaway with her
kids. The boys left and she and Louisa did
some rearranging of boxes, making more
room, until the delivery workers brought in
the last of it. Then, without any argument,
Mallory ran upstairs and packed for the
weekend. It took only a few minutes to
throw some things into an overnight bag.
And truly, being away from this place, even
for just one night, sounded most welcome.
Of course, she knew she would be con-
fronted by her children. She'd have to
explain what she was doing and why things
looked so bad, and then she would have to
convince them that it truly was just temporary . . . and that she hadn't lost her
marbles.

By Saturday morning, Mallory had managed to persuade her children not to have
her locked up in the loony bin. She'd told
them how she was waiting on her house
sale, how it kept getting delayed, and how
that money would pay for an amazing
remodel of the apartment upstairs. She
didn't mention how Thomas had thrown a
wrench in her works or tied up her funds.
She didn't want to give Seth another op-

portunity to lecture her about something she already knew.

Then she talked about the success of her shop, the friends she'd made, and how much she loved living in Portside. "I just feel like I'm paying my dues now," she confessed. "But it's worth it. I feel so at home here."

"It is a cool town," Louisa agreed. "Better than I remembered."

"And you kids will have to come and visit as often as you can. I'll have the pullout sofa bed and maybe a Murphy bed too."

"Or we can rent this place again," Micah told her. "Split three ways, it's been a good deal."

"Yes. It's a handsome house." She glanced at her watch. "Now I should probably get back to my shop."

"Aren't you going to stay tonight too?" Louisa asked. "We thought we'd spend the whole weekend with you. Surely your shop can survive one day without you there."

Mallory considered the mess of boxes, realizing she wouldn't be able to unlock her doors anyway. "I guess you're right. But I'll need to go back tomorrow morning."

"So will we," Micah told her.

And so for the rest of the weekend, she just hung out with her kids in the marvelous house. Of course, the designer in her wanted to make some changes to make it friendlier and cozier. It needed some romancing. But knowing it was a vacation rental, she understood. Better to just keep it clean and cleared and functional. She had better things to occupy herself.

They walked on the beach, played cards, sat by the fireside both inside and out, and ate good food cooked by Marshall. Who knew her new son-in-law was such a great chef? She even took an afternoon nap on Saturday. It all felt unexpectedly luxurious and relaxing.

On Sunday morning, while the guys were tossing a football around on the beach, Mallory and Louisa had their second cup of coffee out on the enormous deck overlooking the ocean. Both just sat quietly, soaking in the beauty of clear blue sky and cerulean waves topped with white foam. The sound of the ocean, the smell of the sea, the warmth of the sun, her children nearby . . . all were heavenly.

"I've been thinking about the name of your shop, Mom." Louisa frowned. "What's up with that? I mean Romancing the Home has a nice sound, but what does it really mean?"

Mallory got her purse and fished out a

business card. She pointed out the definition of romance written there and explained how she wanted to romance people's homes. "By creating a unique haven that provides a beautiful escape from the ordinariness of everyday life or the workplace."

"Seems kind of hypocritical to me." Louisa slid the card into her jeans pocket. "I mean you work in a scrumptious shop then go home to that horrid apartment."

"It's *temporary*, Louisa." If Mallory had to use that word one more time, she might scream.

"Maybe. But it reminds me of the shoemaker's children —"

"Going barefoot?" Mallory finished the line. "Yes. I've had the same thought. Believe me, it's not like I enjoy it."

"Enjoy it? How can you even endure it?" she demanded. "Even if it is temporary. It's creepy and disturbing and just plain weird. I could hardly force myself to be up there, even for just a few minutes."

"I know." Mallory nodded. "I pretty much feel the same way. But like I said, I'm paying my dues, and honestly, I spend all my waking hours in the shop. The only time I'm upstairs I'm asleep. You saw my bedroom. I have my comfortable bed and nice linens, and it is quiet up there."

"Oh, Mom." Louisa looked a bit teary again. "When I think of our house, our beautiful, wonderful, sweet-smelling home — and then I think of you in that nasty apartment . . . well, it just hurts my heart."

Mallory hugged her daughter. "If I had to live in those conditions indefinitely, I would understand your concern. But when you see what I'm going to do to that place, you'll be amazed." Now Mallory began to describe her plans in detail. "Did you notice the ocean view from up there?"

"No."

"Well, it's not like this" — she gestured to the floor-to-ceiling window wall — "but it's not half bad. Really, honey, you won't believe that place the next time you see it. Just be patient." To change the subject, Mallory asked about Louisa and Marshall's new apartment, pressing her to describe how she'd romanced it and made it wonderful.

It was fun to see Louisa's eyes light up as she explained how she'd matted and framed black-and-white photos from both sides of their families. "Then I did this super cool arrangement on that big blank wall in the entryway."

"It sounds wonderful," Mallory said. "Send me photos of everything you've done, honey. And when I'm done, I'll send "after" pictures of my renovated apartment. I know you're going to love it."

The conversation got happier again and by the time Mallory parted ways with her kids, she felt relatively sure they were trying to understand her hard-to-explain situation. Or at least they were no longer discussing how to book her into a nicely padded cell. For the time being anyway. Hopefully she'd get it together before they all decided to pop in on her again.

16

Mallory didn't make it back to her shop until Sunday afternoon. She'd decided to just keep her shop closed until she got everything into place. It wasn't until later that evening that she was finally satisfied — and exhausted. She strolled around slowly, turning off lights and making final tweaks to the fresh displays. The shop looked almost as good as it had for her grand opening. A few fresh flower arrangements, and a good sweeping and dusting tomorrow morning, and she would feel no need to apologize to anyone.

Of course, the back room was a different story. It looked like a hurricane had struck, with empty boxes heaped to one side, some unpacked items and packing materials here and there, and more items yet to be unpacked. But at least she had inventory to last her awhile.

As she went up to bed, she realized, as

much as she'd enjoyed her time with her kids this weekend, she had missed visiting with friends and customers in her shop. Strangely enough, when she went back into her *Rainbow Brite* apartment, she wasn't as aggravated as usual. She was just paying her dues. And it was only temporary. In the end, it would all be worth it. She just needed to be patient.

She felt almost amused as she got ready for bed. All the things she'd been saying to her children these past couple of days must've been what she'd needed to tell herself. Not only that, as she got into bed, instead of shooting up fear-filled prayers, she decided to thank God for a comfortable bed, a roof overhead, and the hope for better things here in Portside.

The next morning, Mallory felt strangely refreshed as she rose early and got ready for her day. With music playing in her shop, she first swept and dusted, making sure the shop looked perfect before she tackled the mess in her back room. By ten o'clock, she'd already unpacked and flattened the last few boxes and was just sweeping up the debris when she heard the dinging bell announcing a new customer.

To her surprise it was Grayson. Seeing his smiling face, she realized how much she had missed him. "Hello, stranger." She returned his smile. "Long time, no see."

"Yeah, I had just been thinking the same thing about you. I stopped by your shop on Friday evening and then again on Saturday afternoon. Looked like you'd blown town."

Pleased to hear of his attempted visits, she told him about her kids' unexpected vacation and the restful time at the beach house. "It's a fabulous five-bedroom Airbnb," she told him. "All the windows look out on the beach."

"Interesting." His brows arched. "What style is the house?"

"The lines look modern from the outside, but it's not cold or austere when you go inside. There's a big rock fireplace. Good neutral earth tones. An open floor plan. Vaulted ceiling. The kitchen is nice but not over-the-top. It's a little sparse on decor, but I really liked the general feeling there."

"Uh-huh." He smiled. "I think I know the place."

"It was called Gull's Wing. I guess that's because of the slope of the roofline. It sort of resembled seagull wings."

His eyes lit up. "Yep, that's the one I was thinking of." He opened a leather satchel and removed a roll of papers. "I wanted to leave these with you, Mallory. They're the plans for my mall and apartments development. I thought you could look them over and see if you have any ideas or suggestions. You know, ways to romance the project." He grinned.

She took the papers from his hand. "I'd love to see them. I'm not sure I can contribute much, but I'll do what I can."

"Keep track of your time," he told her. "This is a paying job."

"Seriously?" She frowned. "That doesn't seem fair considering how you wouldn't let me pay you for hanging my awning."

"You took me to dinner as a payment, remember?"

She nodded. "Yes, I do."

"So, if you won't let me pay you, can I take you to dinner?" He looked hopeful.

"I'd like that."

"Great." He glanced around her shop. "Looks good in here. Different, but good."

"I just got finished getting a bunch of new merchandise set out." She let out a satisfied sigh.

"You look good too," he told her. "More rested and peaceful."

"You know, I feel more rested and peaceful," she confessed. "I guess my kids were right to kidnap me to Gull's Wing. I must've needed a break."

229

"Yeah, even the Lord took a break on the seventh day."

"Point well taken." She knew he was referring to his suggestion that she get some help. "As soon as my house sale is final, I'll hire a sales associate," she told him.

He glanced at his watch. "Well, I need to get going, but I'll be in touch about those plans and my payment for them." As he opened the door, a trio of young women came in, all talking at once.

"Oh, I'm so glad they're open," a short girl with blue hair told the others. "Bree swore we'd love this place."

"We tried to come here the last two days," a girl with tattoos from head to toe told Mallory. "You were totally closed, but we peeked in the windows."

"Sorry about that," Mallory apologized. "My kids were in town, so I took the weekend off."

"A friend told us about this shop," the blue-haired girl said. "We have this bridal shower this week, so we're hoping to find something cool here."

"Well, look around." Mallory gestured to the different displays. "I unpacked all sorts of treasures last night. Let me know if I can help with anything."

"Yeah, we saw all those boxes piled up and

got worried you'd gone out of business already," the tattooed girl said. "Glad you're still here. This place looks so awesome."

Mallory grabbed the broom to finish sweeping the back room, listening with interest as the young trio chatted and shopped. For a moment, she wondered if she needed to be on alert for shoplifters. She knew that happened from time to time, but she couldn't imagine it happening here. Finally, one of the girls called out, announcing they'd found some treasures.

Mallory happily wrote up their purchases, then offered to wrap them, visiting with the girls while she did. Sure, they weren't her typical customers, but they were fun. She told them to enjoy the shower and invited them to come back again.

After they left, a few more customers trickled in, but it never got busy like it had on previous weekends. Mallory used her spare time to spread out the blueprints for Grayson's mall and was pleasantly surprised to see that it was a very thoughtful design. Although it leaned toward modern, she didn't think it was particularly cold looking. The use of reclaimed wood mixed with concrete warmed the exterior, and the outdoor spaces with benches and a fountain and even a stacked rock firepit all looked inviting. All in all, it seemed a smart design and a good use of space, and considering the coastal elements, like salty sea air, the building materials made sense.

By the time she rolled up the plans, she thought some softening around the edges would be simple enough. She jotted some ideas into her Day-Timer and started to daydream about where she'd let Grayson take her as payment.

The week passed pleasantly and peacefully with shoppers and browsers in the store, as well as a couple of design consultations that seemed to promise work. Already Mallory was making plans to transform the back room into a design studio where she could meet with clients. She wouldn't equip it like the one she'd had in her old basement, but she would try to have some basic elements on hand.

Mostly she wanted this to be a more laid-back sort of design business. She wanted to romance the home more than she wanted to completely restyle it. She remembered how many clients she'd served in the past. So many of them had unrealistically high expectations. As if they thought the perfect design and decor would be life-altering. Or even save their marriages and family lives.

Usually, the woman was the driving force behind a redo. Mallory didn't even want to think of how many marriages had been on the brink of disaster. A case of too much money and not enough quality time were the usual culprits . . . a focus on things more than the relationship. As much as Mallory loved a beautiful home, she never wanted to create one that valued possessions more than people. It hadn't always been easy. She was determined to do things differently in Portside.

By Saturday morning, Mallory had to hold back her disappointment that Grayson hadn't come by to see what she thought of his mall design. She considered calling him but knew he was busy and tried to practice patience. So when she saw him entering her shop that afternoon, she was more than a little pleased. But then she spotted the stylish woman with him and felt a little green monster stirring within her. The handsome pair didn't seem to notice Mallory in the back of the store, but she watched as Grayson led the Hollywood-gorgeous blond through her shop.

They took their time, carefully examining every display. What — were they planning to set up house together? Mallory silently scolded herself for her jealous cynicism. She watched Grayson as he led the woman about. He seemed to be enjoying himself. And why not? The stunning woman was impeccably dressed and a serious head turner. Even other customers paused to stare at her. Finally, Grayson and his pretty friend paused by the bedroom display. Grayson showed the woman the framed quote about the meaning of romancing the home. She nodded and beamed at Grayson like he was the next best thing to sliced bread. Mallory had to smile at the thought. Didn't Grandma Bess used to say that? Suddenly she didn't feel quite so jealous. But the curiosity was killing her. Who was this mysterious beauty?

To her relief, an elderly woman needed help finding an evergreen woods candle, forcing Mallory to the back room to unearth it. When she came back, Grayson and Ms. Hollywood were gone. Mallory handed the woman the candle. "Is this the right one?"

The woman took a sniff and her eyes lit up. "Yes. My daughter got me one of these a while back, when you first opened your shop. I already burned the entire thing." She looked a bit surprised by the price. "I guess it's true that you get what you pay for." She put cash on the counter. "I've bought cheaper candles and hated them, but I love this one."

Mallory took the bill and went about finalizing the transaction.

The woman lowered her voice. "Did you see that woman in here just a bit ago?"

"Yes." Mallory tried to appear nonchalant as she made change for the large bill.

"Didn't you recognize her?"

"No." Mallory counted out her change. "Did you?"

"Oh, yes. Of course! She's the host of that new popular TV show. I can't remember her name or the name of the show, but I know that was her."

Mallory carefully wrapped the candle in tissue. "She looks like she'd be good on a TV show."

"Oh, my daughter just loves that show. I've seen it playing at her house."

"Interesting. Do you think she lives around here?" Mallory slipped the bundle into a brown paper bag, then straightened the twined handles.

"I doubt it. She probably lives in Hollywood or Beverly Hills." The woman took her bag. "Thank you, dear. My daughter is right. Your shop is charming."

"You're welcome back anytime. Even if it's just to say hello."

"Lovely. I'll bring my friend Millie next

time," she told Mallory. "She loves pretty things."

Mallory thanked her, then turned her attention to another customer. She always enjoyed helping and visiting, but her mind was elsewhere now. Who was that celebrity woman and what was she doing with Grayson? Wasn't it rather rude for her to come walk around and act very interested then abruptly leave?

Closing time finally arrived and Mallory was still trying to wipe thoughts of Grayson and Ms. Hollywood from her memory. At least the image of that blond beauty pretty much eradicated the image of Corrina in her short-shorts!

It wasn't until the next day that the mystery was solved. Shortly after Mallory opened her doors, Ms. Hollywood walked in, looking just as stunning as yesterday, though a bit more casually dressed. She was dressed in impeccable white jeans, which Mallory knew not everyone could wear for a variety of reasons, and she'd complemented this with a perfectly tailored lemon-yellow blouse and stylish sandals that showed off pearly toenails. Mallory couldn't even remember the last time she'd had a pedicure.

"May I help you?" she asked the woman

with a curious smile.

"I'm Amy Stanton." The woman stuck out a hand to shake, then handed her a business card. "I already know you're Mallory Farrell, the owner of this delightful shop."

"That's right." Mallory blinked.

"Grayson told me all about you."

"All about me?" Mallory noticed the couple who'd just entered the shop. She waved, and they looked on with interest.

"Yes." Amy glanced to the back of the shop. "I don't want to distract you from your customers, but can we talk privately for a moment?"

"Sure." Mallory told the couple to just call out if they needed any help, then led the mysterious Amy Stanton to the back room. Was she here to request a design consultation? It didn't seem likely, although she was carefully checking out the back room, as if doing an inventory. Glad she'd just straightened it up, Mallory invited Amy to sit. "What can I do for you?"

"Well, you might've noticed me in here with Grayson Matthews yesterday. Gray and I are old friends. Anyway, he told me about your shop and brought me to see it and I suddenly realized how perfect you'd be for my show."

"Your show?"

Amy looked slightly disappointed. "*Pacific Design*. It's on the decor network. You haven't seen it?"

"I, uh, I used to watch decor network, before I moved here a couple of months ago, but I still haven't connected cable. To be honest, I've kind of enjoyed life without TV." Not to mention she wouldn't want a cable installer to see her apartment.

"Oh, well, *Pacific Design* is a brand-new show, but we're already getting good ratings. It just started this summer." Amy crossed her legs. "I used to host a morning show in Portland. You probably never saw that either."

Mallory winced. "I'm not sure."

Amy waved a hand. "No problem. But what do you think? Can I feature your adorable shop on my show? I'm particularly interested in the whole romancing the home concept. I think it's very innovative."

"Well, I don't know what to say. I'm honored." Mallory straightened her blouse. "Yes, of course, I'd love to be on your show. What can I do to help?"

"Just say yes," said Amy. "The reason I didn't talk to you yesterday was because I wanted to run it by my producers first. You can never tell what they'll say." Amy shook her head. "Sometimes I think I've found the perfect idea, and they give it the nix." Amy pulled her ringing phone from her pocket and silenced it. "So anyway, I was here to look at the fabulous house Gray built, and after we were done, he told me about you and your little shop. He said you'd worked in design for a long time but had sort of reinvented your life by moving here. Then you renovated your grandmother's tourist shop. Is that right?"

Mallory nodded, still trying to take all this in as Amy continued to talk nonstop about producers and schedules and how the contract had been emailed and was being printed out in Gray's office right now. It was clear why this dazzling chatterbox had worked as a talk show host. Even if she couldn't get a word in edgewise, Mallory liked Amy's energy and enthusiasm.

"You might have to close the shop for a day when we shoot the episode. Maybe even two," Amy told her, "depending on lights and things. But the exposure you'll get will be well worth it. In fact, it will be great for the whole town." She laughed. "You'll be a local celebrity."

"How exciting." Mallory felt like she needed to take a deep breath. Or maybe Amy did.

"Okay, so we're all set for now. We probably won't shoot until late August. I think we're solidly booked for shows until then. Plus, that's when I'm hoping Gray will let us tape a segment about his house too. It's a spectacular home. Have you seen it?" Amy hardly left two seconds for Mallory to respond before continuing. "Anyway, I'll come by with copies of your contract later today."

Mallory finally took that deep breath. "Sounds good."

As Amy shook her hand again, Mallory couldn't help but notice the big diamond ring. Was she engaged or married? And why was Mallory even looking? She smiled nervously.

"I'm sure you'll be just great on the show," Amy continued. "With those dark eyes, you must be photogenic. And I just love your platinum hair. Does someone here in town do it for you?"

"You mean the color?" Mallory laughed. "It's natural."

"No way." Amy actually touched her hair, as if to determine if it was real. "Well, it's absolutely gorgeous. The camera's going to love you." She continued to chatter about how great everything looked as they walked through the shop. "It's jam-packed with eye candy. The film crew will love it." She paused by the bedroom display. "I don't know if you noticed yesterday, but I snuck a lot of photos on my phone. I sent them to my producers, and they loved them. Loved the whole romancing the home concept." She patted Mallory on the back. "You should be proud, girlfriend. This is going to be a really big deal."

"Right now I'm mostly just stunned," Mallory admitted as she held the front door open for Amy. "I'm sure it will sink in later."

"Like I said, I'll get those contracts to you asap. Thanks again." Amy flashed that million-dollar smile and left. As Mallory closed the door, she felt seriously light-headed. Leaning against the door, she took in a slow deep breath. Was that even real? Or had she just been duped big-time? Her kids played practical jokes sometimes, but would they do something like this? She hoped not.

17

"Are you okay?" A petite, dark-haired woman put a hand on Mallory's shoulder. "You look like you might faint."

Mallory forced a smile and stood up straighter. "I'm fine. Just a little stunned, I think."

"Because of that woman?" she asked. "The one who just left?"

"Yeah, who was that?" the man with the petite woman asked. "She looked like a movie star."

"That was Amy Stanton," Mallory told them. "She said she's going to put my shop on her TV show."

"You'll be on a TV show?" The woman's dark eyes grew larger.

"What show?" the man asked with curiosity.

Pacific Design. Mallory still felt like this was dream . . . or a bad joke.

"Oh, yeah, I've heard of that show," the

woman said. "It's on the decor network and is supposed to be good. I keep meaning to record it." She shook Mallory's hand. "Congratulations!"

"Thank you." Mallory recovered a bit and realized she didn't recognize either of them. "I'm Mallory, by the way."

"I'm Gayle." The woman pointed to herself. "And this is my husband, Rich." The trio chatted for a bit and Mallory learned that Gayle and Rich were new to town and, inspired by Mallory's shop, wanted a free consultation for the beach house they'd just purchased.

"I love your shop, and I love the concept of *romancing* a home," Gayle told her. "Right now our home is okay. I mean, there's nothing wrong with it, but other than the ocean view, it doesn't have much zing. Everything is kind of beige-ish."

"No personality," Rich added. "We work from home so we're there a lot."

Mallory tried to stay attentive as the couple told her about what they liked and didn't like about their home, but she was distracted with the idea of being featured on a TV show. Her mind was wandering.

"Well, that all sounds interesting," she finally told them. "How about we make an appointment for later this week?" She reached for her Day-Timer and, after going over some dates, promised to meet them at their house on Thursday morning at eight.

Gayle shook her hand. "This is so exciting."

"Hey, maybe you could get our house all romanced in time to be on your TV show." Rich winked just as Caroline Kempton entered the shop.

"What's this about a TV show?" Caroline's brows arched.

"Did you see that attractive woman who just left?" Gayle asked Caroline. "She's the host of a show on the decor network."

"Interesting. Why was she in Portside?"

Mallory shared about her exciting opportunity with *Pacific Design,* and Caroline's eyes lit up. "Oh, I just love that show. I can't believe you'll be on it, Mallory. Although I'm not surprised. You and your shop will be perfect. Everything here is so photogenic."

"Thanks. It's all just sinking in. I think I need to pinch myself."

Gayle and Rich congratulated Mallory again and headed toward the door, saying they looked forward to seeing her on Thursday.

Caroline rubbed her hands together. "This isn't just good news for you, Mallory. All the Portside businesses could benefit from this kind of PR."

"That's what Amy said too."

"That Amy is so gorgeous," Caroline gushed. "I wish I'd seen her up close."

"Maybe you'll still get a chance. Sounds like she's in town for a while."

"I wonder what brought her here. I heard she's engaged." Caroline peered out the window as if she hoped to spot her. "She revealed it on her show last spring, but she hasn't said who the lucky man is yet. Playing up the mystery, I suppose."

"I saw her ring," Mallory said. "Quite a chunk of ice."

"Well, it's all very exciting." Caroline opened the door. "But I can't stay. I just popped over to invite you to the next chamber meeting. It's Tuesday at noon, and you'll be my guest. It's about time you joined the chamber. And, of course, you must share about *Pacific Design*."

"I'd love to come," Mallory said before Caroline ducked back out. She shook her head in disbelief. Romancing the Home was going to be featured on a TV show!

For the next few hours, Mallory felt like she was walking on clouds as she waited on customers and visited with fellow merchants who'd heard about the TV show through the grapevine — Caroline, of course. There'd hardly been a dull moment all afternoon.

Mallory looked out her front window as she prepared to close up for the evening. It was almost five, but Amy still hadn't returned with the contract. Of course, this only fed into Mallory's crazy fear that this whole thing was a cruel joke. Oh, she didn't actually think so, but the fact that so many people already knew about it was disconcerting. It would be humiliating to have to tell everyone that it was all just a silly prank.

Realizing she hadn't thought to do any research, Mallory pulled out her cell phone to do a quick search of *Pacific Design*. Sure enough, Amy Stanton's pretty face appeared with a description of decor network's most popular new show. It was not a joke! Feeling relieved, she put her phone away and was about to lock the door when she noticed a tall woman hurrying down the street. She carried an oversized bag and was wearing a stylish-looking white trench coat. On closer look, it was Amy.

Mallory opened the door and greeted her. "I was about to lock up," she said as Amy came inside.

"I'm glad you didn't. I got sort of waylaid at Gray's."

Mallory locked the door and stepped away as Amy removed her damp coat.

"That fog is cold and wet." Amy ran her fingers through her hair and looked around. "But it's nice and cozy in here." She extracted a folder. "Here is your contract, Mallory. Three copies. If you sign them now, I'll take them back to my producers to sign tomorrow."

Mallory invited her to sit. "I'd like to read it first."

"Of course." Amy sat down on the new sofa. "Ooh, this is comfy. Take your time."

Mallory walked back to the counter to get her reading glasses, then started to skim the contract. Although she didn't fully understand all the legal language, there was nothing overly concerning and, to her delight, there was a significant payment involved. She hadn't expected that! Half was payable upon signing and half would be payable when they showed up to produce the segment.

She happily signed all three copies, then handed them back to Amy. "This is so exciting," she told her. "I still can hardly believe it."

"Well, I'm excited too. I haven't featured a shop before. I like that it's a different kind of story." Amy pulled her trench coat back on. "You'll get your signed contract back in a week or so, along with your first check."

Mallory beamed at her. "Thanks."

"My assistant, Josie, will give you a call when we know the actual filming dates. We're aiming for the last week of August, but you never know. Anyway, you should hear from her in about three weeks. Any more questions?"

Mallory considered asking about how Amy knew Grayson but decided against it. "I don't think so."

"Great. Well, have fun telling all your friends about this. We love any kind of promotion you can give. Social media, newspapers, friends and family, whatever." She cinched her trench coat belt tighter.

"Don't worry, I'll tell everyone I know." Mallory thanked her again, then unlocked the door to let her out. She watched as Amy hurried down the street. It looked like she was heading back toward Grayson's construction company's office. She shook her head. Why should Mallory care if Amy and Grayson were old friends? If anything, she should be extremely grateful to Grayson for bringing Amy her way.

Still, she wondered about that big diamond ring. Could it have possibly come from Grayson? Probably not. Just because he had attractive women friends didn't mean he was romantically involved with any of them. After all, he was friends with Mallory, and they weren't romantically involved . . . were they?

Mallory was starting to feel like a celebrity by the next day. Local shoppers and fellow merchants dropped in to hear the story and congratulate her. By the time she was introduced as Caroline's guest at the chamber meeting, word of her upcoming TV episode had spread like wildfire. Since the chamber members' interest and curiosity remained high, she told them the whole story and even took questions.

"How did the *Pacific Design* people find you?" Les Howard, owner of Short Stroll Shoes, asked her.

Mallory pointed to Grayson, sitting in the back of the room with Corinna. "That was thanks to Grayson Matthews," she said. "He's a friend of Amy Stanton, the host of the show."

"How'd *you* meet her, Grayson?" Greg Marchetti, owner of the Port Wine Shop, called out. "She's quite a looker."

"How do you know that?" Caroline asked Greg.

He smirked. "Amy came into my shop for

249

a glass of wine. But she never mentioned anything about knowing Grayson or doing a show in our town."

"Amy was a friend of my wife's." Grayson cleared his throat. "I haven't seen her in years. Didn't even know she had this new show."

They asked Mallory a few more questions, including when the big event would happen. She told them late August, and they started discussing the street festival Mallory's grandma had recommended. Enthusiasm grew and eventually they put it to a vote, which passed, though no date was named.

"Let's wait until Mallory knows firm dates," Caroline suggested.

They continued with their planned agenda, including voting Mallory in as their newest member. By the time the meeting adjourned, Mallory felt deeply touched. Grandma Bess had always been involved in the chamber. Mallory could imagine her smiling down on her today.

Mallory's meeting with Gayle and Rich went well. She was surprised to discover that their house was only one house away from the beach house her kids had rented. It was a nice strip of real estate, and as she measured windows and things, she wondered what it would feel like to live here full-time. Of course, that wouldn't be happening anytime soon, but if business continued to increase, and if the TV show gave her an additional boost, well, who knew. Maybe she would be neighbors with Gayle and Rich someday.

"I love your ideas," Gayle told Mallory as she bagged up her things after the consultation.

"Well, I'll work on some drawings and gather up a few things and get back to you, say, next week, if that works."

"Works for us," Rich told her, putting his arm around his wife. "We're almost always here."

"I can see why." Mallory gazed out the window. "This view alone makes the whole house worthwhile. And nothing you want to do should break the bank."

"Just romanticize us," Gayle teased as she slipped her arm around Rich. "We plan to retire in a few years, and I want our happy golden years to be beautiful and romantic."

Mallory smiled. "I'll do my best." She said goodbye, then headed out to her car, pausing to gaze back at the houses along this strip. Gayle and Rich were such a likable couple. They were probably about ten years older than her, but young for their age. She loved how they were looking forward to their retirement years together. Wouldn't it be lovely to grow old with someone you really loved — someone who really loved you?

But, she reminded herself, romancing a home wasn't about that. In fact, she'd already started to romance Sandi's home, and she was single. Well, at least for now. If Sandi had her way, she and Thomas would soon become an item. But Mallory wasn't holding her breath on that one. Thomas was, among other things, unpredictable.

Mallory's happy day continued. Business was good, customers were cheerful, and the weather was surprisingly pleasant for July. The cherry on top came on Friday afternoon when she received a FedEx envelope from the producers of *Pacific Design.* She'd eagerly opened it to discover her signed contract — and a check! With visions of more lovely inventory dancing through her head — hopefully enough to last until the TV show was filmed — she hurried to the bank to deposit it. Then she returned to the shop to start preparing a new order. If it took a couple weeks to get here, which was fairly typical, she would need to get her order in quickly.

She'd heard from Kara, earlier in the

week, that the house sale was scheduled to close in escrow the first week of August. "With no delays," Kara had assured her. "I have my mother's and the buyers' word on that." Mallory hadn't complained for a change. Instead, she'd told Kara her exciting news, holding her phone away from her ear as Kara let out a shrill whoop!

"I'm not feeling quite so financially strapped," Mallory told her. "Not that I don't need that house money. I definitely do."

"You'll have it," Kara promised. "Let me know when you have firm dates for the filming. I'd love to come see it. In fact, I'd love to come see everything in Portside. I've been having serious envy issues. It must be so nice to live at the beach."

"To be honest, I don't get to the beach all that much," Mallory confessed. "I hope that'll change in time. Anyway, Amy said late August for the show, but she warned me it could be later. I'll let you know."

"Thanks. I need a vacation and I can't think of anyplace I'd rather be."

Mallory hoped Kara wouldn't plan to be her houseguest during her visit. "My kids want to come to see the filming too," she told Kara. "They rented this fabulous beach house last time they were here. Maybe we should all look into that again. It's a huge house. I'm sure you could join them there."

"Ooh, that sounds lovely. Sign me up."

Mallory promised to do that, then did a quick design firm checkup with her. Satisfied that Kara was handling things, she told Kara she had to go and they said goodbye.

Now it was Saturday, and Mallory had her next orders for merchandise all ready to go out. Still a bit concerned that her house sale money could fall through again, and that she could be short on inventory when it was time to film, she used every bit of the TV money for her order.

She smiled as she confirmed the purchase. It felt good to know her merchandise would be on its way soon. Having these unexpected funds felt truly fortuitous — a true godsend! Not only could she breathe easier as a businesswoman but she could actually enjoy being a part of Portside. Life was good!

18

It had been almost two weeks since Grayson left his mall plans with Mallory. She'd sketched some drafts of ideas and even created a few on her computer. She always preferred hand-drawn sketches when it came to designs for clients, but she knew not everyone felt that way. Still, she hadn't seen Grayson other than spotting him briefly when he came in with Amy, and then again at the chamber meeting, where he sat in back with Corrina. She wondered if he'd forgotten about leaving the plans with her, or maybe he was extra busy lately.

On Monday morning, she was just turning on the shop lights and some music, doing some dusting, and getting ready for the day when she saw him out front, quietly knocking on the door. Since it wasn't ten yet, she let him in, then locked the door behind him.

"Hey, stranger." She smiled.

255

"Stranger?" His brow creased. "Didn't you call me that once before?"

"Only because I haven't seen you for a while." She led the way through the shop, pausing by the checkout counter.

He ran a hand through his hair. "Yeah, I know. I've been slammed at work. Short-handed and subs backed up."

She reached beneath the cash register to pull out the roll of blueprints. "Then I assume you're not in any great hurry for these."

He sighed. "That project's gotten a little bogged down too. Some glitches in the financing. I'm tempted to put the whole thing on hold until next year." He glanced around her shop. "Honestly, if everyone else in town gets inspired by what you've done, I might just put it on hold permanently."

"Permanently?"

"Yeah, my main reason for wanting the mall was to revitalize Portside, but it almost seems like it's starting to happen organically." He smiled. "You're certainly a big part of that."

"I don't see how. I mean, I love the enthusiasm about the TV show, but that's a ways off."

"It's not just that. I think other merchants are inspired by the facelift you gave Bess's shop, not to mention what you've done in here." He waved a hand in front of him. "Haven't you noticed how others are starting to fix things up too?"

She shrugged. "Maybe it was just time."

"Maybe. Just one more reason to forget about the mall." He drummed his coiled building plans on the countertop.

"Or maybe you just need to let it rest awhile." She reached below again and pulled out her folder of sketches and drawings. "But in case you decide to wake it up someday, here are a few things I dreamed up." She held out the folder to him. "I'm not sure you'll even like them, but it occupied me a few evenings when there wasn't much else going on." She wondered if that sounded pathetic.

He flipped through the pages, studying some more closely than others, then looked at her. "These are good ideas, Mallory."

Her jaw dropped just a bit. "Really? You like them?"

"Absolutely."

"Thanks." She felt a warm rush wash over her. Was it from his praise or from his ocean blue eyes locked with hers?

"If you don't mind, I'd like to keep them. Just in case I decide to revive the mall plan."

"They're all yours," she assured him.

"Thanks, but I can keep them only if you let me take you to dinner like we agreed."

"That works for me."

His eyes lit up. "Is tonight too soon?"

"Gotta eat," she said lightly.

"Do you mind if I make a quick call?"

"Not at all." She went back to readying her shop while he was on his phone.

He hung up, then walked over to where she was adjusting the floral arrangement by the front door. "Okay, we're all set," he told her. "Do you mind if I pick you up this time? There's a place up north I've wanted to try out, and I just made a reservation for seven. Will that work?"

"Of course."

"Is six too soon to pick you up? It's a fifty-minute drive."

"Six is perfect." She smiled. "And a drive up the coast sounds lovely."

He nodded. "Then it's a date."

"Great." She liked that he'd said "date."

"It's probably good we're going there on a weeknight. I hear they're usually booked on weekends."

She wiped her hands on her apron. "Must be quite a place."

"I hope we're not disappointed. See you at six?"

"Yes, six." She paused. "Uh, one question,

is this a formal sort of place?"

"Not formal, exactly, but nice."

She smiled, already planning what she would wear for this "date." "Thanks. See you at six."

The restaurant was better than "nice." It was what Louisa would call swanky, with lovely decor, windows overlooking the ocean, white tablecloths, candles and flowers, and extremely polite servers. As they were seated Mallory was glad she'd put on the dress she'd worn to Louisa's wedding. She loved the tea-length skirt, with layers of sheer fabric in varying shades of blue. It reminded her of the ocean, and she'd hoped to have an occasion to wear it again someday. Tonight seemed the perfect opportunity. Something about the soft fabric and swing of the flowing skirt just made her happy. And she could tell by Grayson's expression when he picked her up in a luxury SUV — not a work truck — that he liked it too. He'd even complimented her on it, saying that the colors reminded him of the sea.

They had visited pleasantly on the scenic drive north. Since it wasn't a weekend, the traffic was fairly light. He even stopped at a lookout location to admire a lighthouse for a few minutes. Even with the detour, they had arrived at the restaurant by seven, where, to her surprise, Grayson ordered a bottle of champagne. "To celebrate," he told her after the server left.

"Celebrate?"

"Your soon-to-come TV show," he said with a twinkle in his eyes. "Congratulations, Mallory. You're the talk of the town."

"Thanks." She blushed. "I don't think I've properly thanked you for telling Amy about my shop."

"Well, she sort of showed up out of the blue," he said. "Amy and Kellie were good friends, but I hadn't seen Amy in years."

"Kellie?" she asked quietly. "Your wife?"

He nodded. "Kellie's parents are good friends with Amy's parents." He smiled. "In fact, Kellie used to babysit Amy when she was a teen, but they got closer when Amy got older. Kellie used to keep track of Amy's career. She was always telling me about it. But when Kellie got sick, Amy never even came to see her." He shook his head. "Didn't attend the memorial service or anything. To be honest, I was pretty surprised to see her in Portside last week." He paused as the server returned with their champagne, uncorked the bottle, and ceremoniously poured it for them.

"Here's to your TV debut." Grayson

clinked his glass against hers, then they both took a sip.

"I'm still dumbfounded over the whole thing. I've had moments when I think I must've dreamt it all up, but the contract and check came on Friday so I'm pretty sure it's real." She smiled. "I'm still curious as to why Amy suddenly showed up in Portside." She knew she was fishing, but really wanted his answer. "I know it wasn't to see me."

"She claimed it was to see me." He shrugged. "Amy told me about her show, then she asked if I knew of any properties that would work for it. I was sort of caught off guard. Anyway, I took her to see the house I built for Kellie . . . before she passed."

"Ah, so that's the house she plans to feature on one of her episodes."

"Yeah, I guess. It's a nice enough house, but I'm not sure it's TV material. I even tried to talk Amy out of it, but she seemed quite determined. My daughter, Lindsey, manages the house for me. Runs it as an Airbnb." A funny expression crossed his face.

"Oh?"

"I wasn't going to say anything, but I think your kids may have rented it when

261

they came to visit."

"*The Gull's Wing?*"

He nodded. "That's it. Kellie named it."

"That's a fabulous house, Grayson. I think it would be wonderful on Amy's show."

He shrugged. "To be honest, I haven't actually seen it for a long time. It was finished before Kellie got sick and then, after that, we didn't use it much. But the kids aren't ready for me to sell it."

Mallory leaned back in her seat. "Is it hard for you to go there?"

He nodded. "Hard to let it go too. Fortunately, Lindsey is happy to manage it, and it supplements her teacher income. Kind of a win-win."

Mallory was still trying to absorb that somehow Louisa had found and rented Grayson's house. She took another sip of champagne, then slowly shook her head. "So when I told you about the lovely Airbnb on the beach, did you know it was yours?"

He looked sheepish. "Yeah, it was kind of awkward." Then he brightened. "But I'm glad you liked it."

"I've never had a more peaceful two night's sleep. I attributed it to being stressed and exhausted, but the house really is amazing."

"You don't seem too stressed and ex-

262

hausted now." He refilled her champagne glass.

"I'm not." She smiled at the memory of her kids' meltdown when they went into her apartment the first time. It had seemed so horribly serious then. Today, it seemed more funny than serious. They continued to visit and enjoy the view. By the time they were done with their meal, Mallory really did feel like it was a date. Oh, maybe not the kind of date where he would walk her to her door and kiss her good night, but she wasn't actually ready for that. Not yet, anyway.

The perfect gentleman, Grayson did walk her to her door and, although she invited him into the shop, he declined. "It's pretty late and I've got concrete guys coming at six in the morning. I should call it a night." He shook her hand and thanked her for a very enjoyable evening. A bit formal perhaps, but she didn't mind.

Enjoying the afterglow of that amazing date with Grayson combined with the delightful anticipation of being featured on *Pacific Design,* Mallory couldn't remember many times when she'd felt this happy. Beyond that, she was nurturing a thriving business and becoming a welcomed member of the community.

By now she'd done numerous free consultations with potential clients, some who decided to proceed with her help and others who didn't. But she didn't even mind when they turned down a design, usually because of finances, and she always told them to use whatever they liked from her ideas. Then she'd invite them to continue visiting her shop and, most importantly, to remain friends.

It was refreshing to be this relaxed about accumulating clients — so different from how she'd approached work early in her career. Now she had no need to pack her schedule too tightly. Maintaining her shop was more than enough to keep her occupied. She was even considering part-time help, if she could find the right person.

She looked forward to loosening her belt and lightening her schedule in due time. But in the meantime, she didn't mind being busy. Even the physically hard work of rearranging her shop every few days was fulfilling. It was a good aerobic workout, and the payoff was a gorgeous shop.

She had just finished up some rearranging on Thursday morning when Grayson knocked on her door. It was still an hour before opening time, and although she felt a bit grubby in her jeans and sweatshirt, she happily opened the door and greeted him.

"I come bearing gifts." He held up a pair of coffees and a bakery bag.

"Just what the doctor ordered." She waved him inside. "I finished my furniture moving workout routine and haven't had breakfast yet."

"You move furniture by yourself?" He looked surprised.

"I have a few tricks of the trade." She pointed to her sliding tools still on the counter. "And I know to use my legs, not my back."

"Wise woman." He set the coffees on her worktable and opened the bag. "I couldn't decide between cheese blintzes and raspberry scones, so I got both."

"Perfect." She reached in to remove a blintz. "I'm starving."

"By the way, I had a good time on Monday night," he told her.

"So did I." She felt a rush of happy nerves as she sipped the drink he'd brought her. He even remembered she liked lattes. "Did your concrete pour come out all right?"

He nodded. "For the most part. Nothing is ever really perfect in construction, but I suppose that's the challenge. It makes life interesting."

She considered this. "That's true in design

265

too. I'll think things are under control, and I've got it all planned down to the smallest detail, then something goes wrong. Hardware isn't what I've ordered, a paint color is a few shades off, a piece of furniture doesn't arrive, or something is damaged."

"Then what?"

"That's when I get to play with it. I actually love to problem-solve. And usually, the end results are even better than my original plan. It's like a perfect imperfection."

"Perfect imperfection." He grinned. "I like that. Kind of like real life."

The sound of her ringtone got her attention. "I'd like to ignore it" — she reached for her phone — "but the mama in me still has to check. You never know." She read the caller ID. "Oh, it's Amy Stanton!" She looked at Grayson.

"Better take it," he said. "Might be important."

"Right." She answered with a cheery "hello."

"Hey, Mallory. How are you?" Before she could answer, Amy continued, her words coming quickly. "So, exciting news here. First of all, everyone is on board with our Romancing the Home episode. The concept is so fresh and new. We couldn't be more thrilled. So that's all great. I hope you're excited too."

"Yes. I can hardly wait until —"

"That's perfect, Mallory. You're not going to have to wait as long. You see, we had another planned episode fall apart on us. It was supposed to be extra special too. I found this awesome historical hotel renovation up in the San Juan Islands in Washington, but their fabulous reno isn't quite finished yet, so we need to do a switcheroo. That's where you come in. The producers want to go with Romancing the Home instead! Isn't that marvelous?"

"Yes. That's great."

"So how does two weeks out sound?"

"Great. Exciting. I'm —"

"I told them you'd be fine with it," she said. "And here's even more good news, Mallory. Because the hotel segment was supposed to be an hourlong episode, well, that's actually forty minutes of film time, but anyway, we were going to split your shop's episode in half with this adorable café down in Monterrey, but the producers came up with this killer idea. The first half of the episode will be about you and your shop and the whole romancing the home concept, and then the second half will be you in your own apartment upstairs, explaining how it all works. Like the rubber meets the road. Isn't that a fabulous idea? The fans are seriously going to eat this up. Anyway —"

Amy continued to talk a mile a minute, but Mallory was struggling to breathe. They wanted to feature the *Rainbow Brite* apartment? She gripped her phone so tight, she worried it would crack as she tried to focus on Amy's words.

"I'm so thrilled about the whole thing," Amy was saying. "I can hardly wait to get back there. Josie will call you with the exact details early next week, but you can put it on your calendar today. Two weeks from yesterday, we'll be there with bells on. We'll arrive on Wednesday night, then we'll film on Thursday and Friday, and hopefully wrap it all up by Saturday. Cool news, huh?"

Mallory struggled to speak. "Uh, yeah, I guess —"

"Great. I knew you'd love it. See you in a couple weeks, Mallory. This is going to totally rock. Now you take care." Amy hung up — Mallory wanted to throw up.

Instead, she set down her phone and stared blankly at Grayson.

"Are you okay?" He peered at her with concern. "You look kind of pale."

"I think I'm going to be sick."

His brows shot up. "The blintz?"

She slowly shook her head. "I wish." She planted her hands on the worktable to steady herself, then tried to take in a calming breath to slow down her racing heart. She was trying to process what she'd just heard, trying to grasp the news that her happy little world was about to crumble. And it was her own silly fault.

19

Mallory was pacing now, almost oblivious to Grayson's presence beside her in the back room. "Two weeks?" she muttered to herself. "No, actually, less than two weeks."

"What's wrong, Mallory?" Grayson asked. "Did Amy cancel your show?"

"No." She paused from pacing to count on her fingers. "Tomorrow is Friday, then Saturday, Sunday . . . Wednesday." She gasped. "Thirteen days. Just thirteen days."

"What's just thirteen days?" He stood beside her, looking concerned.

"I have to get out of doing the show. Have to pull the plug." She reached for her phone.

"Please, tell me what happens in thirteen days?!"

"They're coming to film my *Pacific Design* episode. They moved the date up." Mallory pressed a hand to her throbbing forehead.

"Hey, that's great. You'll get more summer traffic and —"

"That's not it, Grayson. You don't understand. They plan to film my apartment too. And I'm — I'm not ready."

"You can get a lot done in two weeks, Mallory. Isn't your renovation nearly complete by now?"

She felt the threat of tears but hoped to hold them back. "I need to cancel the whole thing. I can't do it."

"Why?"

She looked into his eyes and, realizing this was her awful moment of truth, she took his hand. "Come with me. I'll show you why." She led him up the stairs and flung open the door. "*That* is why."

She watched his face as he stared at her apartment. It looked worse than ever with a heap of clothes piled on the sectional. Beside the loaded drying rack in the kitchen, she'd hung her sheets between a pair of opened doors. Seeing his shock and what had to be disgust, her pent-up tears began to trickle down her cheeks.

"It's absolutely horrible," she choked the words out. "I can't let them in here to film *this.*" The tears came faster now. Sure, no one had died, but it felt like her whole world had been rocked from its foundation. Everything that had looked so rosy this morning now felt black as night.

271

"I feel like such a fool. A total fool." She sobbed harder now as, to her surprise, Grayson gathered her into his arms and just let her cry. Finally, she got ahold of herself and stepped back. "I'm sorry. I'm not usually such a mess."

"It's okay," he said quietly. "Maybe it's not as bad as you think."

"Are you kidding? It's a disaster zone!" She used her sweatshirt sleeve to wipe her damp cheeks, then waved her arms around. "Look at this place, Grayson. Can you imagine Amy up here with her film crew? Honestly, I feel like the village idiot right now."

He gave a weak smile. "You're not the village idiot, Mallory." He started to walk around, examining the kitchen, poking around where plaster had been removed. He even tugged a large chunk off the wall, peering closely to study the wiring underneath. "Thomas is the village idiot." He shook his head. "I can't believe he left you with this mess."

"Is the wiring bad?" She wasn't sure she wanted to know.

He bit his lip. "Doesn't look good. Mind if I take a bigger chunk out?" He pointed to a broken section where an upper cabinet had been carelessly pulled out.

"You can tear the whole place down if you like. I don't think I'd even care."

"That's not necessary." He jerked on the loose piece of plastered lathe, then dropped it to the floor.

She went over to peer inside the gaping hole. There was the telltale tubing. "It's knob and tube, isn't it?"

He nodded somberly. "Thomas must've known. I'm guessing that's why he stopped midstream. He was in over his head."

"And I buried my head." She closed her eyes. "I'm such an idiot."

"No, you're not. But you might've been working with one." He blew out an exasperated sigh. "This is exactly why I was so worried, Mallory."

"I know." She opened her eyes, blinking back more tears.

He pointed up at the ceiling panels. "I'm guessing Thomas didn't get those tested for asbestos either."

"I doubt it." She swallowed hard, a feeling of hopelessness settling over her.

Grayson went around all the rooms, turning off lights and unplugging everything from the outlets. "What about downstairs?" he asked. "Did Thomas open any of your shop's walls before he covered it all with paint?"

"I don't know. I wasn't here when that was done."

"Are you ready to find out?"

"Might as well." She felt even sicker as they went downstairs. Not just about losing her chance with *Pacific Dream* — that was bad enough — but what if her whole building was unsafe? What if she lost everything?

"This is exactly why Thomas needs to have his CCB license and get proper permits and inspections," Grayson growled as he went into the back room. "Any tools around here?"

"The basics." She got her small toolbox out, and he selected a hammer and screwdriver then went to the light switch by the back door.

"I'll poke in here to see what's going on." He used the hammer to pound the end of the screwdriver, which made a small hole. "Just in case, by some miracle, the first floor is okay, we can easily patch this up."

She silently watched him poking and prodding, almost afraid to breathe. What if Grandpa hadn't done it right?

"This is drywall," he said. "That's a good sign."

The tension in her chest loosened a smidge. "No lathe and plaster beneath?"

"Nope." He pulled a fist-sized chunk of

274

Sheetrock out to expose what looked like newer wiring. "Well, I think you're in luck down here." He threw the chunk of drywall in the trash can. "Where's your electric panel?"

She led him over to the panel by the bathroom.

He opened it up and peeked around. "This looks okay too, Mallory."

"That's a relief. But the apartment . . ." She sighed. "I know replacing old wiring is expensive and messy and takes a long time." She picked up her phone from where she'd left it on the worktable. "I should call Amy right now. I'll pull the plug and give her time to find someone else."

"Not yet." He put his hand on her arm. "Give me today to figure some things out, okay?"

"What kinds of things?"

"There's a whole list. I need to talk to the city about permits. Then I need to check on my own project. But most importantly, I'm going to round up Thomas and give him a piece of my mind." He balled a fist at his side.

She felt alarmed. "What're you going to do to him?"

"I might want to punch him." He looked a bit sheepish. "But I just plan to give him the option of making things right with you."

"How?" she asked. "I know he can't pay me back yet."

"He can work."

"But you said yourself, he's not even a contractor."

"*I'm* a contractor. Thomas can labor under my supervision. Not as a sub, because he's not. But he can be my employee. An employee who won't get paid a penny until he breaks even with what he owes you."

"You think you can actually make him do that?"

"He can do that or stand before the contractors' board and face some heavy fines. Not to mention his name will be mud in this town." Grayson picked up his coffee and took a swig.

She blinked. "Well, if anyone can make him toe the line, it's probably you."

"Thanks." He smiled. "Try not to worry about it too much today. I'll let you know how it goes. In the meantime, *please,* do not use any electricity upstairs, okay?"

She nodded.

"Go ahead and open your shop as usual. At least you're not a fire hazard down here right now. I'll send my electrician over as soon as I can. Then I'll stop by later and let you know what's possible and how it goes with Thomas." He shook his head. "If I wasn't so shorthanded right now, I'd pull in my guys to make this right. But I just can't."

"No, of course not. I would never expect that." She felt terrible for being such a nuisance.

"But if Thomas will step up and do what's right, without questioning my direction, it will help a lot. We might even be able to get it done."

"In thirteen days?" She felt pathetically doubtful.

"Yeah, it doesn't seem possible, does it?" She shook her head.

"Well, what's impossible with us is possible with God. Maybe you should do some real hard praying." His smile looked stiff. "Worry less and pray more."

"Believe me, I am praying." And she wasn't kidding. She'd been silently screaming inside, begging God to help her — *help, help, help*! And she didn't just mean with her building. She needed God to help keep her brain from exploding. This was too much. Just too much! Besides the disaster area upstairs, and knowing her shop was at risk, she was worried about Amy's expectations and schedule. Perhaps she was most concerned for the town of Portside. Everyone was so bolstered up and excited about

277

the prospect of being on a national TV show. How disappointed would they be when she let them down? In fact, if Grayson thought Thomas's name would be mud in this town, what would they call her? Slime?

She thought about Grayson. It was so kind of him to want to help, but he had his hands full with his own projects. And after seeing her hot mess upstairs, why on earth would he ever want to come back here or have anything to do with her? She'd seen that horrified expression, similar to her kids' reactions. Who could blame anyone? She hated it up there. And yet she supposedly lived in that squalor. Really, what was wrong with her? Grayson's reminder popped in her head, telling her to pray and not worry. Easier said than done.

God help me, she prayed silently. *Please, help me.* She knew it was past ten now, but she wasn't ready to open her doors. She wondered if, in good conscience, she even should open them. Was this place a firetrap? Was she endangering customers?

She closed the door to the back room and actually got on her knees. It wasn't something she normally did, but she felt so desperate . . . and hopeless . . . it was all she could think to do. She prayed until her knees began to ache. Then, still praying — now for Grayson — she began walking back and forth in the back room. She asked God to help Grayson find solutions, but then felt guilty. What right did she have to drag him into her foolish mess?

He was a good guy to want to help her, but it was futile. Thirteen days was not long enough. And it wasn't worth him short-changing one of his own jobs to try to fix her situation. The responsible thing would be to call Amy back, explain the situation, apologize . . . and then admit to everyone in town that she'd blown it. She could blame it on her enthusiasm and setting her cart in front of her horse, or she could just admit that she should be crowned the village idiot.

Even though Grayson had said it was okay to open her shop, she couldn't. As much as she respected him and believed he knew construction better than anyone, this was her decision, her responsibility. Not only that, but she should probably pack up her belongings and move back to the hotel until she figured things out.

As she penned a sign to hang on her front door, explaining that she was "closed for the day," she wondered if she shouldn't be writing "closed indefinitely." Because the more she thought about that old wiring upstairs, the more she envisioned a fire. It could happen. And her crowded decor shop would become a firetrap to any innocent customers.

Even if Grayson did get a plan together and coerced Thomas into helping — a major miracle — she would still need to be out of the apartment. She went upstairs and, almost afraid to step inside, held back from turning on a single light as she hastily packed up her things. She carried load after load downstairs, piling it all in the back room for the time being. Now that looked like a big mess. Everything in her world felt like a big mess.

She was just picking up her phone to call the hotel when she heard a noise out in her front shop. Knowing it couldn't be a customer since everything was locked up, she peeked out to see. What on earth? Coming into her shop were her aunt and two cousins!

Bracing herself for whatever was coming next, she took in a slow deep breath and called out a loud "Hello?" as she approached them. All three women jumped. "What're you doing here?" Mallory asked them.

Aunt Cindy dangled a brass key as if that

were permission to trespass. "We saw the shop was closed and I have my key, so we just decided to come in."

Keeping herself from snatching the key away, Mallory attempted to compose herself. "May I help you then? I assume you came to do some shopping."

"Don't be silly," Marie said sharply. "We came to talk to you."

"Well, you picked a bad day to do it. As you noticed, I'm closed."

"But you're here," Val said.

Mallory studied her relatives, wondering if they might have some sort of legal letter to frighten her. "Okay, here I am." She leaned against a marble-topped table, folding her arms in front of her. "What do you want to talk about?"

"We want to appeal to your sense of duty and rightness," her aunt began. "We all believe that my mother's intent was to leave this place to Val."

"Yes, you've mentioned that, but I'm not sure how you came to that conclusion."

"It was a phone conversation I had with Mother some time ago. I told Mom how Val lived with me and how wonderful it would be for her to have her own place."

"That's right," Val confirmed. "I remember when they talked."

281

"Yes?" Mallory wondered why no one had mentioned this before . . . and whether it was the truth or just wishful thinking. "But you saw Grandma's will. There was nothing about this in there."

"She was really old, you know how old people forget things," Val said, her voice whiny. "Maybe she forgot."

"Grandma's lawyer didn't think she was forgetful," Mallory said, although they seemed to be ignoring her.

"Anyway, I spoke to Mother about that apartment above her shop," Aunt Cindy persisted, "and she said that was fine — that Val could have it."

"That Val could have it?" Mallory repeated woodenly. She wasn't buying this. Aunt Cindy probably just wanted to relocate her high-strung daughter.

"Yes, that's what she said," Val insisted.

"Did Grandma say Val could have it to use? Or to own?" Mallory asked.

Aunt Cindy rolled her eyes like she thought Mallory wasn't very sharp. "She said Val could *have* it."

"And that's the way I heard it too," Marie confirmed.

Mallory turned to her. "You listened to the phone call too?"

"No, Mom told me about it later.

Grandma Bess said Val could have the apartment."

"And you say that conversation was a while back?" Mallory raised her brows. "Why didn't Val come out here and get it then?"

"Well, we were busy," Aunt Cindy said.

Mallory leaned her head back, looking upward, wishing Grandma Bess could shout down from the heavens what she had truly intended . . . and then, feeling that perhaps she just had, Mallory smiled. "Okay, Val. You want that apartment?"

Val's eyes lit up and she nodded eagerly.

"Fine. It's all yours."

"Honestly?" Val grabbed her arm.

"Absolutely." Mallory walked toward the rear of the shop. "Come see it." As she led them through the back room, she picked up her Day-Timer, flipping it to where she'd been making lists and doing some renovation estimates. She led them upstairs, flung open the door, and invited them in.

Of course, they were all shocked when they saw it. And thanks to Grayson having pulled open the wall and the heaps of things Mallory had been moving around, it looked worse than ever. Seeing Aunt Cindy reaching for a light switch, Mallory shouted at her. "Stop! It's not safe. The old wiring is shot. It could catch fire."

Val's brows shot up. "What's going on here?"

"The whole place needs renovating," Mallory said. "All new wiring, which means all the lathe and plaster will need to be removed. And the plumbing is probably as old as the wiring, so it will have to go." She opened her Day-Timer and started tossing out her cost estimates.

"Naturally, all these things will have to be completed before occupancy." Now she added in her previous costs of renovations, as well as prices for appliances and fixtures she'd already purchased to replace what would be torn out. Finally, she tossed out a rather staggering figure that made even her a bit weak at the knees.

She paused to look up at the ceiling. "Oh, I forgot about that. Asbestos abatement could run another five grand. Just to remove it. And, of course, there are always unexpected expenses. I always add an extra ten percent for a contingency fund, but that's for new construction. For this old building, you should probably add twenty." She looked at Val. "So if you have that much money, the place is all yours. I give it to you."

Val turned to her mother. "I don't have

that kind of money," she whispered. "Do you?"

"Of course not." Aunt Cindy glared at Mallory. "Are you sure about all this?"

"My contractor can confirm everything for you. His name is Grayson Matthews, and he's very well-respected in this town."

"How can you afford that much?" Marie challenged Mallory.

"It will take almost every cent from selling my house, and the sale closes next week. To be honest, I'm feeling a bit shocked myself at the moment. I just heard the bad news today. That's why I'm moving out. It's not safe to live here, and I'll need to close my shop for the time being."

"That's a lot of money for an old apartment," Marie conceded.

"I agree." Mallory sighed. "I'm pretty overwhelmed." She looked hopefully to Val. "But if you can get these funds together, I'll gladly turn it over to you."

"No." Val firmly shook her head. "I can't do that. I don't want it." She walked around, looking closer. "This place is awful. You couldn't pay me to live here."

"Yes." Mallory sadly shook her head. "That's how I feel too."

"Looks like Grandma Bess pulled a fast

one on you," Marie said with a little bit of spite.

Mallory looked upward again and, for a split second, she believed she saw her grandmother winking.

"Let's get out of this firetrap," Marie said.

"Yeah, it stinks up here," Val added as they headed toward the door.

"Probably black mold." Aunt Cindy followed them out.

"Oh, yeah." Mallory slapped her forehead. "I didn't even think about that." Of course, she was fairly certain the bad smell was plain old mildew under the bathroom floor, but who knew what they'd find once they started tearing into it. As her relatives left, she actually felt slightly disappointed that they hadn't taken her up on her offer.

20

Mallory called the hotel she'd stayed in
when she first came to Portside, but they
were booked solid through the end of the
month. She tried another only to hear "no
vacancies." Good for the hospitality indus-
try, but not so good for her. She was about
to call a rather dodgy-looking motel in town
when she heard someone banging on the
front door. She couldn't imagine it was her
relatives again. Besides, Aunt Cindy had a
key. Just the same she approached cau-
tiously.

It was almost noon. She normally closed
shop for the lunch hour, which her regular
customers would know. As she walked
through the shop, she spied a young man
with a tool kit at his side. He didn't look
like a customer. She hurried to unlock the
door. "Yes?"

"Mallory? I'm Brad Kempton." He stuck
out his hand for her to shake. "I'm an

electrician. Grayson Matthews sent me over to look at your upstairs wiring."

"Caroline's son?" she asked as she let him in before relocking the door.

"Yep." He nodded. "I hear you got some old wiring upstairs."

"That's right." She led him to the stairs, glad that she'd removed most of her personal items.

"My mom's shop had the same problem. I rewired it a few years ago."

"That's good to know." She opened the door. "It's pretty ugly up here."

He laughed. "Don't worry, I've seen it all in this town." He started to look around, shaking his head. "Where's the electric panel?"

She walked over to a side wall near the kitchen. "I hid it under this." She removed a picture frame, carrying it over to lean against the sectional.

"Looks like I'll need to shut the power off for the whole building. I saw your closed sign on the front door. Do you mind clearing out?"

"No," she told him. "I think I'd like to get out of here."

He chuckled. "Can't blame you for that."

Although she was grateful Brad was going to do something about that old wiring, she still knew that her timeline was too short. As she finished sorting things in her back room, packing some things in boxes to store here and bagging up others to take to a hotel with her — if she ever found one — she thought through the construction steps she knew it would take to revive her apartment.

She went over her list again, ignoring the estimates she'd made, now imagining a timeline. Even if the rewiring went well, it could take weeks! And what about inspections and approvals? Those always took longer than expected. Thirteen days was not enough!

She hadn't even considered plumbing. Even if her pipes were okay, new drywall and tile and new fixtures would take time — and money. She didn't even know when it would be safe to open her shop again. Being on *Pacific Design* was out of the question. Grayson would have to be a magician to get everything finished in such a short amount of time in a small town like Portside. It was like wishing for the moon. Mallory was sunk.

She parked her car in the back alley and was cramming her clothes and personal belongings into it when her phone rang. Seeing it was Grayson, she eagerly answered. "Thank you for sending your electrician over." She tried to sound brighter than she felt. "That was fast."

"Yeah, it worked out surprisingly well. A shipment of fixtures and exhaust fans seems to be missing, so Brad was at loose ends. But where are you now? I knocked on your shop door — looks like you're gone."

"I'm in the alley, loading my car since Brad suggested I find somewhere else to stay." She leaned against her car. "Which reminds me, I still need to find a hotel or B&B or something. So far, everyone's booked."

"Don't bother with that. I talked to my daughter and our beach house isn't booked this weekend. You can stay there."

"I don't think I can afford that."

"Oh, Mallory, we don't charge friends to use it."

She felt almost teary again but blinked to clear her eyes. "Thanks, Grayson. I really appreciate it." She heard footsteps and turned to see he was just coming around the corner, phone in hand. She smiled and ended the call.

"Here's the security code to get in." He gave her a business card with four numbers scrawled across the top. "If you have any problems, that's my daughter's number. I told Lindsey you'd be there a few days."

She stuck the card in her pocket. "I don't know how to thank you."

"Don't mention it." He waved his hand. "Here's the other news. I filed papers with my buddy Kristin at the city to get a rush on your permit process. She'll have it ready by the end of the day. Can you pick it up?"

"Of course."

"I also talked to Thomas, and he's going to put his current job on hold until he's worked off the remainder of your deposit."

"You make that sound like it was easy."

"Well, I explained his options and he seemed glad to cooperate." Grayson grinned. "And unless you have any objections, I'll be managing this project."

"No, of course not. But can you spare the time?"

"Look, Mallory," he said, "I'm doing this as much for our whole town as I'm doing it for you. Having your shop and your apartment on Amy's show will be a boost for everyone. We've had a pretty good start to our summer tourist season, but that can all fizzle in the fall. If you get that exposure on a big network show, it'll help everyone."

"I'd love for it to happen." She reached into the passenger seat to pull out a roll of design plans she'd hand drawn for the

291

apartment remodel. "I'm not sure this will be much use, but here's what I hoped to do up there."

"That's great." He reached for the plans, unfurling them, and laying them over the hood of her car. "These look good."

"I don't know. I might've been dreaming a little too big. The vaulted ceiling isn't necessary. Right now, I'd settle for just the bare necessities . . . and safety."

He flipped another page, studying her draft for the kitchen. "You've kept this pretty simple and straightforward."

"And my cabinets and plumbing fixtures and tile and light fixtures and everything are all in my storage unit."

"Seriously?" He looked up at her. "That's great news."

"I sort of regretted that I'd ordered them when Thomas first started the job. I mean, since he flaked out on me. I was wishing I still had that money to invest in my shop."

"Well, now you'll have all those items to invest in your apartment. It's giving me hope."

"Do you honestly think it's possible?" she asked. "In less than two weeks?"

"Well, I have a long to-do list and a bunch of questions. First, have you had lunch yet?"

She shook her head even though it felt

like she'd swallowed several bricks for breakfast.

"Let's go grab a burger and go over all
this. Okay?"

She agreed and before long, they were
seated outside at The Chowder House.
While waiting for their burgers, he pored
over her plans, tossing out comments and
questions. She took fast and furious notes
in her Day-Timer. By the time they finished
lunch, Mallory felt better about the future
of her apartment and shop, but she still
knew their timeline was tight.

Grayson rolled up the plans and looked at
her. "We can do this," he declared. "I'm going to pull out all the stops to make it happen."

"What do you mean? What about your
own work?"

"I've decided that losing a week or so isn't
going to make much difference one way or
another with my projects. I'll organize my
crew to get this done, Mallory. I've got some
figuring and scheduling to do."

"And I'll talk to Thomas about the doors
and baseboard." She pointed to her list.
"He's good at refinishing."

"Yeah, the sooner he gets them all out,
the better. It's going to be a mess in there."

"And I heard he's good at tile," Mallory said.

"Great. That'll save a few bucks."

She cringed at the mention of money. "My house sale is supposed to be final next week," she said. "But maybe I should look into a building loan in the meantime —"

He held up a hand. "Let's talk about money later. I plan to keep costs down as much as possible. And since you've already got a lot of the expensive stuff in your storage unit, it might not even be too bad. What we need more than anything is time."

She looked at her watch. "Well, I can get started on my list."

"Me too." He grinned. "Too bad *Pacific Design* doesn't have cameras here now. Might be interesting to get this whirlwind remodel filmed."

"Or it might just slow down the works." She reached for her bag.

"Yeah, you're probably right." He held up a finger. "One more thing. I got to thinking you should keep your shop closed until we resolve the old wiring."

She nodded. "I already decided to do that."

"Smart woman."

"You mean smart for the village idiot."

"Aw, Mallory, you gotta quit saying that."

He reached for the check, but she beat him to it.

"I won't say that again, as long as you let me get this."

"Fine." He grinned. "Gives me more time to get busy."

They parted ways with an agreement to stay in touch. She promised to get the building permits, and he asked her to drop them by the building so he could post them before tomorrow. As Mallory left, she knew they both had a lot to get done. Could they get it done in time? That remained to be seen.

By the end of the day, Mallory had dropped her things off at the beach house and visited her storage unit to gather the light fixtures, sinks and faucets, and anything small enough to fit in her SUV. Then she'd dug out her original sketches of the kitchen and bathroom plans, driven about an hour to visit the countertop company Grayson had recommended, and asked about a rush order for countertops. The woman there let Mallory walk through their scrap yard and measure pieces until she found some slabs of quartz that she thought would work. She explained the urgency of their plan, and the woman promised to do her best. Finally, on her way back, Mallory used the Bluetooth on her phone to talk to Thomas.

"I'm so glad you agreed to work with us," she said as she drove down the beach road.

"Not like I had much choice," he replied in a grumpy tone.

"Well, in the long run, I think you'll be glad you did." She worked to keep her tone cheerful. "Your finish work is exceptional, and I don't know if you heard it or not, but my shop and apartment are going to be featured on a popular design show."

"Oh, yeah." He perked up. "Sandi mentioned that."

"Well, I remembered the tile you did for Sandi's powder room, and it looked good, Thomas." She slowed down for a curve, glancing out to the bank of clouds sitting on the ocean's horizon. Might be a good sunset night.

"You saw the powder room?"

"Yes, and I was impressed."

"Hey, thanks."

"So you might remember that I wanted my whole bathroom tiled, but now that time is of the essence, I'm willing to just do the shower and floor. It's not a terribly big space."

"I might be able to get the whole bathroom done."

"That and still get all the doors and wood trim refinished?" she asked.

"Well, let me think about that. You know, I could always install the HardieBacker on your bathroom walls. Then I could just do the shower and floor, for starters. And if you want I could do the walls later."

"I love that idea," she told him.

"Cool. When do I start?"

"Well, you'll have to coordinate that with Grayson."

"Yeah, he's got some other stuff for me to do too."

"Well, once you've worked out what I already paid you, I'll consider you on the clock, Thomas. It's not like I want to take advantage of you." She controlled herself from adding "like you took advantage of me."

"Okay, that sounds fair. I'll call Gray and find out where to start." He actually thanked her before he hung up.

Mallory was back in town by then and headed straight for the city to pay for the permits. Feeling like the wheels of progress were turning, she drove back to her shop and was surprised to see several pickups parked on the street, as well as Caroline Kempton peeking in the front window. Though tempted to duck around to the back alley, Mallory decided it was better to just face the music.

"Brad told me he's doing some work for you." Caroline's brow creased. "In your apartment?"

"Did he tell you it's a hot mess?" Mallory forced a smile.

"Yes." Caroline nodded with wide eyes. "What's going on?"

Mallory put a hand on Caroline's arm. Knowing whatever she said would probably go through town on the Caroline hotline, she spilled the beans.

Caroline's mouth gaped. "Oh, my. That would've been embarrassing. I had no idea."

"I thought it would've been all done by now. I made the plans and got most of the pieces. I just didn't have anyone to do the work. Until Grayson stepped in."

"You couldn't get anything better than Matthews Construction." She frowned. "But I thought you said all the builders were busy."

Mallory nodded. "They are. Grayson is really going the extra mile here." Her thoughts stuck on how her holding on to Grandma's shop had put the brakes on Grayson's big plans for a mall. Not that it particularly mattered anymore. Grayson could've held that against her, but he hadn't.

"Well, my boy Brad is the best electrician in town," Caroline boasted. "He already took care of everything in my building."

"He told me. That will make your remodel so much easier. I wish my grandma had hired him here." She unlocked her door, curious to get in and see what was going on inside. Hopefully her shop wouldn't suffer too much.

"I'll let you get to it. I'm sorry about your troubles, but hopefully you'll get it all resolved in time for the show." Caroline's expression revealed that she had her own doubts.

"We'll do our best." Mallory went in, then locked the door behind her. To her relief, someone had taped plastic sheeting over the door between the shop and back room. That was something. More protective plastic sheeting was taped over her shelves of merchandise in the back room, and another piece of sheeting was draped over the entrance to the stairway. Someone cared about dust control here. But it didn't appear to be due to asbestos. She knew what that looked like. It'd be a much heavier kind of protection, and no one would be allowed in until abatement was done. She slipped through the slit opening of plastic and went upstairs, feeling hopeful.

"Hello," she called as she went into the apartment. White dust was everywhere, on the floors and in the air, and the workers wore masks and protective goggles. To her relief someone had moved all her furnishings to the center of the room and draped them in more protective plastic.

"You shouldn't be up here," Grayson said as he emerged from the bathroom with a pile of rubble in his hands. He tossed it into one of the wheelbarrows.

"I'm already pretty grubby." She waved to the jeans and sweatshirt she'd been wearing all day.

"You need a mask." He pulled one out of his pocket. "Put this on."

She put it on, then gave herself a mini tour of her own place. "I can't believe how much you've done already. Just getting rid of those horrible painted walls is a huge improvement. I can't imagine what the tenant who painted them was thinking." She looked at all the walls, now stripped down to the studs. All the old wiring was gone. "This is absolutely amazing."

"I've got a good crew." He frowned. "But you really shouldn't be up here. I don't want OSHA coming after me."

"Okay." She headed for the stairs, and he followed. Down in her back room, she removed the particle mask. "I'm almost spellbound by what you've accomplished in less than a day." She handed him the permits, then told him about her conversation with Thomas.

"He already called me. That's why I started tearing into that bathroom. He's bringing over HardieBacker tomorrow."

"Tomorrow?" She blinked. "What about the plumbing?"

"The drains are good, but my plumber's going to add fresh water lines. He'll probably start that tomorrow as well. And Brad will start running wires too."

Mallory felt almost breathless, and not due to the dust. "I just can't believe it, Grayson, you're like superman."

"I've got a super team. But we still have a long way to go." He pursed his lips. "To be honest, I'm worried about that ceiling. I've called in a guy to test it. If it's asbestos, it will set us back."

"I wondered about that too."

"Well, it is what it is." His smile looked strained.

"Right. I've got some stuff to unload from my car. I thought we could use this room as sort of a holding area." As he followed her out, she told him how she'd found some good quartz pieces. "Fortunately, there aren't a lot of countertops in my plan. I think we can make it work, but they can't do anything until we make templates. Of course, we can't make templates until the cabinets are installed."

They made a couple trips to get the boxes into the back room, then Grayson put a hand on her shoulder. "I think you've worked hard enough, Mallory. How about you call it a day?"

She reluctantly agreed. But then she grabbed his hand. "I don't know what I would've done if you hadn't jumped in like you did." She let out a long sigh. "I felt so hopelessly helpless."

"Get some rest," he told her. "We'll regroup in the morning. I still have some design questions to talk over with you."

Mallory thanked him again and, realizing she was more tired than she thought, she drove back out to the beach house. She'd felt guilty for the way she'd literally dumped her belongings on the living room floor earlier, but she'd been eager to accomplish the chores on her list. Now she was eager to get everything straightened up. Her fear had been that Lindsey would pop in. She didn't want Grayson's daughter thinking she was a total slob.

Mallory sighed. Although that news may

already have circulated through town by
now. Not that she particularly cared . . .
anymore.

already have circulated through town by
now. Now that the particularly card
anymore.

21

Mallory arrived at the shop at six on the morning of day three. She thought the construction crew wouldn't have started work this early, but as she entered her shop, she could hear pounding upstairs. Grayson had informed her yesterday that his team needed to move all her boxes and furniture pieces downstairs to have room to work and not damage any of her stuff.

She'd assured him that was fine, but as she walked around her shop now, seeing random pieces stacked and stowed and shoved wherever they'd found a space, her heart sank. Even the plastic sheeting over doorways was torn in places and some pieces were completely torn down. Her previously pretty shop now resembled a poorly packed storage unit. But she reminded herself not to complain. She quietly snuck up and peeked around the apartment. It looked like all the plaster and lathe hadn't just been removed from the walls, the messy piles had been removed from the apartment entirely. And the wall that had separated the living and kitchen areas had been removed.

The floor creaked behind her and Mallory turned as Grayson came in.

"What do you think?" he asked.

"Wow!" She shook her head in amazement of the room's transformation. "This is awesome."

"We're making good progress with the demo, but don't worry, things will slow down." He chuckled like this was a good joke.

"It's good to see the old wiring is all gone," she said.

"And the fresh water pipes too. They were pretty nasty." He nodded toward the bathroom. "That's what they're doing in there right now. Unfortunately, we had to rip into the bathroom downstairs. That's where the water and sewer pipes connect to the street."

"Oh." She nodded, trying not to imagine how her stylish powder room must look right now.

"I told the plumber you'd talk to him about fixtures down there. I know it wasn't on your list, but you might as well switch them out while it's a mess."

She felt a nervous tightening in her stomach. She didn't want to question Grayson, but she honestly couldn't imagine how this was all going to be done in time — or within her budget. Still, it would be good to have it done. Even if she had to cancel being on the show.

"I do have some good news," he said in a slightly apologetic tone.

"Oh, it's all good news," she assured him. "Just a little overwhelming."

"I'm sure it's hard to see your shop looking like that."

"It's okay. I understand." She crossed her arms in front of her. "Now what's your good news?"

He pointed to the 1950s ceiling panels. "My asbestos guy texted me last night to say these are *not* asbestos."

"That is good news! I actually woke up in the middle of the night thinking about asbestos."

"Guess I should've let you know last night, but I didn't want to wake you." His brows arched. "Are you comfortable at the beach house? Sleeping okay?"

"Are you kidding? It's heavenly. It's my own anxious thoughts that wake me up."

"Well, you can rest well tonight. I didn't want to say anything before, but asbestos would've blown my work schedule to smith-ereens."

"I figured it would." She sighed.

He walked her through the apartment, explaining what was on the day's agenda. "Brad will install the electric panel and start running wire. I showed him where you made changes on your plans for more lights, but I told him if he has any questions, he can just call you."

"Great. Tell him I want to keep things as simple as possible. If he needs to tweak a can light location for his ease, that's fine. I never expected them in the first place. Mostly I don't want to waste his or anyone's time on anything. Keep the wheels rolling."

"Not going to play the temperamental artiste decorator card?" he teased.

She wrinkled her nose. "Even when there's all the time in the world, I try not to be a nuisance."

"That's the kind of designer I like." He grinned. "And I'm glad you're here this morning because I wanted to run something by you." He pointed to the small living room window that looked toward the ocean.

"What're you thinking?" She wiped dust away from the sill, then peered out the small window. "I just hope you're not going to tell me there's not time for a bigger window."

"No, but I have a *bigger* idea." He explained how he had a lot of patio sliders in storage. "I got a great deal on them last winter. Anyway, I got to thinking, what if we set a pair of them right here? A right slider and a left slider, with a post in between. They would open all this up." He moved his hands apart. "It'd make this wall look like one huge window."

"I would absolutely love that!" she exclaimed. "Can you actually do it? I mean, on our timeline?"

"I know we can do it. Timing is another story, but opening that wall up will save my crew a ton of work. Literally."

"How's that?"

"As you know, we need to move a lot of Sheetrock up here. We'd have to come through your already crowded back room and then up the stairs. It'll be a pain. But if this wall was opened up, we could park a lift down in the street. Then we'd raise the Sheetrock up and pass it right through this opening." He patted the wall.

"Wonderful!"

"But because of the sliding door openings, we'll need some kind of little terrace out there. For code and for safety. Are you okay with that?"

"Grayson, I'm way more than okay. I dreamed of doing something like that *someday*. But won't building a terrace eat up even more time?"

"Nah, I have enough guys to have some working on the exterior and the others in here. Unfortunately, the exterior of your shop will be a mess for a while."

"Well, it's not like I'm going to be open anyway."

He picked up a stray board, then leaned it against a wall. "Since the terrace will sit just above your metal awning, I was thinking you might want a metal railing to keep it looking like it belongs here."

"Perfect. That'd keep the Parisian vibe."

"Exactly. I have a good friend who's a metal fabricator. Actually, I'd call Jake more of an artisan. He could probably get it done in time, if he's not busy, but you'd need to meet with him asap. I'll text you his number."

"I'll call him as soon as I leave here," she said as some of the workers clomped up the stairs. "And now I'll get out of your hair."

She waited for the guys to come in then scurried back down, but before she left, she took a peek in the powder room. Of course, it was a mess. Her pretty touches, as well as the old fixtures, had been removed. Her lovely dark green walls were torn apart and there was broken plaster and lathe all over. Oh, the price of progress.

But, again, she would not complain. To anyone. She knew they were simply doing what needed to be done. To show her gratitude, she stopped by the bakery and got a big box of assorted pastries. She was just going in the back door of her shop when she noticed Thomas driving his pickup down the alley. She waited for him, calling out a friendly greeting. He waved and got out. "I'm here to pick up the doors and wood trim," he told her. "I'm going to refinish them in my garage to stay out of their way."

"Good idea." She held out the bakery box. "Mind taking these up for me?"

His eyes lit up. "Not at all. But what if they think it's from me?"

She shrugged. "What if they do?"

As he took the box, she reached for her phone and, although it wasn't even eight yet, she called Grayson's metal guy, Jake, to explain what was going on and their very short deadline.

"Oh, yeah, I heard about the shop that's going to be on *Pacific Design*. That's you?"

"Yes. The production team will be here in

ten days. You're familiar with that show?"

"Sort of. My wife loves it. I pretend not to watch, but if I see some metal going on, I might sneak a peek." Jake laughed.

"So do you think you could make a railing in a week?" she asked tentatively. "That's about all you'd have."

"That's pretty tight, kinda like my schedule." He paused. "But if my wife hears I blew a chance to be involved in a *Pacific Design* project, she'd probably kill me."

Mallory laughed. "We wouldn't want that."

"No, we wouldn't." Jake invited her to drop by his studio to work with some designs. They agreed to meet at ten.

By the time she went to meet Jake, Mallory had gotten measurements from Grayson, made some rough sketches of what she'd like, and even found a few photos online. She figured anything she could do to streamline this process would help.

Jake's wife, Emily, met her at the door, inviting her into the studio to show off samples of her husband's craftwork.

"Grayson was right in calling Jake an artisan." Mallory ran a hand over a metal sculpture.

"This is so exciting," Emily said. "Jake's work on *Pacific Design*. I'll be posting it all over the place." She listed all the social networks she used.

"Maybe I should hire you to do my social networking," Mallory said.

"Hire me? I'd do it for free." She led Mallory to a shop in the back of the studio. "Hey, Jake. Our local celeb's here."

Mallory laughed. "You don't know how close I came to pulling the plug on everything." She quickly explained to them about her living space challenges.

"Well, Jake is going to do everything he can to make sure your terrace looks fabulous, aren't you, Jake?" Emily elbowed him.

He nodded then led Mallory to his worktable where they started to discuss the design. They decided on a railing that was both easily constructed and pleasing to the eye. "You know, I was worried when you told me you were a designer," Jake told her as he walked her back through the studio. "I thought you were going to be difficult. Some interior designers have pretty big egos."

"Well, I think my ego's been kicked around some lately." She smiled. "Probably a good thing." She thanked him.

They shook hands, and he promised to send photos of how the project was coming. As she left, she felt grateful for making even more new friends. As hard as it was to get so much done in so little time, there was an upside too. By the time she was done, she would know half the town!

But as she drove through Portside, she felt at loose ends. Because of the demands of the shop, she wasn't used to having this much spare time. And according to her Day-Timer, she didn't have any consultations until Thursday. She parked in front of her shop, sadly looking at her "Temporarily Closed for Repairs" sign. And then she got an idea. Since Grayson was doing so much for her, maybe there was something she could do for him. Or, at least try.

She went into her shop and began to look around . . . trying to find an inspiration piece. She was going to romance his beach house. She picked up a soft throw in shades of pastel blue and turquoise, knowing it would warm up his sand-colored sectional. Plus, it would be cozy on a cool night. Liking the idea of using beach tones in his house, she started to gather up other things. A vase she could use to arrange beach grass in, a couple of pillows, some candles, a pretty lamp to warm up his kitchen counter . . . and a number of other things.

She wasn't worried about depleting her inventory since her shop was already well packed and not even open for the time being. Not to mention she had another large order scheduled to arrive next week. Hopefully, she'd find room to squeeze in all the new boxes and furnishings when her delivery arrived. Unpacking everything and getting it all together would be another story. A story she couldn't think about right now!

She was just putting the last load into her SUV when she saw a woman rapidly approaching her. As she got closer, Mallory realized it was Corrina, and, judging by her serious expression, she was on a mission.

Mallory closed the back of her SUV and smiled, greeting Corrina.

"Hello," she replied crisply. "Have you seen Gray?"

"Earlier this morning." Mallory nodded toward the apartment. "Up there."

"Well, he's not answering his phone."

"Oh?" Mallory studied Corrina, wondering if she'd done something to upset the woman.

"According to Mike, who's working on your apartment right now, Gray's not up there."

Mallory shrugged. "Then I guess I can't help you."

"I guess not." Corrina stepped closer, looking intently at Mallory. "But you're pretty good at helping *yourself.*"

"Helping myself?"

"Yeah, helping yourself to other people's help. You don't seem to mind that Gray is putting his own business and building projects at risk for your sake. As long as he gets your work done, that's fine, right?"

Mallory stepped back. "Grayson assured me his projects would be fine."

"Fine?" Corrina scowled. "Mrs. Hampton is not fine. She's already called twice today, demanding to know why no one's working at her beach house today."

"Oh . . ." Mallory slowly nodded. "Well, that happens sometimes, doesn't it? I mean, I've worked on remodels and new builds. I realize that some homeowners can get impatient when workers aren't there for a day or two. They don't understand that schedules can change, but that doesn't mean anything is wrong. Sometimes two or three weeks will go by without anything changing on a site. Homeowners hate those snafus, but that's just how it goes. I'd think you'd know that by now, but maybe you're new to the construction business."

"I'm not new. And it might go like that on *your* projects. But not on Gray's. He's always on time. He's known for that."

"Well, I'll admit I'm very impressed with

315

Grayson's work ethic. And he's amazing at scheduling his crew and subs, but he's not a magician." Mallory smiled stiffly.

"Maybe *you're* the magician." Corrina tilted her head to one side. "Somehow you've gotten Gray under your spell, and it looks to me like you're taking advantage of him."

Mallory felt like a pot that was about to boil over. She tried to remain calm. "I'm not sure why you're this upset at me, Corrina. Are things really that stressful at the office? Or is something else troubling you?"

"*You* are troubling me." Corrina narrowed her eyes at Mallory.

Mallory lowered her voice. "Is this personal?"

"I know you've gone out with Gray. Is *that* personal?"

Mallory was speechless.

"You're living at Gray's beach house. Is that personal?"

"I really don't think that's your business."

"Gray *is* my business," Corrina declared. "I've been looking out for him ever since Kellie died, and I'm not about to let some selfish out-of-towner come in here and mess everything up. Gray deserves better."

"Maybe you need to talk to him about that."

"Maybe I will."

"If I see him, I'll be sure to let him know you're trying to reach him." Mallory moved toward the driver's door. "If you'll excuse me, I've got a lot to do."

Corrina actually rolled her eyes before storming off.

Mallory felt shaky as she got into the driver's seat. She never enjoyed confrontations with anyone, but for whatever reason, this one seemed worse than normal. Clearly, Corrina had more than a business relationship in mind for Grayson. Hadn't Mallory suspected that some time ago? But had Grayson done anything to make Corrina believe he felt the same? Did he feel the same?

22

Mallory still felt somewhat rattled when she got to Grayson's beach house. Was she being selfish and taking unfair advantage of him? Had she put his construction business at risk? Or was Corrina just extremely territorial about her relationship with Grayson?

By the time she finished unloading her SUV, Mallory figured it was most likely the latter. Corrina was probably jealous, but the harsh words of her accusations still stung. To distract herself, Mallory began to rearrange and decorate. As she set out various decorative items, she got even more ideas. An area rug here, something for the wall there. She didn't want to get too carried away or offend Grayson's sensibilities, but anything he didn't like could easily be undone later.

As she "played house," Mallory realized that her efforts here could become something of a backup plan. In the event that her apartment project wasn't done on time, she could suggest to Amy and her crew that Grayson's handsome home could be filmed instead. Hadn't they been considering his house anyway?

Mallory would explain to Amy that this was simply an example of romancing the home. Why not? Excited at the prospect and genuinely having fun, she soon had a fairly comprehensive list of ways she'd like to romance the beach house. With little else to occupy her, she made another trip to her design shop to gather up even more pieces.

She pulled away from the shop with her loaded SUV, relieved not to have crossed paths with Grayson for a couple of reasons. The first was the conversation she'd had with Corrina. The other was her mission of romancing his home — she wanted it kept secret until she was all done. Hopefully Grayson would like it, or at least understand her motivation.

She was trying to maintain a more masculine vibe in this house — no frills or froufrou. Not only would that not fit Grayson, but it would not fit the house, and Mallory always tried to respect the place she was decorating. She was once teased for saying she didn't want to "embarrass" the house.

That was when a homeowner wanted ruffled floral curtains in the living room of a rustic ranch-style house. Fortunately, they appreciated her design when it was finished, but Mallory never talked about embarrassing a house again — not in front of a client anyway!

It was late afternoon when Mallory finished the last of her project. Pleased with the result, she took photos on her phone, thinking she would have them ready just in case she needed to send them to Amy. It probably wouldn't make for as good of a show as seeing the shop and upstairs apartment, like Amy planned, but it would be better than nothing.

She was just taking pictures of the back deck, where she'd placed a few items, when she heard a female voice calling her name from inside the house. Her stomach flipped. Hopefully it wasn't Corrina again. Bracing herself for the worst, she slid open the back door and went inside.

A pretty, young brunette was standing by the island in the kitchen. "Hi, sorry to just walk in," she said, then walked over and stuck out her hand. "I'm Lindsey Matthews, Grayson's daughter. I was gone last weekend when you moved in here. I just wanted to come check on you and make sure you have everything you need."

Mallory shook her hand. "You're probably wondering what's going on in here." She gestured toward the decorative items she added.

"Yeah, I'm kind of curious." Lindsey's brow creased. "Dad said you'd only be here a week or two."

Mallory smiled. "Yes. And I'm so grateful for your hospitality. This is such a delightful house. I wanted to show my gratitude by putting a few items here. Just to sort of personalize the house, you know?"

Lindsey nodded with wide eyes. "Yeah, I've wanted to do that myself, but I'm not good at this sort of thing."

She explained about the backup plan for the *Pacific Design* show. "Anything you or your dad don't want in here can be easily removed."

"No, I totally love what you've done," Lindsey gushed. "Seriously, it looks like something for *House Beautiful.* But I was worried that you thought you were moving in here permanently."

Mallory laughed. "I'm sorry. I can see how you'd think that. I'm probably feeling extra antsy since my shop is closed. The designer in me wanted to come out to play so I brought this all in today. It's sort of my way

321

of saying thanks. Sorry for not asking first. I can take it down if it's a problem."

"It's not a problem for me. I think it's gorgeous." She pointed to the area rug in teal and taupe tones. "I tried a couple of rugs there, but they just looked silly." She also nodded to the mantle. "And those glass balls and candles look amazing. But I'm worried they could get broken by rowdy guests."

"I had similar thoughts," Mallory admitted, "but if they use the house for *Pacific Design,* I thought it would be nice."

Lindsey walked around to admire what Mallory had done. "It's amazing how a few well-chosen items can change the place."

"That's why I call my shop Romancing the Home." She explained the concept and Lindsey grinned.

"You know, when Dad told me you and he were friends, I was curious. And when I saw the name of your shop, I got a little worried. I thought maybe you were romancing him too."

A rush of anxiety washed over Mallory and, suddenly reminded of Corrina's confrontation, she was at a loss for words.

"Not to suggest there's anything wrong with that." Lindsey looked uneasy now. "I mean, I'll admit I'm overly protective of my dad. But I do understand that his personal life is his personal life. I didn't mean to offend you."

"No, you didn't offend me." Mallory turned to look out the window.

"I think I did." Lindsey came over to face her. "I know by the way Dad talked about you that he totally respects you so if anything I said hurt your feelings, I'm sorry."

"It was nothing you said, Lindsey." Mallory attempted a lighthearted smile but felt a heaviness beneath. "I'm feeling a bit thin-skinned because of what someone else said this morning," she said, choosing her words wisely. She had no intention of revealing the source. "No big deal."

"I think I know who you mean." Lindsey pursed her lips with a frown. "Did Corrina say something to you?"

"Oh, I don't know." Mallory turned back to the ocean. She took in a deep breath and slowly released it.

"Well, you don't have to say anything. I'm certain it was Corrina. She called me yesterday and went on and on about how you were taking advantage of Dad and she was going to do something about it. I wasn't sure what to say to her. I mean, I like her well enough, but sometimes she oversteps. So, anyway, I called Dad and he told me not to worry about it, so I didn't. I'm sorry if Corrina said something hurtful to you."

"Thanks." Mallory faced Lindsey. "Your dad is right. You shouldn't worry about it. You know, you remind me of my daughter, Louisa. She's very thoughtful and sensitive to other people's feelings." She smiled. "I'll bet you're a great teacher."

Lindsey blushed. They moved over to the couch, and she told Mallory how she'd only been teaching for three years, but she loved teaching grade school, especially second graders. They chatted pleasantly for almost an hour, then Lindsey remembered she had a date. "It's not anything serious . . . yet." She extracted her car keys from her purse. "I only met Joel a week ago, but I do like him. And he seems to like me, so you never know."

Mallory walked her to the front door. "Well, I hope you and Joel have a delightful evening."

"Thanks, Mallory. And I just want to say once more that I love what you've done with the place. I hope Dad does too. It all seems to go perfectly with the house."

Mallory beamed at her. "Nothing you could say would've pleased me more." She waved as Lindsey went out to her car. Once Lindsey was out of the driveway, Mallory went back inside. She kicked off her sandals and poured herself an iced tea, feeling the most at home she'd felt since moving to Portside. She turned on the music system, which she'd already tuned to a classical station, then returned to the back deck where the afternoon sun was still beaming down.

A band of fog was rolling across the horizon, but until it blocked the sun, she planned to soak up some sunshine and vitamin D. She rolled up her sleeves and pant legs, then sat down on a deck chair and just leaned back and relaxed. For a bit, she imagined what it would feel like to be out here with Grayson. But then she remembered the emotional connection he had with this house. He'd built it for his wife, but they'd never really had the chance to appreciate it. She wondered if he'd ever sat out here and enjoyed this view. Probably not. Maybe he never would.

She had nearly drifted off to sleep when she heard footsteps in the house. She sat up straight. Hopping up from her chair, she rolled down her sleeves and pant legs. Already that band of fog was starting to block the sun and a cool breeze was blowing. "Who's there?" she called out, hoping it was Grayson.

"It's me." Corrina stepped out onto the deck.

"Oh." Mallory took in a breath, bracing herself. "What are you doing here?"

"I thought I was coming to apologize," Corrina said in a stony voice. "You left the door unlocked, so I let myself in and saw that you've now taken over Grayson's house too. Now I'm not sure you deserve an apology."

"Well then, don't let me keep you." Mallory went inside and Corinna followed. Locking the sliding door behind them, Mallory headed for the front door, which she meant as a hint. She turned back to her uninvited guest.

Corrina narrowed her eyes. "You're like a hermit crab."

"Huh?"

"You know, hermit crabs push others out of their shell and take over. Isn't that what you're doing here?"

Mallory couldn't help but laugh. "Look, Corrina, I know you're upset because I'm friends with Grayson. That's what this is all about. But I wish you'd give it a rest."

Corrina picked up a handblown vase, holding it in the air like she planned to hurl it into the fireplace. "You can bring in all your fancy decorations, like you're queen of the castle, but it won't work. Gray will see right through you."

Mallory considered explaining her backup plan to Corrina, but thought, why bother. This woman was determined to believe what she wanted to believe. Instead, Mallory removed the expensive vase from Corrina's hand, then nodded toward the door. "Thanks for the reminder to lock up. I'll be more careful next time. Now, I don't want to keep you." She actually took her by the arm, directing her to the exit. "For the time being, this shell is mine and since I prefer being a hermit, I'll ask you to leave." She opened the door and gently pushed her out.

The surprised look on Corrina's face made the theatrics almost worth it, but as Mallory leaned against the closed door, she felt unsettled. That woman did not give up easily!

The next morning, Mallory went to check the progress on the apartment early. Once again, the workers were already there. To her surprise, they were tearing into the front wall, making space for the sliding glass doors. She learned that Sheetrock was being delivered by eleven and they needed to open it up before the shipment arrived. Not wanting to get in their way, she walked around the other rooms. All the doors and woodwork were gone, making the place look more naked than ever. New wiring was in all the walls and hanging out of the ceiling where lights would go. The kitchen was wired too, and it looked like the fresh water pipe installation was in process.

She peeked into the bathroom to see that not only was the rough plumbing in but someone had started to put HardieBacker on the floor and in the shower. It reminded her that she still needed to pick up the tile from her storage unit. Things were progressing at a breakneck speed. But the clock was ticking too. Would they make it in time?

She heard more guys coming up the stairs and, not wanting to distract anyone from their work, she got out of the way and headed down. Hoping to see Grayson, she lingered in the back room, trying to reorganize the mess and make some more space for people to maneuver. She wished there were more ways to help, but realized she was probably most helpful by not being underfoot during this stage. When it came time for lights and fixtures and hardware, she would make herself useful. In the meantime, she might as well enjoy her downtime at the beach house. Good grief, most people would welcome such a break.

Not seeing Grayson or his truck, she got

in her car and went to the grocery store. It was the first time since moving to Portside that she'd gotten real groceries, not just microwave meals and easy-to-fix food. The beach house kitchen inspired her to cook, and she loaded her cart with fruits and vegetables and a fresh salmon fillet. At the checkout stand, she selected a pretty bouquet of fresh flowers from a grab-and-go container, and feeling like a real citizen, she checked out.

As she drove back to the beach house, she was determined to savor this unexpected "vacation." She reminded herself it was just a matter of days before she'd have to throw herself into high gear and get everything shipshape before the film crew arrived. Well, that was only if Grayson's team finished in time.

Putting that thought out of her mind, she planned her day. She decided she would put her groceries away, do some housekeeping, and make good use of the spacious laundry room. Then she would take a nice long walk on the beach and maybe find some interesting shells or driftwood or other treasures. After that, she'd just relax. Fortunately, someone, probably Lindsey, had stocked the built-in bookshelf in her bedroom with a tempting selection of novels. Her afternoon goal would be to just lose herself in one. Then she would make herself a real dinner of salmon with a side of new potatoes and asparagus and a salad and a slice of the lovely boutique bread to top it all off.

It was just past five when, after falling asleep reading a novel, her ringtone woke her. To her pleasure, it was Grayson.

"We're almost ready for your plumbing fixtures, and your kitchen cabinets and appliances are just a day or two off," he said. "Anyway, if I could get your storage unit key, my guys can load up a truck and bring everything over to the site."

"Sure. Of course." She stood up. "Want me to bring the key to you now?"

"Tomorrow morning is soon enough."

"Great. I'll bring it by."

"Or . . . I could pick it up."

"I don't want to put you out."

"No trouble. I wouldn't mind some time at the beach."

She opened the sliding glass door and stepped inside. "I'm grilling salmon for dinner, would you —"

"I'd love to join you," he said, interrupting her.

She smiled at his eagerness. "Then consider yourself invited."

"Is six too soon?"

She glanced at the clock. It was just past five now. She wanted to tell him seven to give herself more time but then she heard herself say, "I, uh, I guess not."

"Great. I've been working since five a.m. and only had an apple for lunch so I'm feeling pretty hungry."

"Six is perfect," she assured him.

"If it helps, I can manage the grill for you. I'm pretty handy with a barbecue."

"Perfect. See you at six." Mallory hung up and checked the clock again. Just forty-five minutes to get dinner ready. Her mind blanked and it felt like she'd forgotten how to cook. She still wasn't well-acquainted with this kitchen yet, so that was an added challenge. She changed the music to a more lively station, then went to work making a salad and prepping the other food. In a groove now, she decided that cooking was like riding a bike.

She set the table, placing her grocery store flowers in the center, then, worried that looked *too* romantic for an impromptu dinner, she moved the arrangement to the breakfast bar, right behind the small charcuterie board she'd thrown together. Just crackers, cheese, nuts, and olives, but at least it looked nice.

Feeling pretty good about what she'd accomplished — and with a bit of time to spare — she was headed to the bath to do a little primping when she heard the front door open. "Hello?" a voice called from the entryway. "Hope you don't mind that I let myself in," Grayson said as she came around the corner to greet him. "I've got my own key."

Surprised to see him clean and out of his work clothes, she was even more aware of her own grubby condition. "Well, at least one of us looks nice." She stuck out a bare foot, still gritty with beach sand. "I haven't had a chance to clean up."

"You look good to me." He held out a bouquet of flowers that were much prettier than the ones from the grocery store. In his other hand was a bottle of rosé. "I come bearing gifts."

"Thanks." She took the flowers then led the way through the house.

"What's been going on here?" he asked as they entered the great room. "Things have changed."

"It was meant to be a surprise," she said sheepishly. "I've been romancing your house a little as a thank-you for letting me use it."

"Oh?" He continued exploring, looking all around him with a creased brow that worried her.

332

"And it's sort of a backup plan too," she said nervously.

"A backup plan? For what?"

He sank onto a counter stool, and she explained her idea. "It's not that I think my apartment won't be done in time, but I realize anything could happen between now and then."

"That's true." He was still looking over the room, a hard-to-read expression on his face.

"I remembered how Amy had originally wanted to use this house for the show. And, Grayson, it's such a beautiful house. Even without any extra touches. But I'm a designer and, well, I just couldn't help myself."

He barely nodded, not meeting her gaze.

"And anything you don't like or don't want can be easily removed," she continued anxiously. "It can all be removed if you like. Tomorrow, if you want."

"No, no, I don't want it removed." He turned back to her. "Just taking it all in."

"Right . . ." An uneasiness swirled in the air, like something foreign had invaded their previously friendly relationship. Had she offended him? Overstepped her bounds? She wanted to apologize but couldn't quite put together the words.

"It's just that I haven't been here in a

while," he said quietly. "Everything looks different now."

"Oh . . . I realize this house has memories." Trying to ignore the tension, she busied her hands by hurriedly seasoning the salmon. She slid the platter toward him. "You might want to get this on the grill."

"Yeah." He picked it up and stood, still looking around his house with a slightly confused expression.

She watched him head to the back deck and around the corner where the grill was tucked into the outdoor kitchen area.

As she put the potatoes on to cook and laid asparagus in the steamer basket, Mallory wondered what he was thinking. Why had he gotten so quiet? Was he upset with her changes? Did he regret allowing her to stay here to occupy the house he'd built for his wife? Did he resent that she'd made herself too much at home?

Perhaps he would agree with Corrina's cruel metaphor . . . that Mallory was a selfish hermit crab who'd sneaked into someone else's cozy shell, shoving out everything else, including his dead wife's memory.

23

What Mallory had hoped would be a delightful evening with Grayson felt awkward and clumsy and disappointing. The salmon was overdone, and the potatoes were on the crunchy side. Not that it mattered much because it seemed neither of them had an appetite. The bottle of wine remained unopened, and Grayson excused himself before eight. He apologized for not being good company, blaming it on tiredness. But Mallory silently blamed herself. Both for his exhaustion, since it was her demanding project he'd been working on nonstop, and for him being offended, because of the changes she'd brought to his beach house.

Shortly after he left, she sent him a quick text, apologizing for overstepping her bounds. She promised to clear everything out by tomorrow afternoon and said she'd seek other accommodations. Even though he didn't reply, she felt a bit less stressed as she got ready for bed. Resolved to get out of his hair, she would do whatever she could to make his life less complicated.

Mallory woke to the sound of her phone chiming at 5:00 a.m. Groggily reaching for it, she saw several messages from Grayson, and suddenly felt wide awake.

Sorry I was such a stinker last night. Please don't move out of the beach house.

And don't change anything you did there.

Your backup plan makes total sense now. I'll explain more later.

Most of all, forgive me for being the village idiot!

On one hand, she felt better. At least he wasn't mad at her . . . or hurt. That had been her biggest concern. On the other hand, unless she misread his messages, he seemed to be hinting they might actually need her backup plan, after all. Perhaps something had gone wrong at the apartment or with his scheduling. But even if that were true, she would rather lose her apartment than his friendship. She texted him back something to that effect and, as she showered, she decided to take his team another big box of donuts this morning.

A couple more days passed without an actual conversation with Grayson. She saw him in passing when she checked on the state of her apartment, but he was always so busy, and she hated being in the way. She decided to just wait it out. With less than a week until the scheduled show date, Mallory felt a smidgeon of hope that miracles did happen. Thanks to Grayson's full crew working, literally, around the clock, it looked like they might finish on time. Of course, it would take just one mishap or slip of the schedule to derail everything.

On the Friday before the show, her kitchen cabinets and appliances were in, and she'd installed hardware and switch plate covers over all the outlets. Wanting to help however she could, she was now assisting Thomas with the backsplash. She buttered the backs of the tiles with an adhesive and handed them to him so he could work much faster. When she'd ordered tiles, weeks ago, she hadn't dreamed they'd be installed in such a mad rush. Otherwise she would've gotten easy to cut and install tile sheets instead of these subway-sized glass tiles in varying shades of pale blue and aqua and azure that went up one at a time.

"Maybe I should hire you as my assistant," Thomas teased as he pressed the last rectangle into place. "You make me work more than twice as fast as usual."

Mallory stepped back to admire their work. "I love how the tiles look with the driftwood-colored cabinets," she said. "Reminds me of the ocean."

"What color is your countertop?" he asked as he gently sponged the face of the shiny tiles clean.

"A little paler than the cabinet color. Like bleached driftwood."

Thomas stepped back to look, nodding. "That'll be nice."

"It's scheduled to be set on Monday."

"Great. I'll have the grout finished by then." He rinsed his sponge in a bucket of water. "Ready for the bathroom tiles?" he asked hopefully.

"Sure, if you want help."

"Well, you do make me work faster."

She tilted her head to one side. "I'll help with one caveat," she said. "Don't accuse me of rushing you. I don't like being called bossy."

"Okay, *boss*." He grinned. "Anyway, I'm starting to enjoy your company. And I think

338

we've gotten our pace figured out now."

"Great." She picked up the bucket of adhesive. "Ready when you are."

As they started working together on the shower, Mallory was glad she'd chosen an easy design for this project. Just basic oyster-colored tiles with an accent strip of glass tiles that matched the ones in the kitchen. They jokingly bantered back and forth as they worked, and the tiles went up even faster than she'd imagined. They'd just started to do the glass strip when Grayson stuck his head in the bathroom.

"I thought I heard your voice in here," he said to Mallory. "Thomas got you helping him?"

"It really speeds things up," she told him.

"Come on, assistant." Thomas held out his hand. "I'm waiting on ya here."

She quickly buttered an azure glass tile, trying to read Grayson's expression. He seemed troubled . . . or maybe just tired.

"Keep up the good work." He jerked his thumb behind him. "I gotta get back to it."

After he left, an uneasiness settled in her gut. She knew this rush job was stressful. She hated to think how most of the weight rested on Grayson's shoulders. She was doing everything she could to help. Mostly as Thomas's assistant since his jobs were things she was comfortable with. She'd helped him paint and install baseboard and even hung doors. She knew that good finish work was important to the TV show. If only they could finish in time.

"So no backsplash on the vanity?" Thomas asked as she handed him the last glass tile.

"No. Just the paint. I'm using an elegant old dresser with a vessel sink for the vanity. The plumber will put it in place when he installs the shower fixtures and kitchen sink early next week."

"A dresser there should look pretty cool."

She nodded. "How about if you help me hang the mirror above it today. It'll be easier to get it up before the dresser's installed."

"What kind of mirror?"

"Nothing fancy. Just beveled glass with a carved wood frame. But it's big and heavy."

As they worked, she imagined the other touches she would place in this small room. Besides the usual amenities that make a bathroom luxurious, she would hang a peaceful seascape opposite the mirror. That alone would make the room feel grand and special. Her original plan didn't include a bathtub, but after enjoying the slipper tub at the beach house, she wondered if that had been a mistake. Too late now.

Grayson's voice interrupted her thoughts.

"Come on out here, Mallory," he called loudly.

She handed Thomas a buttered tile. "Hope it's nothing gone wrong."

"Hurry back," he called as she left. "I need you."

Grayson stood in the living area. "I want you to see this." He pointed to where several of his guys were securing the two sliding glass doors in place. For days that big opening had been covered with sheets of plywood, making the apartment look extra dark and gloomy.

"Oh my goodness!" She literally gasped. "That is drop-dead gorgeous." Once the men finished the installation, Mallory went closer to check out the view. "You can really see the ocean now." She gazed over the rooftops across the street in wonder. It was like a completely different apartment. "It's amazing, Grayson. I'm so glad you thought of this." She pointed to the terrace that ran the width of the doors. "And that's up too. I hadn't even noticed it from the street." Her designer wheels were spinning. Although it was narrow, the terrace was wide enough to hold a couple of small chairs and a side table, with room along the edges for a potted plant or two.

"I heard from Jake this morning," Grayson told her. "He's almost done with the railing."

"Fabulous." Her mind filled with ideas of how she'd arrange the great room furnishings to make the most of this view. What fun she would have. "This is so exciting," she said. "I can hardly believe it's all falling into place. For the first time, it's feeling very real to me."

"We're not out of the woods yet."

"But it seems like we're very close," she said cheerfully. "The biggest projects are done. I know we're racing the clock, but everything else seems doable. More so than it did last week."

"We still have that final inspection. Anything can happen with that."

"Meaning?"

"Well, plumbing and electric . . . this is an old building." He shrugged. "You never know."

"But the plumbing and electric are new," she said.

"New meeting up with old," he reminded her. "And done in a rush."

"Oh. Yeah . . ." She forced a smile. "I guess this is where prayer comes in."

He nodded. "Yep. Keep the prayers coming, Mallory."

"I better get back to help Thomas." She

pointed to the glass doors. "But those really do look fantastic. Thank you for going the extra mile there. I would've settled for a large window, but it never would've looked this nice." She stepped out of the electrician's way as he moved his ladder in place to install a ceiling fan. "I better get out of here before I slow down the works."

As she returned to the bathroom and buttered the next tile for Thomas, she silently prayed, begging God for mercy with the building inspectors. Probably more for Grayson's sake than her own. She hated to imagine how stressed he would be if the remodel failed. He'd invested so much into this. It wouldn't just be the time and energy spent. It was almost like his reputation was at stake too. Even more so than hers. Everyone in town was watching the renovation.

She couldn't count how many people she'd bumped into during the past week. Everyone was enthusiastically cheering the project on and hoping for the best. Of course, there'd been a few naysayers too. Debbie Downers who thought she and Grayson had bitten off more than they could chew, doubting that *Pacific Design* would actually show up, or that Mallory would even stay in business. But she tried not to listen to them. Still, she knew that if they were right, if the project unraveled at the end, Grayson could receive a professional black eye for it. He would suffer more than she would. And that was what gnawed at her at three in the morning. She spent the nights praying more than ever, for Grayson's sake more than hers, that the project would succeed.

The morning before Amy and her team arrived, everything was miraculously in place. Well, except for Mallory's furnishings. Grayson wouldn't allow her to put anything up there until the inspector gave them a pass. Just to be safe. Everything looked great — on the surface, anyway. The painted walls looked clean and solid, the old woodwork of the doors and trim gleamed. The wood plank floors were stunning, the terrace railing was in place, and the kitchen and bathroom had never looked better.

Best of all, everything was working. The electric and plumbing and mechanicals had all been running for a few days now. But like Grayson pointed out, anything could happen. "You never know with an old building," he'd reminded her while they'd waited for the inspector to arrive that morning.

"It's one reason I like to avoid these remodels."

Now Mallory was waiting on pins and needles. She'd gone downstairs with an excuse to "putter in her shop," while Grayson walked the inspector through the apartment. She'd been through plenty of inspections with remodels before, but none had been as stressful as this one. All along, she'd hoped that small town inspectors weren't as nitpicky as what she was used to, but according to Grayson, they could be worse. Unfortunately, he told her, it sometimes depended on the inspector as well as their mood. But he'd sworn her to secrecy on that bit of info.

As she sat on the cream-colored sofa, with unopened boxes crammed into places all around her, she prayed. *Desperately.* Even with her backup plan, she'd still need to find spots to store all of the apartment furnishings, which littered the shop and back room.

Even if the inspector passed them and her furnishings got to move upstairs, she'd still need to unpack the shipment that had arrived yesterday, then she'd have to scramble to clean and put everything in an attractive order. It would be no small task, but she felt up to it. She'd made a long list, creating

345

a step-by-step plan for how things would be moved and put into place. She'd lined up Thomas and a couple of Grayson's team members to help. Now, if only the inspector was in a good mood today.

She could hear footsteps coming down the stairs now. Grayson was telling the inspector goodbye and letting him out the back door. Afraid to move, she stayed glued to the sofa, waiting. But when she heard a loud whoop from Grayson, she leaped to her feet and hurried to meet him in the back.

"We passed!" Grayson grabbed her into a bear hug, swinging her off her feet. "We did it!"

"Thank God," she cried. "And thank you, Grayson." She actually had tears of relief and gratitude in her eyes. "I can hardly believe it."

"Me too." He set her down. "I was prepared for the worst." He shook his head. "The way the plumber patched into existing drain pipes could've sunk us, but we're okay."

"And the drain pipes?" she asked.

He waved a hand between them. "They're fine. Probably last another hundred years."

"I owe you big-time," she told him.

"You already paid me."

"I'm not talking about money, Grayson. I

owe you more than I can ever repay."

"Well, now it's up to you, Mallory. There's a lot to get done before tomorrow. How can I help?"

"You can help by going home and taking a day off." She gently nudged him toward the door.

"But I —"

"I can tell you're exhausted. You've been working night and day. Please, go home and take a nice long nap. Once you're good and rested, I'll consider letting you help me."

He held up his hands. "Okay, if you insist."

"I do." She looked into his face. "But thanks so much. I never ever, in a million years, could've done this without you. I'm going to try to think of some fabulous way to return the enormous favor."

"How about you fix me dinner again," he suggested. "Only this time, we'll do it right."

"Yes," she said. "As soon as I'm done with the TV show and have time to catch my breath, I will fix you the best dinner you've ever had." She walked him to the door, opening it and gently nudging him out toward his pickup. "But, please, go home and have a good long nap."

He yawned. "I'm halfway there now."

"Drive safe," she called before closing the door. She turned to face her disaster of a

347

shop. Now it was time to get to work. She texted Thomas and the others, letting them know they were officially and quite literally on the clock now. And the clock was ticking.

24

The moving crew got all her furniture and boxes upstairs by noon. But, not trusting Mallory's ability to arrange large pieces by herself with her sliders, they insisted on getting the heavier items in place. Even after Mallory was mostly satisfied with the arrangements, Thomas refused to leave.

"You're going to hurt your back." He rushed to her aid when she picked up a big box. "Let me get it."

She thanked him but didn't admit that her back had been aching some. Not that she had time to give it any thought. After several rearrangements of the larger pieces, she was grateful for Thomas's help. Finally, she was happy with the layout. Everything, including the big area rugs, was balanced and in place.

"I can handle the rest myself," she assured Thomas. "It's mostly just making it look pretty now. But I do want to thank you for all you've done, Thomas. Not just today but with the tile and painting and all that. We never would've finished without you."

He shrugged. "Least I could do."

"I appreciate it."

He looked down at his work boots. "Well, I'm glad you gave me a second chance, Mallory."

"You're a good worker. If I have other small design projects that need finish work or tiling, I'll be sure to call you."

He raised his head and smiled at her. "Thanks."

"I'm glad we ended this well." She stuck out her hand and they shook. Of course, she still wanted to encourage him to get his contractor's license, but she knew Grayson had sufficiently lectured him on that topic. No need to keep beating him over the head with it.

After Thomas left, she put some music on and went to work. She realized that not every single thing had to be in place. Just camera ready. They'd have no need to film behind closet or cupboard doors, so acting more like this was a staging than an apartment she was eager to occupy, she focused her attention on the visible spaces.

She was just setting up the kitchen area when she heard a woman's voice calling up the stairs. She peeked her head around the corner and spotted Lindsey in the stairwell. "I feel like I'm always intruding on you. I knocked on your back door, but you didn't answer. It wasn't locked so I let myself in." Lindsey held up a drink. "I brought you an iced mocha."

"You're an angel of mercy." Mallory invited her up the stairs and eagerly took the drink, leading her into the apartment.

"Wow, wow, wow!" Lindsey walked around the living room, admiring every tiny detail. "This place is absolutely brilliant."

"Your dad's a miracle worker." She sipped the mocha.

"And this terrace! It's awesome." She looked out the sliding doors. "You actually have an ocean view up here. Who knew?"

"Your dad. It was his idea to put those doors there."

"Well, I totally love it. I love every bit of it. If you ever want to rent it out, I'm first in line."

Mallory laughed. "I'll keep that in mind. Right now, I can't wait to move in myself. I considered sleeping here tonight, but then I'd have to fix everything up again for the film crew and I still have my shop to get looking pretty."

Lindsey bit her lip. "Yeah, I noticed it

looked kind of chaotic down there."

Mallory nodded. "I'm trying not to think about that yet. I have until tomorrow night to get it in shape, but if I wrap this up, I might go after it tonight."

"Are your kids and your friend still coming to stay at the beach house?" Lindsey asked.

"Yes. But I don't want them to pay this time. I plan to cover the cost for their visit."

"No. Dad said no charge. I only asked if they were coming because I have a load of clean linens to drop off."

"You can just leave them with me. I'll take them over when I'm done here."

"Sounds good." Lindsey nodded to some boxes that were still waiting to be unpacked. "Do you need any help here?"

"Well, if you want to put away the dishes and glassware, that'd be great. The other boxes of kitchenware don't matter so much. I was considering just hiding most of them in the coat closet."

"I'm happy to put them all away if you like." Lindsey opened a box of dishes. "These are pretty. Any directions for where they go?"

"In the glass front cupboards. Dishes can go left of the dishwasher and glasses on the right." Mallory tweaked a display on the countertop. "What I really need are some fresh flowers," she said absently.

Lindsey set some plates in the cupboard. "I can get them for you."

"Seriously? You wouldn't mind?"

"Not at all. My friend Gina has a flower business. She sells arrangements at the farmers market on Saturdays. Want me to call and see what she's got available?"

"That'd be fabulous. Thanks!"

"She's also got this great greenhouse with houseplants too. Could you use any of those?"

"Absolutely. Do you think Gina would have any filled flowerpots to spare? I wanted to put some out on the terrace but haven't had time. I'll take them, even if they're just loaners, although I'm happy to buy them as well."

Lindsey was typing on her phone. "I'll ask."

"You truly are an angel of mercy."

Before long, they had made a long list and Lindsey called to arrange for Gina to deliver the plants the next day. As they continued putting the kitchen together, Mallory asked how things with Joel were going.

"I really like this guy," Lindsey said. "It's almost scary."

"Scary?"

"Well, I've had some letdowns with some guys. You know, the ones that act like they're something then turn out to be something else."

"Ah, yes, I've had some of those too." Mallory sighed. "In fact, I've decided I'm not the greatest judge of men."

"But you like my dad, don't you?"

Mallory didn't know what to say. She opened her mouth, then closed it.

"I just meant that he's a good guy. Of course, I'm biased."

Mallory smiled. "He is a good guy, Lindsey. And I do like him. And I respect him. A lot." She thought about what Lindsey said about that being "scary." Maybe that's how Mallory felt too. It was scary to like a person as much as she liked Grayson. "So, tell me, what is it you like most about Joel?"

She thought about this for a moment. "Well, he's not very flashy. I mean, he's good looking, but not in a way that stands out. You can tell he doesn't care about that. He's not a slob or anything. I guess he's just comfortable in his own skin."

"That's a good trait." Mallory remembered how vain her ex used to be. Maybe he still was. She didn't know for sure.

"Joel always seems more concerned with how I'm doing and feeling than he is for himself. He's very thoughtful . . . and kind."

"Sounds like he likes you a lot."

"I guess he does."

"What's he do?"

"He's a teacher too. High school. History."

"Uh-huh. So you both get summers off?"

"Yeah. That's convenient." She set the last of Mallory's water glasses in the cupboard. "I mean, if it developed into something, not that I'm planning on that. You never know."

Mallory leaned against her new countertop. "Well, I think Joel sounds like a very nice guy. I haven't even met him, and I already like him."

Lindsey closed a cabinet door. "I guess he reminds me of Dad."

"Well, that sounds like pretty high marks. What does your dad think of Joel?"

Lindsey laughed nervously. "They haven't met."

"Why not?"

"Well, Dad's been so busy lately and this thing with Joel is pretty new. I just didn't want to rush things, you know?"

"Yes. My daughter, Louisa, was in a similar boat a couple years ago. Right after her longtime boyfriend Charlie broke up with her." She plucked a vase from one of the boxes, then walked to the sink. "They'd been together all through college and everyone assumed they'd get married, but out of the blue, Charlie found someone else. Louisa was devastated and I felt sorry for her, but I was also relieved. I didn't think Charlie was so great." Mallory rinsed the dust off the vase, then wiped it until it shone.

"What happened then?" Lindsey asked.

"Yes, you probably wonder what I was getting at." Mallory laughed. "It seems Louisa met Marshall just a few days after Charlie dumped her. She liked Marshall a lot, but she was convinced he was a rebound. She didn't think things with him would ever last so she kept him a secret. She didn't introduce him to me or her brothers until they'd been dating for almost a year. She brought him home for Christmas and they got engaged on New Year's Eve. We thought it was crazy fast, but then we found out they'd been dating for a whole year." Mallory tossed an empty box into the coat closet. "I'm not even sure why I'm telling you all this." She laughed. "I guess I'm just feeling chatty."

"I'm glad you did." Lindsey peered curiously at Mallory. "Did Dad tell you about me?"

"About you?"

Lindsey's brow creased. "About my bad breakup with Flynn?"

"No. He never mentioned a thing about it." Mallory studied her.

"Well, Flynn broke up with me. It was about three weeks ago. He was my first serious boyfriend. We'd been together a year and a half, and I guess I really thought he was the one."

"Oh." Mallory nodded. "I'm sorry. I know that's hard."

"That's why I didn't want to mention Joel to Dad yet. To be honest, you're the only one I've told." She looked at the oversized clock above the sink. "In fact, Joel and I are going out again tonight."

"Well, he sounds like a good guy. Give him a chance and who knows? I've heard that the second time around is sometimes the best."

"Interesting." Lindsey nodded with a thoughtful expression. "Maybe it'll be like that for my dad." She winked. "And maybe for you too?"

Mallory was speechless again. Not knowing how to respond, she patted Lindsey on the back. "You're very fortunate in that you've got a good male role model in your dad. If Joel is even a little like him, you'll be fine."

"Thanks." Lindsey smiled. "I better go."

"Thanks for your help. And for connecting me with your flower friend."

"Do you need help setting up your shop tomorrow?"

Mallory eagerly nodded. "Yes! I would love an extra hand. And I'll gladly pay you!"

After they arranged to meet up in the morning, Lindsey left and Mallory set up the bedroom and bathroom. Fortunately, those rooms were easier than the kitchen and living room. Other than a few more items she'd gather from her shop, the flowers scheduled to arrive tomorrow, and some fresh produce to put in the kitchen, the apartment was almost completely romanced. Mallory was exhausted.

But she wasn't ready to leave this sweet space just yet. Kicking off her sandals, she sat down on the sectional and just looked all around, critiquing her design and simply enjoying the ambiance. It wasn't a large room, but with the big windows, doors, and vaulted ceiling, it felt spacious. She'd just leaned back to relax when she heard more footsteps coming up the stairs. Wishing she'd asked Lindsey to lock up, Mallory peeled herself off the couch and went over to see who it was.

"Hello." Grayson popped his head in and

held out a brown bag. "Cheeseburger?"

Mallory clapped her hands. "Between you and your daughter, I'm very well taken care of today." He looked confused, so as he came inside, she told him about her visit with Lindsey.

"I have to say, Grayson, you've raised a very sweet young woman." She pointed to the island bar, then went to the cupboard to grab plates. "Have a seat."

He removed his ball cap and followed her order. "So Lindsey's been here." He nodded. "How's she doing? I haven't talked to her much lately."

"Because you've been so busy with my project," she said. "Don't worry. Lindsey's doing great." Mallory set out plates and ice water, then removed the burgers and fries from the bag. "These smell delicious."

Grayson glanced around the living room. "Hey, it's looking great up here. Good job romancing your home." He grinned. "If you took before pictures, I bet you could enter a contest and win some sort of most-improved space prize."

She slid a plate in front of him and sat on the stool to his left. "Well, I didn't take before photos. I think I was too humiliated."

"It was bad." He picked up his burger. "There were moments I had my doubts that we'd ever get done."

"Well, you were good at maintaining a poker face."

He reached for a few fries. "I'm impressed with how Thomas stepped up."

Mallory nodded, then told him about how he'd even stuck around to help her today. "I think giving him that second chance really meant something to him."

"It could've gone a lot differently."

"I know." She picked up a fry, looking all around the kitchen and living area, trying to determine if she'd missed anything. "I'm mostly done up here, but I still have a lot to do."

"Your shop?" He grimaced. "We meant to keep it tidier down there, but you get to moving fast and things don't always go as planned."

"No worries. That's on tomorrow's agenda." She hoped she sounded more energetic than she felt.

"Well, I'm sorry." His shoulders sank a bit. "We don't normally leave jobsites in that kind of shape."

She waved off his apology. "I should've put some drop cloths or plastic sheeting on things myself. By the time that occurred to me, it was too late."

"You probably could use some help with

360

the dust removal."

"Well, your lovely daughter has offered to come tomorrow. And Sandi said she could probably give me a few hours of her time as well."

"I could send Corrina over to lend a hand if you'd like. She hasn't had much to do while my other project was on hold."

"Oh, I think we can handle it." She picked up her ice water and took a slow sip.

His brows arched. "Not a fan of my assistant?"

"More like she's not a fan of me."

He pursed his lips. "Did she say something to you to make you think that?"

She evaded eye contact. "I think Corrina is just extremely protective of you." Mallory wanted to say "territorial" but knew that was a bit harsh. "She was worried that I was taking advantage of your generosity."

"Seriously?" He looked surprised. "She *said* that?"

"Something to that effect." She sipped more water.

"Well, Corrina can be outspoken sometimes. We blame it on her Irish roots." He smiled. "But her heart's in the right place. Still, I'm sorry if you were offended by her."

Mallory considered this. Was he suggesting that she shouldn't have been offended?

That she had overreacted to Corrina's temperament? For some reason this rubbed her all wrong. Maybe she was just tired. Probably the latter.

"Well, it's water under the bridge now." She wiped her mouth with a paper napkin and stood. "I'm sure Corrina is relieved that my project is all finished and you can be done with me." She carried her glass to the sink, taking her time to refill it.

"Well, that might be overstating —" He was cut off by the sound of a male voice calling up the stairs.

"Delivery for Mallory Farrell."

"I wonder what that could be." Relieved by the interruption, Mallory set down her glass and hurried down the stairs to see a young man holding out a florist box. She thanked him, then carried the box back up. Grayson was still seated at the island.

"Looks like flowers." She set the long white carton on the counter. "Maybe these are from Lindsey's friend Gina. Although I thought her flowers were coming tomorrow." She lifted the lid and was shocked to see several long-stemmed red roses. "Oh my. How pretty."

Grayson leaned over to see what was inside. "Talk about *romancing the home*," he teased. "Who sent those?"

"I have no idea." As she removed the small envelope, she wondered if they were from Grayson and he was just playing coy. She removed the card, then read it aloud. *"Thank you again for the second chance. Yours, Thomas."* She blinked in surprise. "Well now, go figure."

"That was certainly nice of him." Grayson's tone sounded cool.

"Yes, very thoughtful." She felt a bit off balance as she extracted a tall crystal vase from a lower cupboard. Was Grayson jealous? Or was he aggravated at her for questioning his assistant earlier? She placed the heavy vase in the sink, running water from the tap. "Red roses aren't exactly my favorites, but these are elegant."

"And *romantic.*" Grayson tossed the paper bag and napkins from their dinner in her trash and set the dishes on the counter beside the sink.

"I can probably place this in the shop." She put the roses into the vase, then turned to face Grayson.

His expression was cloudy. "Looks like you've made quite an impression on Thomas."

"I think he's just grateful for the second chance. Like the card says." She set the heavy vase on the island.

"Don't be so sure about that. I saw you two working together on the tile this week. Thomas seemed to be enjoying himself a lot. It's only natural he should be attracted."

"Attracted?" Mallory wanted to ask Grayson if he was jealous, but it sounded so silly.

"Whether you meant to or not, it seems you sent him all the right signals, Mallory. Maybe he thought you were romancing him." Grayson smiled but it didn't reach his eyes.

"Well, as you know, I was trying hard to win Thomas over." She straightened the roses in the arrangement to have something to do, even though they looked perfect already. "We needed his cooperation and help to get this place done."

Grayson crossed his arms. "That's true."

"My grandma used to always say you catch more flies with honey than vinegar, although I never understood that. Who wants to catch flies?"

"Well, if Thomas was a fly, it looks like you caught him." Grayson attempted a laugh, but it sounded hollow.

Mallory had to control herself from pointing out that Grayson had probably caught his assistant in a similar manner. Was *that* intentional?

Grayson checked his watch. "I should

probably go. I know you've got a lot to get done and not a lot of time to do it."

"That's true. Thank you for the cheeseburger and —"

"No problem." He grabbed his hat and headed for the door.

She wanted to say something . . . but what? He was clearly bothered. Was it because of Thomas's gift? Or was this related to Mallory's take on Corrina? Maybe she was just making a big deal over nothing. She couldn't be sure, but one thing was certain, she didn't have time to sort it all out now.

25

Mallory entered her shop early the next morning. Like Grayson had warned, everything was covered in a thick layer of construction dust. Her plan was to deep clean the back room first.

Sorting and dusting was tedious, and the shop needed to shimmer and shine before Amy and the *Pacific Design* camera crew arrived late that night.

By eight, Mallory had the back room all cleaned and sorted out and was unpacking boxes when she noticed a redhead poking through the opened back door. "Anybody home?"

"Corrina?" Mallory dropped a large box of pillows on the floor. "What're you doing here?"

"Gray sent me on a mission of mercy." Corrina looked around with a slightly intimidating intensity. "Looks like you really *do* need help. So, what can I do?"

"Seriously?" Mallory felt suspicious. "You *want* to help?"

"Gray wants me to help." Corrina's smile looked forced. "And he's the boss."

Mallory looked at Corrina's cream-colored pants and silk blouse. "It's dirty work. You'll ruin your pretty clothes."

Corrina shrugged. "I can keep myself clean."

Mallory studied her face. "If you're only doing this for Grayson's sake, I can —"

"Look," Corrina cut her off. "Gray doesn't need me in the office today, and I can use the hours so I'm helping you. Unless that's a problem?"

"It's no problem." Mallory huffed out a breath. She explained how everything needed to be carefully cleaned. "Some things require a damp rag and several wipings and rinsings to get rid of that fine plaster dust." She pointed to a pile of rags and a couple of buckets. "The worst of the dust is in the rear of the shop, but everything got coated. Why don't you start up in front, where it's not as bad, and work your way to the rear?"

Corrina nodded to the vacuum cleaner. "How about if I vacuum the floor first?"

Mallory wasn't surprised that Corrina was already questioning her plan. Not wanting

367

to alienate her or lose out on free help, she explained how gravity pulled dust down and the most sensible way to clean was from the top down.

Corrina pointed to the hose attachment on the vacuum cleaner. "But we could use that to vacuum the merchandise first."

Mallory considered this. "Well, you could be on to something. At least for the soft surfaces." She tapped her chin, grimacing as she felt how dusty her hands were. "Sure, why not give it a try and see how it works. Honestly, I don't care how we do it. I just know we need to make this place sparkling by the end of the day."

Corrina took the vacuum cleaner and Mallory started to unpack another box, selecting some items to go up front in the shop, and some for the shelves back here. She could hear the vacuum roaring out in front, and she hoped, and prayed, that Corrina was being careful. Hopefully, she knew that some items needed more TLC.

"Hello there?"

Mallory turned to the back door where Lindsey was coming in. Dressed in jeans and a flannel shirt, she looked ready to work. Mallory explained her plan, and Lindsey grabbed a bucket of water and some rags and headed out. She'd been gone only a few minutes when Mallory heard a loud crash. After rushing out to see what happened, she could tell by Corrina's face that she had broken something.

"I was vacuuming a lampshade" — Corinna pointed to a pile of glass shards and a crumpled lampshade — "but the whole thing tumbled over. I think this old table is wobbly."

Mallory took in a deep breath. "If you want to vacuum a lampshade, you should probably remove it from the base first. Don't you think?"

"I suppose you're right. Sorry about that." Corrina didn't actually look sorry, but maybe Mallory was overreacting again. Then again, she had really liked that lamp! She took another deep breath and reminded herself that people were more important than things.

Mallory felt Lindsey's eyes on her. They exchanged glances, and Mallory attempted a smile for Corrina's sake. "Don't worry about the lamp," she told her. "How about you clean up that mess, and I'll take charge of the vacuuming." She reached for the still-whirring machine.

Corrina shrugged. "If that's what you want."

"After that, if you still want to help, how

369

about you get started on dusting?" She waved a hand. "As you can see, there are plenty of hard surfaces to be cleaned. And it'll take more than one go-round to clear everything too."

The three women worked together with no more mishaps for about an hour. It was slow going, but then Sandi showed up and there were four sets of hands. Having Sandi chattering away happily helped brighten the atmosphere, and before long it was noon and they'd made good progress. Mallory was just offering to order some food when Caroline Kempton showed up with a very nice lunch spread.

"I asked my girls at the Chic Boutique to make salads." She set out three large bowls on the worktable, as well as paper plates and utensils. "I'm free all afternoon to help," Caroline told Mallory as the five of them took turns filling plates. "And if we're still not done, I can close my store at four o'clock, and my girls can come over to lend a hand."

Mallory was deeply touched. "It's so kind of all of you to give your time today."

"Well, it's somewhat self-motivated." Caroline winked. "I want your shop to look so fabulous on TV that people will come from all over to check out our town. That will be good for my business too."

As the five of them worked into the afternoon, Mallory noticed several things. Sandi preferred talking to working. Corrina was slow, but meticulous — and careful not to get herself dirty. Caroline was steady and thorough. And Lindsey was by far the most valuable worker. She was fast and careful and not given to chatter. Mallory knew she'd do something special to thank all of them, but she wanted to do something extra special for Lindsey.

At four o'clock Kara showed up with Louisa in tow. "We left the fellows at the beach house," Kara said. "We're here to help."

Knowing she had two workers with an eye for design, Mallory assigned them specific tasks. Louisa's job was to put the powder room back together. Mallory pointed out the items that had gone in there, then turned to Kara. "I know this is only a back room," she said, "but the cameras might come through here, too, so I want it to look as attractive as possible." Mallory grabbed some fresh rags and went out to help the crew in front. A moment later, Caroline pulled her aside.

"We girls were talking just now, and Sandi pointed out that you'll be on camera tomorrow." Caroline glanced down to Mallory's stained sweatshirt.

"You're right." Mallory frowned at her haphazard appearance. "But I'll clean up by then."

"Well, I just called my friend Maddie. You know about Madeleine's on Main, don't you?"

"I've seen the sign. Isn't it a beauty shop or something?"

"It's a *salon.* Maddie is the owner, and when she heard about you being on *Pacific Design,* she adjusted her schedule. She can take you *right now.*"

"Oh, I couldn't possibly —"

"Yes, you can, Mom." Louisa called out as she came over to Mallory. "I'm not trying to be mean, but you are in desperate need of some help." She pointed to Mallory's hands. "Look at those dirty nails and —"

"I've been working and cleaning for days."

Louisa pouted. "That's my point, Mom. You have to do this."

"She's right," Kara said from her place by the kitchen display. "You better take this opportunity while you can. I can manage things here for you. After all, I am your design partner."

"And we all want you to look your best

372

tomorrow," Caroline insisted. "You owe it to yourself and the entire town."

"They're right, Mallory. You have to go," Lindsey chimed in, a fresh bucket of water in her hands. "Madeleine's is wonderful. You'll love it. We have your to-do list, and everyone is working hard."

"But I'm a mess," Mallory protested. "Look at my filthy jeans and —"

Caroline cut her off. "You'll be wearing one of their robes."

"I'll bring you something to change into after you're done," Louisa promised. "Just go, Mom. No more excuses!"

"Fine, fine." Mallory realized she was outnumbered and too tired to fight their good intentions. She picked up her handbag and headed out the front door. It felt surprisingly good to be outside in the cool ocean-scented air. Madeleine's on Main was only two blocks away, and Mallory was curious about the place with the pretty sign, but the windows were always heavily curtained. She'd never been overly indulgent with spas or salons. In fact, she could count on one hand how often she'd had a mani-pedi. And the only time she'd had a facial, she'd broken out the next day. The only thing she did regularly was get her hair trimmed, and she was overdue for that. So if ever she needed some beauty assistance, it was probably now. Hopefully Madeleine wouldn't be too overwhelmed.

With some trepidation, Mallory opened the door and entered the elegant reception area, where she was immediately greeted by a sophisticated gray-haired woman who introduced herself as Madeleine Bouchet. "You must be Mallory." She grasped her hand then flipped it over to study her nails. She grimaced. "Looks like we've got our work cut out for us." Her tone was serious, but her smile was warm. "Right this way."

Madeleine escorted Mallory to a large dressing room, explaining that all their products and procedures were made from natural ingredients. "And from old recipes from my family in France." She handed Mallory a soft terry robe. "First you will soak and then you'll be gently exfoliated. After that, we have a few more treats in store for you." She introduced Mallory to a younger woman. "Brittany will take care of you."

In her fluffy white robe Mallory decided she was either being pampered beyond imagination — or a sheep being led to the slaughter. "I'm a little nervous," she admitted as she and Brittany entered a room lined with bathtubs. All but one was occupied with very relaxed-looking women of various ages. Each of them wore a head wrap and an eye mask.

"Our herbal soak will help you unwind." Brittany opened a container and held it out for Mallory to smell. "This contains lavender, hyssop, basil, chamomile, and elderflower. Do you have allergies to any of these?"

"No."

"Lovely." Brittany swirled a generous portion of herbs into the tub.

Mallory sniffed the aromatic bath as she untied her robe. "It smells lovely."

"That's great to hear." Brittany set a towel on a wood bench, then helped Mallory tuck her hair into a stretchy protective wrap. "Here's some lemon cucumber water to hydrate you." She pointed to a tumbler by the towel.

Mallory felt a bit self-conscious as she slipped off her robe and stepped into the tub, but the other women seemed completely oblivious. Once she was settled, Brittany handed Mallory a silk eye mask. "This is filled with chilled barley and herbs. Now, you go ahead and relax until I come get you."

Mallory understood why the other women were so relaxed. Before long, she was too.

Even if she did nothing more than enjoy a good soak, the soft music, and the lovely aroma, it would be enough. Everything was heavenly!

The water was just starting to cool when Brittany returned. "Time to get out." She gently removed the silk eye mask and gave Mallory a hand as she climbed out of the water. She helped her into the terry robe and handed her a towel. "Now it's time to massage and exfoliate," Brittany informed her as she led her to a different room. "Again, we use all-natural ingredients."

By now Mallory felt too relaxed to question her. She allowed herself to be rubbed and oiled and massaged. By the time Brittany finished, Mallory's limbs were as limp as spaghetti. Could she even walk? As it turned out, she could.

"Next is your facial." Mallory followed the young woman to a reclining chair. Despite being relaxed, Mallory suddenly remembered her last facial. She told Brittany about the breakout. "I have to be on TV tomorrow."

"Don't worry. Madeleine told me to pick out our gentlest procedures," Brittany said. "No one ever breaks out from our yogurt and honey facial. No allergies to those, right?"

376

"Right." Mallory leaned back, then forced herself to take in a deep breath. It helped and soon she was back to her formerly relaxed state. She could get used to this!

After her facial, Mallory was treated to a manicure and pedicure by a young girl named April. Though tempted to try a more exciting color, Mallory finally decided on a conservative pearly shade — and was pleased with the results. Although she was curious about the time, she even accepted the offer of an herbal shampoo and conditioning treatment and a quick trim.

By the time she was sent to the dressing room, Louisa had already dropped off a clean set of clothes. As Mallory got dressed, she truly felt like a new woman. And as she walked back to her shop, she almost didn't care how things looked in there. Oh, she did care, but even if there was still loads of work to be done, she wasn't worried.

As soon as she opened the door, her heart soared. At first glance, everything looked shiny and clean and nice. At second glance, she knew she needed to do a little rearranging and tweaking, but that would be easy. And fun. Hearing voices in the back room, she went back to discover Lindsey and Louisa and Kara still at work.

"Shoot. We thought we'd be done before

you got back, Mom." Louisa went to hug her. "Wow, don't you look refreshed and pretty."

"We were just getting rid of the evidence." Kara stowed the vacuum cleaner in the closet.

"And the flowers arrived." Lindsey gestured to the worktable where a few lovely assortments of blooms sat in buckets of water, waiting to be arranged.

"Thank you all so much." Mallory hugged each of them. "I couldn't have done this without you."

"You're welcome. By the way, Amy came by a little bit ago," Kara informed her. "But Lindsey did a great job keeping her at bay."

"She wanted to check into her hotel, anyway," Lindsey said.

"Thank you all so much," Mallory told them. "I can't believe how much you got done. It looks great."

"We also peeked into your apartment, Mom." Louisa's smile widened. "It's even better than you said it would be."

"I love it," Kara confirmed. "It should look great on TV."

"Thanks to Lindsey's father." Mallory put a hand on Lindsey's shoulder.

"Speaking of Dad, he wants to take me to dinner." Lindsey checked her phone. "See you later, everyone."

"You ladies are the best." Mallory thanked them again as Lindsey took off. "I want to hang out here awhile and do some staging and flower arranging." She pointed to Louisa and Kara. "But you two need to go relax and enjoy the beach house. You're probably starved. Don't wait for me. I'll catch up with you later tonight."

Finally, with her shop and apartment to herself, Mallory slowly walked around, taking her time to view every display from all angles, tweaking and rearranging and making some spots for flower arrangements.

She set the last bouquet in place and knew this was as good as it gets. The shop and the apartment had never looked more beautiful. She truly had romanced them both. But as she turned off the lights and locked up, she realized that something even more important had happened. She had romanced the town.

She thought of all the friends she'd made since moving to Portside, many who'd helped her today. She even considered the women at Madeleine's her brand-new friends. And it was for the sake of all these new friends and fellow business owners that she wanted tomorrow's filming to go as perfectly as possible.

26

When Mallory finally got back to the beach house, the guys were locked into a loud war movie, and Louisa and Kara were out on the deck with a pot of decaf coffee. Although she would've preferred going straight to bed, Mallory got herself a mug and went out to join the women.

"You missed a gorgeous sunset," Kara told Mallory as she sat down.

"I actually saw some of it from my apartment." Mallory filled her mug. "I was putting some flowerpots on the terrace just as the sky got colorful. It made the terrace look so pretty. I even snagged a couple of pics on my phone."

"That apartment, Mom," Louisa said. "It's killer."

"Yeah, I want to meet this Superman." Kara sighed.

Mallory added creamer to her decaf. "Superman?"

"Yeah, that Grayson Matthews. You told me the condition of the apartment just two weeks ago. I can't believe how much he got done in such a short time. It doesn't seem humanly possible."

"Yeah, it felt miraculous to me too. Grayson set all his projects aside, then orchestrated his entire construction crew to work around the clock." Mallory leaned back to look up at the dark sky where stars were just coming out.

"I want to meet him," Kara said. "I hear he's a bachelor."

"Yeah, and according to Corrina, he's *dreamy*." Louisa giggled.

"Dreamy?" Mallory bristled. "Did Corrina actually say that?"

"Yeah, that and a lot more. Lindsey was getting a little irritated." Louisa set her mug on the table with a loud clunk. "What's wrong with you, Mom?"

"What?" Mallory sat up straight.

"Yeah," Kara jumped in, "this amazing guy bends over backward to help you and you don't even give him the time of day?"

Mallory stared at her daughter and friend. "What are you talking about?"

Lindsey rolled her eyes. "We're talking about the fact that it seems obvious that dreamy Grayson is into you."

"You guys have never even met him and yet you seem to know all about him," Mallory protested.

"We have ears," Louisa said.

"And I'm a pretty good sleuth," Kara said. "Between Grayson's delightful daughter and his entitled blabbermouth assistant, well, I can put two and two together."

"Me too!" Louisa jabbed her mother with a finger. "Grayson is into you, Mom."

"And I like him too," Mallory admitted.

"Then why don't you let him know?"

"Let him know?" Mallory considered this. "Well, I think I've been trying. I romanced this beach house, after all. Did you even notice the difference, Louisa?"

"Yeah," she said. "It looks way better, Mom. But that's your work. What else have you done?"

"Well, if you haven't heard I've been a little busy. But I did, uh, fix him dinner here once." She sighed. "Although that was kind of a disaster."

Kara refilled her mug. "A disaster?"

Mallory briefly described the botched dinner. "But we did have a very romantic dinner date a few weeks ago. I actually thought we were getting somewhere."

"Then what happened?" Kara asked.

"I'm not sure." Mallory tried to remember. "But Corrina hasn't helped. It feels like she'd trying to derail anything between us."

"Of course she is." Louisa sounded exasperated. "You do know that she's already laid claim on Mr. Dreamboat? Lindsey clued me into that."

"Not that she needed to." Now Kara sounded fed up. "Corrina made it crystal clear herself."

"At least you guys know what I'm up against," Mallory told them. "What would you suggest I do differently?"

"Lindsey did mention that her dad hasn't dated anyone since her mom died," Louisa said.

"What about Corrina?" Kara asked. "I got the impression they were dating before Mallory showed up."

"That's probably the impression Corrina wants you to have." Louisa rolled her eyes. "That woman sounds totally delusional to me."

Mallory couldn't help but laugh.

"Take it from me, Mom. That chick clearly does not like you."

"She's probably just jealous," Kara said.

"She's protective of Grayson," Mallory explained. "She's been looking out for him ever since his wife died."

"Seriously, Mom? I honestly thought she

was going to sabotage your shop a few times today."

"It might not have been intentional," Kara said. "She's pretty klutzy. She kept bumping into things and eventually she knocked over a glass vase. Fortunately, it wasn't an expensive piece."

"I caught her starting to wipe down a parchment shade with soapy water," Louisa tattled. "I stopped her just in time."

Mallory felt more amused than angry. "I'm just glad you two watchdogs were around to keep an eye on things."

"Lucky for you, after the vase incident, Sandi stepped in and suggested Corrina call it a day." Kara giggled. "Good thing too. I was about to read her the riot act."

"But back to Grayson, Mom. What're you going to do about him?"

Mallory let out a yawn. "I'm going to think about that after the *Pacific Design* film crew finishes up two days from now."

"Good idea." Kara stood, reaching for Mallory's hands. "Off to bed, girlfriend. You're probably exhausted, and tomorrow's a big day."

Louisa stood too. "You should get your beauty sleep."

Mallory didn't argue with them, but as she got ready for bed, she couldn't help but mull over what her friend and daughter had said. It was both comforting and concerning that they had observed the same things about Corrina as she had . . . but what could she do about it? Nothing right now. And maybe nothing ever. An old adage came to her as she was falling asleep. "Let go and let God." For now, that was good enough.

Just like every morning these past couple of weeks, Mallory woke up early the next day. The house was still and silent, so she quietly but carefully got ready for the day. She dressed in shades of gray and picked plain silver jewelry. She knew her colorful friend Sandi would find the neutral ensemble boring, but she didn't want to compete with the decor in her shop or apartment. Besides, the tunic top over slim pants felt comfortable, and it would probably be a long day.

She considered making coffee before slipping out of the house but didn't want to risk waking anyone and getting delayed with socializing. She wanted to feel clear and focused when the crew arrived. To that end, she planned to go to her shop and do her final tweaking and checking. Meanwhile, she would walk around and pray for the day. She would pray for Amy and her film crew, as well as her own family and friends. It would be a good beginning to a good day.

Since she'd already told Amy's assistant that their crew could use the back alley to park their vehicles, Mallory planned to park right in front. That way, when the time came to film the exterior of her shop, she could simply move her car and allow them an uninterrupted shot of the pretty façade. But she had a weird feeling in her gut. Even before she saw the vandalism, she sensed that something was wrong.

As she pulled up, a horrified shudder ran through her. Both of the front planter pots had been tipped over. The metal bench was also on its side. But worst of all, hot pink spray-painted words were splayed across the clean white stucco. The kinds of words that made her feel sick inside . . . and filled her eyes with tears. Who could've done this? Who hated her this much? Oh, she knew Corrina disliked her, but she wouldn't stoop to anything this low. Right? It must've been teenagers. But why today? Why? Why? Why?

Feeling like she was in a bad dream, Mallory got out of her SUV and just stood on the sidewalk, staring in horrified shock. What should she do? Call the police and report the vandalism? She pulled out her phone and dialed 911 with shaky fingers.

Of course, when the woman inquired about her emergency, Mallory felt silly.

"It's not exactly an emergency." She explained the situation and gave the address. "I haven't gone inside yet." Her voice caught in her throat with the realization this could be more than just a surface problem. "But I-I'm worried the damage could be even worse in there. I'm just v-very upset and a little scared."

The woman told her to wait outside and that police were on their way. Feeling shaken, frightened, and shocked, Mallory got back in her SUV to wait. She was relieved the police cars were coming, but it was a bit embarrassing to hear their sirens and see the flashing lights, as if this were a life-endangering emergency. Although, for all she knew, the perpetrator could be inside her shop or apartment right now.

The officers questioned her briefly, then asked her to unlock the door. Her hands were so shaky as she handed the keys over to them. Bracing herself for what was inside, she watched as they entered her shop. Following them, she was relieved to see things were intact. Nothing was damaged. They checked the back room and upstairs, then assured her that she was safe.

"Unfortunately, it just looks like a bad

case of vandalism," one of them told her.

"And bad timing too." She explained about the filming today.

They questioned her about suspects, and she told them she didn't know anyone who would do such a thing. They took photos of the outside and looked for fingerprints. Then the officers even helped her set the planters and bench upright. They promised to let her know if they uncovered anything, then told her to have a good day and to call if she needed any more help.

Mallory was just reviving her ruffled flowers and plants — pinching off broken parts, tucking them back into their pots, packing the loose soil around them — when she heard another vehicle pull up. She glanced at the clock. It was still too early for tourists, so she thought it might be the police again. But she looked up to see Grayson's construction truck parking behind hers. He leaped out with a stunned expression on his face, and she met him by the front door. "What on earth happened here?"

She hung her head. "Vandals."

"Why would anyone do this?" he demanded.

"Kids with an ax to grind?" She sighed. "That's what the police suggested. They just left."

"Yeah, I heard the sirens from my office earlier. Then I got curious as to what was going on." He looked up at the spray-painted words. "Why would kids write *that*? No offense, but it seems kind of personally aimed at you, Mallory."

She worked to hold back the tears threatening to spill over. "Yeah."

"Do you have any enemies?"

"That's what the police asked too. I don't expect everyone in town to like me or my shop, but I never expected this."

"What about your relatives?" he asked suddenly. "You said they were pretty angry about you inheriting your grandma's property."

She considered this. "I guess that's possible, but it seems so childish. I just can't imagine three grown women with spray paint, sneaking out to do this in the middle of the night. Besides, the last time they were here I showed them the apartment — when it was a wreck — and I even offered to sell it to them for the cost of my investment. They couldn't get out of here fast enough."

"Yeah, now that you mention it, I recall you telling me about that."

"Besides, they have a key, and I still haven't changed my locks. If they wanted to hurt me, they could've let themselves in and made a mess in there."

"And it's okay in there?" He pointed toward the store.

"Thank God." She gently tucked a broken geranium back in and dropped the broken parts next to the pot.

"It just seems so senseless." He checked his watch. "Hey, when does your film crew arrive?"

"Amy's assistant said nine-ish."

"Well, we're burning daylight here." He ran his hand over the stucco. "Do you have any leftover paint that matches this?"

"Yes, I was just about to go look," she said eagerly. "I'm pretty sure there's a partial gallon of exterior paint in my cleaning closet. I'll get it. And a brush."

"I've got some spray primer in my truck. Let me get one coat on to cover that horrid color. We'll give it time to dry then hit it with your paint." He put a hand on her shoulder. "It's going to be okay, Mallory."

She just nodded, but as she went back inside, she couldn't help but smile and mumble, "Superman to the rescue *again.*" It wasn't that she liked playing the helpless victim — she knew she wasn't helpless — but it was nice to have a good friend when you needed one.

By the time she unearthed the paint from

the packed cleaning closet and located a paintbrush, Grayson had already covered and concealed the nasty words with smoke-colored primer that almost made it look as if there'd been a fire. "I know it's not very pretty, but it'll ensure that the pink paint doesn't bleed through."

"Thank you." She set the bucket down. "I wouldn't have even thought of that."

"While that's drying, how about I get us coffees?"

She sighed. "Coffee sounds heavenly. Thank you."

"Latte?" he asked.

She nodded and thanked him again. Then, feeling hopeful, she went back inside and started tweaking . . . and praying. Despite the bad beginning, she asked God to bless the day and everyone who would pass through her doors. Finally, upstairs on her wonderful terrace, she even asked God to bless whoever had tried to hurt her.

She leaned over the railing and spotted Grayson walking up the path. He was holding two coffees and a brown bag. "Come on up here," she called out.

Before long, they were sitting on the terrace, enjoying coffee and bagels with cream cheese. To Mallory's relief, Grayson didn't bring up the vandals again. Instead, they talked about the day ahead. "Are you nervous?" he asked.

"Yeah, but I'm trying not to think about it." She looked out over the ocean. "I just keep reminding myself that I'm doing it for the team. You know, for the whole town, the businesses . . . For some reason it makes me less nervous."

"I like that." He nodded. "I know everyone appreciates the exposure you'll be giving Portside."

She wanted to add, "Everyone but the vandals," but she didn't want to go there. As a distraction, she started to gather up the remains of their quickie breakfast. "Do you think the primer is dry enough?" she asked as she put everything into the paper bag, then brushed the crumbs off the metal table.

"I checked it on my way up and it looked good."

"Great. I can finish it before —"

"You're not going to paint it." He shook his finger at her. "Not in your good clothes. By the way, I meant to tell you how pretty you look, Mallory. Hopefully Amy won't get jealous of you for stealing the show."

She laughed then thanked him.

"No one would ever guess that you were

splattered with paint and tile grout just days ago."

"I thought about saying something about that in the interview. I do plan to mention the folks in town, like you, who lent a helping hand. I want the viewers to understand these things don't happen by magic."

"You're going to do great," he assured her. "Now I want to get that paint on before any of your fellow merchants start getting nervous."

"Yes, I can just imagine Caroline opening her shop and freaking out over seeing the mess down there. And I still need to sweep up the flower debris and wash the windows. I want to make the entrance sparkle and shine."

As they set out on their separate tasks, Mallory loved the camaraderie she felt when she and Grayson worked together. When she completed her little project, she stepped back to watch Grayson finishing with the paint.

"I'm grateful the vandals didn't get paint on anything but the stucco." She leaned onto the broom handle.

"Yeah, I hate to think how that could've messed up the awning or your front door."

"That paint is covering perfectly," she told him. "And I have to say that I always enjoy working with you, Grayson. You're so good at whatever you put your hand to. I even enjoy watching your paint dry."

He chuckled as he finished the last swath of paint. He blended the edges so it didn't look patched on, then turned to her. "I know you enjoyed working with Thomas too. How do I compare?" his tone was teasing, but his eyes looked serious.

She shook her head. "There is no comparison. I'll admit I was trying to humor Thomas at first. Just because I was so worried he'd walk out on us. Then as his attitude improved, I tried to keep things light and cheerful. But to be honest, I never felt that comfortable with him. Like I needed to be on my guard because he is so unpredictable. Like a loose cannon. I just didn't want him going off at me."

"Well, your tactics must've worked or he wouldn't have sent those roses." He wiped the excess paint off the brush.

"Yes, that is awkward," she admitted. "Especially since Sandi is trying to so hard to catch his eye."

"Does Sandi know about those roses?" Grayson's brow creased as he put the lid on the can.

"No, of course not. No one knows. Well, except you."

"Because that could ruin a good friendship." He nodded to the freshly painted stucco. "I don't think she'd do something like this, but you know what they say about a woman scorned."

"Oh, Sandi would never do that." She firmly shook her head.

"And what about Thomas? Did you say anything to offend him about the roses?"

"No. I haven't spoken to him at all."

"Because you said he was a loose cannon."

"I just can't believe he'd do this." Mallory sighed. "To be honest, I don't even want to think about it anymore."

Grayson nodded. "I'm sorry. I should just forget it too. But I'm still irked about it."

"I'm going to play the Scarlet O'Hara card," she told him.

"What's that?"

"I'm going to think about it tomorrow. Or the day after. But not until the filming is done. And by then, I suspect I won't even care."

He grinned. "Yeah, I like that. Me too."

As they went their separate ways, Mallory pushed all thoughts of this morning's vandalism away, focusing instead on her shop and apartment. The film crew would be here any minute now. It was time to turn on the lamps and music and light a few candles. It was time to romance the whole building.

27

The first day of filming felt seriously nerve-
racking to Mallory, but she tried to maintain
a cool and calm demeanor as the film crew
moved and rearranged, it seemed, every
single thing in her shop. Oh, she understood
their reasoning. Amy's production assistant
gently explained it was to position lighting,
make way for cameras, and get the best
angles and shots. Still, it wasn't easy seeing
her previously pretty shop so disheveled and
dismantled. By the time they finished, Mallory was emotionally exhausted, but not too
tired to put everything back into its rightful
place. She knew it was silly, but she also
knew she would rest better knowing that
her shop didn't look like Portside had
experienced a major earthquake.

As for the apartment upstairs, she knew
she had to let it go. The film crew had
already moved all their equipment up there,
getting everything all set to shoot tomorrow

morning. Mallory felt fairly certain the place would look like a great big mess too.

She was just moving a chair back into place when she heard knocking at the front door. Peeking at the entrance, she spotted Grayson and eagerly unlocked the door to let him in.

"Welcome to my world." She waved her arms to the disaster area.

"What happened?" He looked around with a furrowed brow.

"Everything is from the camera's perspective. They have to set everything up to get the most from each shot, plus have room for Amy and me and their lights and everything." She sighed. "It was quite an education. But to be honest, it's something I hope to never participate in again."

He still looked perplexed. "I hope it was worth it."

"Oh, yes! Absolutely. It's a wonderful opportunity. I shouldn't complain."

"Want some help putting it back together?"

"I would love your help." She pointed to the sofa that had been wedged between the window and a buffet. "Let's get that back over here."

Neither of them spoke much as they worked together. But once again, she was reminded of how much she enjoyed Grayson's company. Even while doing something as mundane as moving furniture in silence. Remembering Kara and Louisa's challenge to show Grayson her feelings, Mallory struggled to think of something to say. But the more she tried to put words together inside her head, the cornier it all sounded.

Finally, she was almost uncomfortable with the silence. "You're awfully quiet this evening," she said. "But maybe, like me, you're just too tired to converse intelligently." She attempted a laugh, but something about his expression suggested he was not amused.

"Sorry." He pushed the last dining chair into the table they'd been rearranging and stepped back. "Looks like the big pieces are in place now."

"Yes." She looked around. "Thank you. That made it go lots faster."

"Glad I could help." His tone sounded flat.

She tried not to frown. "Is something wrong, Grayson?"

He didn't answer, but just looked down at the table, fiddling with the edge of a runner.

"Did I do something?" she asked meekly. "Did I offend you somehow?"

He looked up. "No, no, not at all, Mallory."

"But you seem different. Like something is troubling you. Do you want to talk about it?"

"Yes." He nodded. "It's why I stopped by, actually. But then I immediately regretted it. I realized what I had to say could wait since you're probably tired. But then I saw the shop all messed up and you have more filming tomorrow and the timing is —"

"No, it's fine," she told him. "Whatever you came to say, I'd rather you just say it, Grayson. Especially since you've got me extremely curious now. Even if it's something horrible." She felt a tightness in her chest. "Like you don't want to be my friend anymore . . ."

"No, that's not it." He actually reached across the table to take her hand. "Nothing like that, Mallory. I'm sorry. I didn't want to upset you."

"But you seem upset." She'd never seen him like this before. Her mind filled with things that would put him in such a sour mood. "I feel like something terrible has happened. Is it Lindsey? Is she okay? I know about Joel. Is that —"

"Who's Joel?" His brow creased even more as he released her hand.

Her jaw dropped. "I'm sorry. I wasn't supposed to say anything."

"Now you have to tell me," he said firmly.

"Only if you promise not to mention this to Lindsey."

"I'll do my best."

"Well, she told me about her breakup with Flynn. We talked a lot about that sort of thing. And she really likes this other young man, Joel. He sounds like a great guy, but she's worried it could be a rebound romance, and she wasn't ready to tell you about him. Not yet."

He looked relieved. "Oh, well, that's understandable. No, I won't let her know you told me." He almost smiled. "I think it's nice she confided in you."

"She's such a sweet girl, Grayson. But you know that." She frowned. "So, please, tell me, what's up? What's troubling you?"

He pulled out a chair for her. "Sit down."

"Okay." She sat, bracing herself for whatever he had to say.

He sat down across from her, inhaled deeply, then released it. "I know who vandalized your shop, Mallory."

"Oh?" She felt a weight lifting. It wasn't really the end of her world, after all.

"Yeah." He put his elbows on the table, wrapping one hand around his fist.

"And?" She drew out the word.

"I found empty cans of pink spray paint in the dumpster outside my office."

"One of your crew members?" She felt her eyes opening wide. "They're such nice guys."

His expression was somber. "Not my crew."

"Well, that's good." She was on pins and needles now.

"Corrina came in to work late this morning." He pressed his lips together. "And she clearly had a hangover."

"Oh." Mallory suspected where he was going but didn't want to believe it.

"By then I had set the empty paint cans on my desk, thinking I'd call the police. But when I noticed Corrina's bloodshot eyes and puffy face, and when I saw her expression as she noticed the spray cans, well, I knew."

"She admitted to it?" Mallory felt sick inside.

He simply nodded. "She denied it at first, but when I mentioned that I planned to hand the cans over to the police as evidence, she caved."

"Oh, dear." Mallory actually felt a tiny bit sorry for Corrina. "Did you call the police?"

"Not yet."

"Are you going to?"

"I'm leaving that up to you."

"Oh, Grayson." She stood up, pacing back and forth as she talked. "I can't do that. I mean, there must be another way to deal with this. She would be so humiliated. You say she'd been drinking? She was probably intoxicated. Not that it's an excuse, but it's an explanation. And I know she doesn't like me. In fact, I'm sure she hates me."

Grayson was standing now too. "But hating someone doesn't give you the right to break laws."

"I know." Mallory looked into his eyes. "But you must realize why she hates me, don't you?"

He nodded. "I do now. She said she felt threatened by you, because she thought you were stealing me from her and it wasn't fair. She wanted to get back at you and getting drunk with her girlfriends gave her the courage to step over the line. But she's very sorry about it now. And embarrassed."

"I can imagine."

"So, it's up to you. If you want, I'll call the police and make a report. You won't have to be very involved."

"I don't know. I mean, as crazy as it sounds, I do feel sorry for her."

"Sorry for her?"

"Oh, Grayson, can't you see she's in love with you? I think she must've been in love with you for years."

"How did you know about that if I didn't?" he asked.

"Corrina pretty much told me." Mallory straightened the already perfect place setting in front of her. It was part of her autumnal display. She suddenly wished they were in a real dining room. Just her and Grayson sharing an intimate meal together. She looked up at him. "Remember that time I mentioned Corrina had said some things to me out on the street? I didn't go into it much because I didn't think you believed me. To be honest, it kind of hurt my feelings that you dismissed me."

"I do remember that now. I just couldn't imagine how Corrina could be like that. I was totally blind to it, Mallory. I'm so sorry. I should've believed you. I might've prevented this whole mess by confronting her then."

"Or it might've made her do something worse." She picked up a soup spoon and stared at the upside-down image in the curved metal.

"You could be right." He slowly shook his head.

"I'm still a little stunned you couldn't see

that she was in love with you."

"I can see it now. Twenty-twenty hindsight, I guess. But I was oblivious to it before. Corinna stepped in after Kellie died. She was so helpful and smart and capable. I just thought she was an extremely loyal and diligent employee. To be honest, it's not easy to let her go. You don't find employees like that every day." He held up his hands. "But I guess you only get that kind of attention if they're in love with you. Go figure."

She set the spoon down. "You fired her?"

"Of course. I can't have an assistant who's in love with me. Not to mention one who vandalized a jobsite. That's dangerous and Corrina just proved it." He rolled his eyes. "In fact, I must've been nuts not to see it. You thought you were the village idiot once. Now I think I've earned the title."

"You're being too hard on yourself."

"Well, Corrina laid into me. She thought I knew how she felt. She even imagined I returned her feelings. But I swear to you I never did. And I never said anything the least bit romantic. I'm sure I didn't."

"Perception is in the eyes of the beholder."

"Did you just make that up?"

Mallory sighed. "When you love someone, well, you know what they say . . . when your heart's on fire, smoke gets in your eyes."

405

She attempted a feeble laugh.

"I don't think it's like that with me."

"What do you mean?" she asked.

"I mean, I don't think smoke gets in my eyes. I think I can see more clearly when I'm in love. Kind of like blue sky and sunshine."

She smiled. "Yeah, I'd prefer that to smoke any day." Mallory jumped at the sound of someone pounding on the door. Hoping it wasn't Corrina, she hurried up front, trailed by Grayson.

Seth, Micah, and Louisa were clustered outside the door.

"It's my kids." She unlocked the door and opened it wide.

"We called your phone, but you didn't answer," Seth said as they all rushed in.

"We got worried," Micah told her.

"I silenced my phone for filming and forgot to turn it back on." Mallory apologized, then introduced her three kids to Grayson. "Well, you told us you'd be done by now. I hope you didn't forget that Marshall is making a celebratory dinner," Louisa said.

"Oh, I definitely did." Mallory looked at Grayson. "I'm sorry. I need to go."

"So do I." He looked at her kids. "Nice to meet all of you."

"Why don't you join us for dinner?" Louisa asked.

"Thanks, but I have some things to attend to." He smiled. "How about a rain check?"

Louisa frowned. "I'd say tomorrow night, but we're leaving in the afternoon."

"Then you'll all have to come back again," he told them.

"For sure," Micah said. "Especially if we can rent your beach house. It totally rocks."

"My daughter handles that for me, but I'm sure she can accommodate you." He reached for the doorknob. "Good luck tomorrow, Mallory. I'll catch up with you after the filming is all done."

She thanked him, then turned to her kids. "I'm so sorry my phone was off. You kids run along while I shut things down in here. I'll be back at the beach house ASAP."

The boys took off, but Louisa insisted on staying back and riding to the beach house with Mallory. "So that was Mr. Dreamboat." She followed her mom around the shop like a puppy dog as she turned off lights and locked the back door. "He *is* good-looking, Mom. What was he doing here?"

"He just came by to check on me."

"Because your phone was off?"

"Maybe." Mallory grabbed her purse from

the closet.

"I think he really is into you, Mom. No kidding."

Mallory opened the front door. "No kidding?"

"I think you're holding out on me. Is something going on between you two? It almost felt like we interrupted something."

"We were just talking." She locked the door after Louisa stepped outside.

"About?"

Mallory wondered how much to say. Less seemed to be more in this situation. "Well, he did tell me that he had to let Corrina go."

"Grayson fired Corrina?" Louisa sounded happy.

"Yes." They climbed into her SUV. "He finally figured out that she was in love with him."

"You mean he honestly didn't know? I was only with that woman for a few hours and I knew."

"Well, men and women are different."

Louisa laughed. "I'm glad you finally figured that one out, Mom."

Mallory laughed too. Now, instead of talking about Grayson or Corrina like Louisa wanted, she filled her daughter in on the afternoon. Her kids and Kara had lurked along the sidelines during the morning filming, but eventually they all got bored and responded to the luring call of the beach.

Of course, the afternoon filming hadn't been any more exciting than the morning, but it was something to converse about, and she tried to make it sound more interesting than it actually was. But as she told Louisa about Amy's bloopers that required retakes, she was actually thinking about Grayson. She wished they'd been able to finish their conversation. It had almost felt like they were getting somewhere. Or was she as silly as Corrina and needed to heed her own words . . . because it was true, women and men often did perceive things differently. Mallory could be all wrong about where she thought Grayson had been going. For all she knew, the blue skies and sunshine line could've been about Kellie. Perhaps he'd never be ready for another love in his life. Not everyone was capable of a second time around.

28

To Mallory's relief, the second day of filming went smoother than the first. And it went faster too. She no longer felt disturbed at the sight of her picture-perfect designs, at least in her opinion, torn completely apart and rearranged by the energetic film crew. She knew it could all be put back together again. Tomorrow.

Today, she wanted to get back to the beach house in time to say goodbye to her kids and Kara. She knew that, for various reasons, they all wanted to be on the road by three, but she hoped to spend a little time with them before they took off, and she wanted to thank them for their help. But by the time she arrived, they were already loading their cars. After the hugs and promises to return ASAP, all that was left was to wave goodbye and watch them drive away.

As she went back into the house, she felt

like an inflatable pool toy that someone had slipped a needle into. Exhausted, she was fading fast, but she still wanted to straighten up the beach house before moving into her new apartment. When she'd left the house this morning, it had been pretty messy. But as she walked through now, she was pleasantly surprised to see everything neatly in place. Probably the work of Kara and Lindsey.

Although the sky outside was still blue, the fog bank on the ocean's horizon was rolling in. Determined to catch some sun, she grabbed a cozy throw and a pillow and went outside. Feeling worn-out but relaxed, she sank into a comfortable lounge chair and quickly drifted off.

A tap on the shoulder woke her. By now the damp fog had blocked out the sunshine. Grayson was standing over her.

"Aren't you cold out here?" he asked.

She stretched her arms above her head. "Come to think of it, I am."

"Then come inside and get warm." He extended his hand and helped her to her feet.

"What're you doing here?" she asked as she gathered her pillow and blanket.

"Well, I knew your guests were leaving today, and I figured you'd be exhausted after all the filming, so I thought I'd fix you dinner." He opened the door, leading her inside.

She noticed a crackling fire in the fireplace. "You must've been here awhile."

"Long enough." He led her to the island, where he'd already set out a tempting plate of sushi.

"Wow, this is totally unexpected."

"I have to admit, I didn't make that myself." He smiled. "For the record, I'm not a bad cook, although I don't make sushi. But I was in such a hurry, I just nabbed some things from the deli."

"Well, you did arrange it nicely on the plate."

"Thank you. I wanted to make it look good for you."

She smiled as she picked up a small plate and a pair of chopsticks. She popped the latter apart with a loud snap. "Even if it didn't look good, I would appreciate it."

"Before I forget, I want to tell you the rest of the Corrina story." He reached for a small plate too.

"The rest of the story?" She picked up a piece of sushi.

"I told Corrina that you didn't want to press charges and she was grateful. She even asked me to thank you."

"That's nice." She set the sushi on her plate.

"I also gave her a pretty stern warning." His face grew serious. "I told her if she ever pulls a stunt like that again, not only will I report her to the police but I will inform them of her responsibility for the spray paint job she pulled yesterday."

"Thank you." Mallory sighed. "It had occurred to me that she might be even angrier at me now, and I wondered . . . if she got drunk again . . . well, who knows."

"My thoughts exactly." He nodded. "But I think we can rest easy. Corrina told me she's moving back home. Back to Portland. I already wrote her a letter of recommendation."

"With a warning that her new boss might want to watch that old *Fatal Attraction* movie before hiring?" she teased.

He laughed. "Well, enough about that. The rest of the evening is for us to just relax and enjoy." But as he reached for a piece of sushi, his phone rang.

"Sounds like you're wanted." She took a bite of a California roll, pleasantly surprised that it was flavorful.

He wrinkled his nose as he pulled his phone from his jeans pocket. "I guess I should get this."

"Of course." She put another piece of sushi on her plate and tried not to listen when he answered.

"Hi, Amy. Yes, I happen to be with Mallory right now. Did you want to speak to her?" He paused. "She had her phone's volume off during the filming, I'll bet she forgot to turn it on again." He winked at Mallory.

Mallory could hear the sound of Amy's fast-paced chatter from a few feet away but couldn't make out the words. Maybe that was a good thing.

Grayson turned his face away from her. "Oh, well, we're actually here right now. I brought some dinner from town." He paused again, rubbing a hand over his neck. "Yeah, sure, come on out. We'll see you soon." He hung up and turned back toward Malory. "So, as you probably heard, Amy has been trying to reach you. She wants to come out to see you."

"Me?" Mallory got worried. "Did I do something wrong today?"

He shrugged. "I don't think so. She didn't sound unhappy."

"She *never* sounds unhappy." Mallory smirked. "Even if she does ten blooper retakes in a row and her crew starts grumbling, Amy keeps smiling. Nothing seems to rattle her."

"Guess that's why she's so good at what she does."

Mallory nodded glumly. What could be so important that Amy had to come here and interrupt their plans? Didn't she have her own life? "I'm curious, Grayson. You're good friends with Amy. Do you know her fiancé?"

He chuckled. "She's not engaged."

"Really? What about that massive ring she wears?"

"She told me it's a fake. Just something to help her show's ratings." He winked. "But keep it under your hat."

"Interesting." Mallory glanced down at the uneaten sushi on her plate. "So what about dinner?"

"I guess it can wait. Or" — he looked uncertain — "I guess we could invite Amy to join us."

"It's up to you." Mallory tried to sound nonchalant, but she wanted to stomp her feet and say "no way!" Why couldn't this dinner be just the two of them? She noticed Grayson's casual attire compared to her "filming" outfit and felt overdressed. "If you don't mind, I'd like to get into some comfier clothes." And hopefully a comfier attitude too.

"Of course. Take your time."

As Mallory headed back to the master bedroom, she realized this would be her last night in this house. And, really, she was eager to make the move into her apartment. Just spending time in front of the cameras with Amy today, talking about the transformation the place had undergone, made her even more thrilled about taking up residency there. She could imagine coffee on the terrace, sunsets from her sectional, and just the freedom of being under her own roof. She'd miss the beach just outside the doors here, but living above her shop and in town was a pretty fair trade-off.

Dressed in her favorite faded jeans and a loose cable-knit pull-over, she was just slipping into her loafers when she heard Amy's cheerful voice down the hall. That was quick. Mallory headed toward the sound of the voice, then paused in the doorway. She forced herself to forget that she'd spent more than enough time with Amy these past two days, pasted on her happy face, and went out to join them.

"This place looks fabulous," Amy was telling Grayson. "I absolutely love what you've done since the last time I was here. You just have to let me feature this house in my episode about Oregon beach homes. In fact, we could probably shoot your segment while the crew is still in town. Would that work for you? We could start at eight tomorrow and probably wrap by noon." Amy flashed a brilliant smile in his direction. "Oh, Grayson, please, tell me you'll let me do it." Just inches from his face, she folded her hands in a pleading posture.

Mallory, unobserved in the shadows of the hallway, watched Amy cajoling with amused interest. She had changed from her filming clothes too. But instead of something casual, Amy wore a fitted white sundress that showed off her tan and her curves. She'd also donned high-heeled sandals that didn't look the least bit comfortable. Perhaps she had a big date tonight. Mallory's heart soared at the thought. Hopefully she wouldn't stay very long.

"Please, Grayson," Amy continued begging as Mallory joined them in the great room. "It would save my show both time and money, and I promise we'll be in and out so fast, you'll hardly know we were here. Please, say you will."

"I don't know what I say." He put a hand on Mallory's shoulder. "But you'd have to give this talented woman the credit for romancing my home. She's been living here during her apartment renovation, and she's the one who brought in all the color and life. I could hardly believe the transition myself." He smiled at Mallory. "You really romanced this place."

"Thanks," she murmured.

"I suppose Mallory could be part of this segment too." Amy pursed her lips, her eyes still fixed on Grayson. "Although I wanted to focus more on architecture than decor in this particular episode. I mean, it's definitely a plus that the place is staged, but it's this gorgeous architecture that needs the real spotlight. And since you built this house, I'd like to have you play the host for this segment."

"Well, I don't know." He glanced at Mallory, as if he wanted her opinion.

"You should definitely do it!" She couldn't help but smirk. "After all, remember what you told me, 'Do it for Portside.' "

He chuckled. "Our words do come back to haunt us."

"Then you'll do it?" Amy's big blue eyes lit up. "Oh, Grayson, you're the very best." She threw her arms around him, hugging him tightly. "I'm so excited."

Feeling awkward — and a little jealous — Mallory went into the kitchen area. She poured herself a glass of water and took a long cool drink while Amy chattered away

418

at Grayson, making a plan for when her crew would arrive and what he needed to do to prepare for them. While they were talking about Amy's big plans, Mallory slipped back to the master bedroom and prepared to leave. She'd already packed most of her things that morning, so it'd be easy enough to slip out unnoticed now. It wasn't that she was mad at Grayson, but if Amy's crew was coming early in the morning, it just made sense to leave tonight. Fortunately, thanks to her kids and Kara, the master bedroom and bath were clean and neat and ready for filming.

She carried her bags down the hallway, setting them by the front door, then returned to the great room where Amy was still detailing tomorrow's agenda. Poor Grayson, with his back to the fireplace, almost seemed trapped. But Mallory reminded herself that he was a big boy. He could take care of himself.

"Hey, you two," Mallory interrupted. "Since you'll be filming tomorrow morning, I'm just going to clear out now."

Grayson's shoulders slumped. "But what about —"

"I can take a rain check on dinner," she said. "If Amy doesn't have plans, she might like to stay."

Amy brightened at this. "I don't have plans."

"But I —"

"I'm pretty worn-out from getting up super early these last couple of days. Sleeping in tomorrow sounds lovely." Mallory went over to Grayson, stepping past Amy to get to him. "Thank you so much for sharing your beautiful beach house with me, Grayson." She hugged him. "Thanks for everything."

"No problem," he said quietly.

She leaned back and looked him in the eyes. "I'll catch up with you later."

He nodded. "Yeah. Okay."

Mallory turned to Amy. "I just remembered. Grayson said you had something to talk to me about."

"Oh, yeah." Amy crossed the room to grab her expensive-looking purse, then carried it back to their place by the fire. "I brought your final payment for your involvement in the show."

"Oh, that's nice." Mallory watched Amy dig through her bag. "You could've just put it in the mail."

"I know it's in here someplace." Amy extracted a bottle of wine, handing it to Grayson. "I meant to give you this last time, Grayson. It's from my sister's vineyard in

420

Napa. But now we can have it with dinner." Next she pulled out a wrinkled envelope. "Here you go." She handed it to Mallory. "Thanks so much for allowing us to film your darling shop and apartment." She flashed her million-dollar smile. "My assistant will let you know the air dates."

"Thank you." Mallory slid the check into her bag, then started to gather up her luggage.

"Here, let me help you," Grayson offered, stepping toward her.

"I can handle it," she said briskly. She bent her knees and picked up the biggest bag. "If you could just get the door —"

"No, I'll get this." He wrestled it from her. "And I'll get the door too."

She just nodded, allowing him to accompany her out to her vehicle. After her bags were loaded in back, he reached for her hand. "I'm sorry about this evening, Mallory. It wasn't what I had planned."

She forced a bright smile onto her face as she unlocked her car. "I know. But I really am tired, Grayson. The idea of settling into my own sweet apartment, and sleeping in tomorrow, sounds very good to me."

"I can understand that." He glanced back at his house. "The idea of dining alone with Ms. Chatterbox sounds torturous to me."

She couldn't help but giggle.

"You sure you won't change your mind and have something more to eat? You must be hungry."

"I'm more tired than hungry."

"Yeah, you're probably tired of Amy too." He glumly shook his head. "Thanks for inviting her for dinner."

Mallory shrugged. "Well, if I hadn't, she probably would've invited herself anyway." She affectionately patted his cheek. "You're just too darn irresistible, Mr. Matthews." Before he could respond, she dropped his hand and got into her car. She waved goodbye, but as she drove away, she questioned her choices. Had she been a fool to abandon poor Grayson like that? Leaving him in the hands of gorgeous, gregarious Amy Stanton? But then again, she reminded herself, if Grayson couldn't be trusted with another woman, it might be painful, but it would be better to discover it sooner than later. By the time she was climbing the stairs to her apartment, she was resolved. If Grayson cared as much for her as she did for him, she had no reason to worry. Whether it was pretty Corrina or dazzling Amy, if Grayson was the man she thought he was, it didn't matter. Despite its disheveled appearance after today's filming, her apartment still felt welcoming as she dropped her things by the door. After some quick re-arrangements, she got the place pretty much back to normal.

Her stomach grumbled as she fluffed the last throw pillow. She remembered the attractive cheese and cracker platter that she'd arranged for staging earlier. The crew had nibbled on it some, but the leftovers were still in the fridge. She made herself a small plate and, happy to be home, took it to her comfy sectional. She sank into it with a long, satisfied sigh. She leaned back and noticed that the fog bank on the ocean had broken up into clouds now. A glorious sunset was just beginning.

As she munched on her snack-like dinner, she wondered what tonight would've been like if Amy hadn't shown up at the beach house. Would she and Grayson be making a fire outside, bundled up in blankets, watching the colorful sunset together? Maybe someday . . . if it was meant to be.

It wasn't until she was getting into bed that another image popped into her head. Now, instead of envisioning herself on the back deck with Grayson and the colorful sunset, she saw him out there with Amy. Amy was filling wineglasses with the bottle of her sister's wine, looking deeply into

Grayson's eyes, and proposing a toast to their future! Too tired to dwell on this most unwelcome image, Mallory punched her pillow, turned off the lights, and turned the whole thing over to God.

29

By the next day, Mallory's worries about Amy putting the moves on Grayson felt silly. Reconciled that what would be would be, she set out to have a carefree day. So glad to have the filming all behind her and her whole building useable and livable, she planned to practice an attitude of gratitude for the entire day — hopefully for her entire life. She had never felt so much at peace.

As new customers and recently made friends came and went to her shop, she realized how much she loved living in Portside and how much she looked forward to getting more plugged in to the community. All her hard work and investment had been so worthwhile. Not just materially either. And even if what she hoped would happen with Grayson never got past the starting gates, she was content. She would continue on this path.

Even when Thomas showed up, Mallory

felt at peace. She politely thanked him for the roses, showing him where she'd placed them in the dining section of her shop. "It was so sweet of you to want to celebrate the filming of *Pacific Design,*" she told him, hoping he'd take the hint that she didn't see his flowers as more than just a friendly gesture. "I even mentioned your name during the filming. I pointed out the floors and woodwork and said how you did such a professional job on them."

"Hey, thanks. Maybe I'll be famous now." He chuckled.

"I'll let you know when the show is scheduled to air," she said lightly.

"Cool."

"And I told Sandi that I'd love to have you and her and a few other people over for a thank-you dinner in my apartment. Since you and Sandi are neighbors, maybe you can compare your schedule with hers, then she can let me know what dates are good."

He appeared surprised by her suggestion but didn't respond. To her relief, a pair of women entered the shop. She politely excused herself, and since he didn't linger, she hoped he'd picked up on her clues.

Caroline came in just before closing time. "How did it all go?" she asked. "I've been dying to hear the details."

Mallory filled her in some, then Caroline suggested she lock up. "I'll take you to dinner and you can tell me all about it."

Mallory agreed and Caroline suggested they meet up at The Chowder House. As Mallory closed up her shop, she checked her phone, hoping Grayson had left a message, but seeing nothing, she told herself it did not matter and got ready to meet Caroline for dinner.

The two women dined on chowder as Mallory detailed the past two days of filming. "I'm not complaining," she finally said, "but it was not all fun and games like people think."

"It sounds a little grueling to me."

"Honestly, I'm just glad it's over." She sighed. "And poor Grayson was put through the same wringer today."

"How's that?"

Mallory explained how Amy had twisted his arm to include his beach house in a different episode. "I'd brought in some decor while I was there so it looked pretty nice," she told her. "It was my way of thanking Grayson for letting me use his house during my renovation, but I hate to think of what it must look like now." She took her head. "The way the crew moves everything around, I can only imagine."

"You'll have to go fix it up for him again," Caroline said.

"I guess. Well, if he asks, anyway. Don't want to overstep my bounds."

The server brought their check and Caroline grabbed it before Mallory had the chance. "I heard that Corrina has left town." Caroline lowered her voice. "Seems kind of sudden, don't you think?"

Mallory just shrugged. "Grayson said she was going to move back home to Portland. Must've been missing the big city."

"Or she figured out that Grayson has his eye on you." Caroline's brows arched. "That's the scuttlebutt around town."

Mallory laughed. "Well, I think Grayson has had his hands full today. Unless I'm mistaken, Amy was putting the moves on him last night."

"Are you kidding? Amy Stanton is some serious competition, Mallory. I had sort of hoped that you and Grayson —"

"Yes, I am kidding." Mallory jumped in, realizing she'd said too much. "Amy was just very enthusiastic in persuading Grayson to feature his house on her TV show. You know, I can't blame her, it's really a spectacular house. Have you ever seen it?"

Caroline shook her head. Seeing her opportunity to segue the conversation, Mallory began to describe Grayson's impeccable home. After that, she started to talk about plans for Caroline's apartment and how she hoped to get started on it soon. To Mallory's relief, by the time the two women said good night, the topic of Amy and Grayson had never risen again.

As Mallory went home, she admired the quiet street, the quaint shops that had improved their appearances in the past couple of weeks — with hanging flowerpots, freshly painted shutters, and outside seating in front of some stores. It all gave her a sense of sweet satisfaction. Portside was changing. Not in the big way Grayson had envisioned before Mallory had shown up and thrown a wrench in the works. But the town seemed to be evolving in a way that would be good for everyone. And she felt like she'd played a part in it. Like she would continue to play a part in it. And it was exciting!

When she went to bed later that night, without one single word from Grayson, she refused to allow worrisome visions of him and Amy to disturb her peace. Even if he and Amy had eloped right after filming the segment of his beach house, Mallory would be just fine. Oh, sure, she might be a little blue at first, but she would recover.

Mallory was happily flitting around her shop on Monday morning, turning on lights and music and lighting an aromatic candle. It wasn't opening time yet, but she'd made an early appointment with Lindsey, and she looked forward to reconnecting with her.

While they'd been cleaning the other day, Mallory had mentioned her need for part-time help. Lindsey had expressed interest, but Mallory had been too distracted to follow up. Then Lindsey texted a reminder yesterday, asking if Mallory was still looking for an employee. They'd scheduled to meet this morning to discuss it.

Mallory spied Lindsey at the front door and hurried to let her in. "You're early," she told her. "Always a good sign."

"That's because I'm excited." Lindsay grinned.

"Come on upstairs. I've got a fresh pot of coffee and some blackberry scones waiting for us."

"Sounds good to me."

After they were seated at the island, Mallory told her the days and hours she felt she needed help and what she felt she could pay.

"I'd love to work weekends, especially

after school starts. But I could manage an afternoon here and there," Lindsey said. "And don't worry. I didn't expect much more than minimum wage."

"But I want you to have more than minimal responsibility," Mallory explained. "I want to feel comfortable leaving the shop in your hands. I know you're a responsible person. I'd see you kind of like an assistant manager. I think that deserves more than minimum pay."

"Well, it all sounds good to me."

"And you may change your mind about your hours when you're back to teaching, so I might need to hire another employee. I hoped you might even be able to help me train whoever I hire. That is, if I find the right person. I don't particularly want to place an ad for it." She smiled at Lindsey. "I wouldn't just hire anyone."

"I might be able to help you find someone before school starts."

"Fabulous."

They talked awhile longer then shook hands on it. "When do I start?" Lindsey asked.

"Today, if you like."

"I like." She nodded eagerly.

"Well, then let's start training you."

Mallory took her through the usual steps

431

of getting ready to open shop. Then she showed her how she handwrote receipts for each purchase. "I put one copy in the customer's bag and the other goes into the books once a week. I know it's old-fashioned, but I like it this way."

"And if a computer crashed, you'd still have everything right there." Lindsey pointed to the receipt book.

"My thoughts exactly." Now she showed her how to use the credit and debit card machine. "It's probably easier than using the cash register, but most purchases are made with plastic."

"It all seems pretty simple and straightfor-ward," Lindsay said.

"It really is." She explained about custom-ers asking for items she didn't have or was out of. "I make notes of that here." She pulled out her notebook. "Get their name and phone number and jot down the item they're wanting." She led Lindsey to the back room. "As you can see, I keep some of the faster-moving small items back here. If you see we're running low on soaps or lo-tions or things in the front, just restock them." She shrugged. "It really isn't a very complicated business."

"I think that's why I like it."

"And, as you know, I like to keep everything looking clean and pretty out there. I clean the powder room every morning." She held up a finger. "Except I totally forgot today."

"Let me do it," Lindsey insisted.

Mallory left her to it while she went to unlock the front door. She stepped outside to check the flowerpots. The soil was still moist so she was about to go inside when she heard a voice calling from down the street. It was Grayson, hurrying toward her.

"Just who I wanted to see." His smile warmed her as usual.

"It's good to see you too. How's it going?"

"Okay, I guess. But I want to apologize again for the other night. What a fiasco that turned into."

"Fiasco?"

"Yeah, that Amy." He shook his head. "She wanted to party and was acting like we were going to wine and dine and dance the night away. I had to put my foot down. I told her if she didn't leave, I'd pull the plug on filming my house the next day. That got her out."

Mallory couldn't help but laugh. "Well, I have to admit, she looked dressed to kill, Grayson. That should've been your first clue."

"I guess I'm a little clueless."

"Yes, you've proven that before." She leaned against the stucco. "So how did it go yesterday? Did Amy still come to film your house after that?"

"Oh, yeah." He actually rolled his eyes. "It was quite a day. Exhausting and painful and, please, don't ever let me agree to anything like that again."

She liked that he seemed to include her in his future decisions. "Sorry to hear that, but I'm not too surprised. That's pretty much how I felt. I think I'm still recovering."

"And my house! It's turned upside down." He shook his head. "That film crew — it felt like they wouldn't be satisfied until they'd rearranged every single thing. I honestly don't understand it. I thought it looked great the way you had it."

"It's all about camera angle and light. But at least it's over." She poked him in the shoulder. "And remember, it was all for Portside, right?"

"I guess." He frowned, and for a long moment neither of them said anything. They just stood there on the sidewalk, staring at each other.

Mallory glanced to her shop. "I should probably go in."

"Right." He nodded, not breaking their eye contact. "I really am sorry for how my dinner plans got ruined the other night. Amy really is a force to be reckoned with."

"So did you reckon with her?" Mallory teased.

His frown turned to a scowl. "As a matter of fact, I did."

Mallory blinked. "How's that?"

"Well, Amy, I discovered, is used to getting her own way. And that's probably an understatement." He sighed. "The filming that was supposed to wrap up by noon wound up taking the whole day. And then, even though her production crew packed up and left, Amy wouldn't go. She actually wanted to fix me dinner. In my own house! Somehow she'd gotten the impression that I was interested in her. It was weird considering I practically threw her out the night before. She kind of reminds me of Corrina." He scratched his head and peered at Mallory. "What is it about me? Do you think I do something to lead women on?"

She laughed. "Maybe it's just your irresistible charm."

"Charm?" He grimaced. "I don't like that word."

"Yeah, charm's the wrong word. Personally, I don't care for charming men. Maybe it's because you're polite, Grayson. You're thoughtful and kind. Women are attracted to that."

"So, I should be more of an ogre?"

She smiled. "Even if you were an ogre, you'd still be an intelligent and rather good-looking bachelor. Playing hard to get appeals to some women so you'd probably still be considered quite a catch." She shrugged. "Maybe you're hopeless, Grayson. You'll always have a trail of single women chasing after you."

"That's discouraging." His expression softened. "Especially when I'd rather have just one."

Mallory heard the door open behind her.

"Lindsey," Grayson said, "what're you doing in there?"

"I work here, Dad." She came outside, looking her dad up and down. "What are you doing here?"

"Just visiting with Mallory." He grinned. "Seriously, you're working at the shop?"

"I just hired her," Mallory told him. "Couldn't ask for better help."

"Someone just called about a design consultation," Lindsey told her. "She sounded pretty urgent, and I promised to have you call her right back. I hope that was okay."

"Perfect." Mallory smiled at Grayson. "If you'll excuse me."

"Under one condition," he said.

"What's that?"

"Have dinner with me tonight. At the beach house. I'm cooking."

She glanced at Lindsey, then back at Grayson. "Under one condition."

"What's that?" His brow creased.

"Let me go straighten up that beach house first."

"I'd love that." Grayson told Lindsey how the film crew had messed the place up.

"That's too bad," she told him. "Mallory had romanced it so nicely too."

"It should be easy to put back together." She turned to Lindsey. "Would you be okay on your own for a couple hours while I'm gone?"

"I don't see why not. I can always call you if I need to." Lindsey looked from her dad to Mallory. "And just in case I forget to say this later, I hope you two have a very nice evening together." She winked, then went back inside.

"That's a sweet daughter you have," Mallory said.

"Don't I know it." He grinned at her. "Well, I've got to get to work. Want to meet me at the beach house at, say, six thirty?"

"It's a date."

He nodded. "That's right. It *is* a date."

437

She was ready to go, but he was still lingering. "Anything else?" she asked.

"Yes," he declared. "It's more than a date. Let me make my intentions clear, okay?"

She blinked. "Okay."

"I don't just want to date you, Mallory Farrell. I want to *romance* you."

She felt her heart racing. "Romance me?"

He nodded. "Yes. It's like that quote on your business card. I want to share with you that feeling of mystery and excitement, and I want us both to live in that remoteness from everyday life. That and a whole lot more. Are you okay with that?"

"I'm more than okay with it, Grayson. I've been waiting and dreaming of being romanced by you."

And there, right in front of God and everyone coming and going on Main Street in Portside, Oregon, Grayson Matthews gathered her up in his arms and passionately kissed her. "This, I hope, is the official beginning of you and me romancing each other for the rest of our lives."

Mallory had no argument with that.

ABOUT THE AUTHOR

Melody Carlson is the award-winning author of more than two hundred books with sales of more than seven million, including many bestselling Christmas novellas, young adult titles, and contemporary romances. She received a *Romantic Times* Career Achievement Award in the inspirational market for her many books, including *Finding Alice,* and her novel *All Summer Long* was made into a Hallmark movie. She and her husband live in central Oregon. Learn more at www.melodycarlson.com.